"I don't need your help."

"But you do, for you will not be looking into the ordinary things with these men. Rather you shall ascertain their individual personalities to determine their compatibility with mine."

Gideon laughed, though she could not tell whether it was with amusement or disbelief.

"I have been thinking, and we must figure out a way," Ingrid continued firmly, "for you to accompany me or be nearby when I speak with these men. Note their flaws, their incompatibilities. My parents want me to marry for love."

His head tilted. "But you do not wish to do so?"

A tiny clench tugged beneath her breastbone, but she ignored it. "I'm inclined toward monogamy, and the piano stole my heart long ago."

"Stolen hearts, unsuitable beaux. I find myself in agreement with you. Love is far too overrated. All right, my lady." He pushed to his feet. "Send a missive with the time and day that I am to rescue you from your parents' nefarious plans."

He winked before strolling off, and once again, Ingrid's breath shallowed and her heart raced.

Jessica Nelson believes romance happens every day and thinks the greatest, most intense romance comes from a God who woos people to Himself with passionate tenderness. When Jessica is not cleaning up after her teenagers, she can be found staring into space as she plots her next story. Or she might be daydreaming about a raspberry mocha from Starbucks. Or thinking about what kind of chocolate she should have for dinner that night. She could be thinking of any number of things, really. One thing is for certain—she is blessed with a wonderful family and a lovely life.

Books by Jessica Nelson

Love Inspired Historical

Visit the Author Profile page at LoveInspired.com.

The Husband
Dilemma

JESSICA NELSON

LOVE INSPIRED
INSPIRATIONAL ROMANCE

LOVE INSPIRED®
INSPIRATIONAL ROMANCE

Recycling programs
for this product may
not exist in your area.

ISBN-13: 978-1-335-49847-2

The Husband Dilemma

For questions and comments about the quality of this book, please contact us at CustomerService@Harlequin.com.

Love Inspired
22 Adelaide St. West, 41st Floor
Toronto, Ontario M5H 4E3, Canada
www.LoveInspired.com

Printed in U.S.A.

Now unto him that is able to do exceeding abundantly above all that we ask or think, according to the power that worketh in us, Unto him be glory in the church by Christ Jesus throughout all ages, world without end. Amen.
—*Ephesians* 3:20–21

To my wild teenagers, who eat all the food and complain about my cooking skills, but still let me hug you... My heart would be empty and incomplete without you. And to my amazing Jesus, Who has been my ever-present help and joy, both in shadowed valleys and on sun-kissed mountaintops.

Chapter One

Gideon West had seen many strange things in his life as a detective with Bow Street.

He did not count a woman hiding behind a curtain in an office during a ball as one of those strange things. In truth, the emerald green slippers peeking from beneath the curtain's satin hem were most certainly a new experience for him. Curiosity piqued, he quietly placed his completed investigative report on Lord Bunsworth's massive, teak desk and then backed out of the private office.

He had merely stopped by to close the investigation, but he'd found a fancy ball in progress. Thankfully the butler knew him and let him into Lord Bunsworth's quarters in order to drop off his findings.

He had not expected to notice someone hiding behind curtains, and he doubted the servants knew of the deception.

The woman obviously did not want to be found. That did not mean he would give her what she wanted.

It was not outside the realm of possibility that she might

be a thief. He'd seen his share of those, and they came in all shapes and sizes.

He stood in the long hall, debating if he should leave without notifying the servants of her presence.

Balls often offered the perfect opportunity for a thief to sneak in and filch jewels. The height of the Season, springtime, provoked a spike in criminality.

At the far end of the hall, a door opened and an older woman sporting a turquoise gown emerged from the ballroom. As she neared, her violet-eyed gaze flicked over him, briefly lingering. Not with feminine interest, but something he couldn't put a finger on. Almost…recognition? Then she glanced away, bored disinterest pasted on her face. Doubtless she considered him a servant, unworthy of her attention.

She dipped her head into the office he'd just left. "Ingrid?"

No response.

Gideon bit back his grin. The woman made a wide berth as she passed him. He heard her calling into other rooms, but no one by the name of Ingrid answered. When she came back, she paused as if to ask him a question, but then thought better of speaking to someone who was clearly a commoner. Irritation tightened her expression, and her stride to the ballroom looked stiff.

Amusement curled his lips. If she'd bothered to speak with him, he might have helped her. As it was, the snobbery of the *ton* never failed to irritate him and he remained mute.

He glanced at his stopwatch. Perhaps a minute, and he'd postulate the girl ventured out on her own. Perhaps she was a young lady who had snuck down to watch the ball, dreaming of her own Come Out one day, followed by her subsequent search for a wealthy, titled husband. Silly rich people.

He stayed away from them.

As expected, a moment passed and then a head of raven hair peeked out from the office.

"Ingrid, I presume," he said in a casual tone. His grin widened as she turned to face him. What arresting features she had. Piquant nose, big eyes the color of violets, and a mouth unconventionally wide that bestowed upon her face a certain individuality.

"It is rude to presume." She straightened and stepped into the hall. Her pristine gown bespoke wealth, and so did her perfume. Jasmine, perhaps?

This was definitely no schoolgirl. He pushed off the wall to join her, noting her tall height. All the more attractive, in his book.

"It is also rude to speak to one you have not been introduced to." Her gaze raked him from head to toe. "You are?"

"Call me Curious. Why were you hiding behind office curtains, ignoring your mother?"

A flush scurried across her skin, deepening the hue of her cheeks to rose. One finely drawn black brow lifted, and then she stepped back into the office and closed the door.

In his face.

That was certainly a surprise. He did not recall any woman ever shutting a door on him. He chuckled. Sassy lady. He should stay, indulge his curiosity by investigating the mysterious Ingrid's identity. After all, the evening held little entertainment to look forward to. The orphans who sometimes sheltered in his lodging were probably scattered about London, causing a ruckus. They wouldn't come straggling in until after midnight, though he'd tried his best to keep them safe.

He should see himself out of this fancy town house

filled with the wealthy peerage. Go home. Find a way to save more money so that he could rent a bigger home for his growing brood of adorable miscreants.

"Ah, Mr. West." Lord Bunsworth, a portly baron with a penchant for gambling, lumbered into the hall. "Did you have any troubles with gathering that information?"

"None at all. My investigative report is on your desk. I was just leaving." His stomach rumbled loudly.

Lord Bunsworth's broad face split into a smile. "Come to the ballroom for a moment. We've teacakes and punch. You sound hungry."

"I could use food," Gideon admitted. He'd been working all day and the kids were growing so fast he could barely keep fresh bread in the house. "I am not dressed for a ball."

Bunsworth laughed. "My wife told me it was to be a musicale." He waved a hand through the air. "She underestimated her popularity, I believe. Come, come. No one shall notice nor question your presence."

Gideon shrugged. Though at odds with propriety, it wouldn't be the first time he'd ventured into a ballroom for information. He often eavesdropped on conversations, filing away slips of information for future cases.

And there did remain a tempting chance he'd run into the lady with the cheekiness to close a door in his face.

Grinning, he followed Lord Bunsworth through the press of guests in the modest ballroom. The polished wooden floor gleamed beneath mirrored wall sconces that reflected candlelight throughout the room. At the far end, open doors showcased a refreshment room filled with those of the uppercrust, drinking and enjoying biscuits and sandwiches. Women clothed in their finest jewels and most exquisitely cut gowns flashed him coy smiles as he walked by, despite the low quality of his clothing. He returned their smiles. He tended to like people, even the superficial people of the *haut monde*. And beautiful women whirling about in shimmering, sumptuous gowns proved no exception. There had been a time in his life when he'd lived a wilder existence, irresponsible, commitment-free.

But not anymore. He'd since settled into bachelorhood, vowing away from any relationship that might careen toward marriage. His career fulfilled him, and caring for orphans from the slums took all of his extra time.

They wove through the crowd and when Lord Bunsworth abandoned him at the punch table for more interesting conversations, thoughts of the woman named Ingrid tickled Gideon's mind.

She intrigued him.

Perhaps because she spoke in a direct fashion. Clear words without simpering. Quite at odds with what one expected from a woman hiding behind a curtain. He'd noticed in his work that pretentiousness often surrounded the nobility. As did expensive perfumes, French confections and secrets. So many secrets. The *beau monde* espoused wasteful madness. Who better to know of their vices, their selfish expenditures, than a detective? His orphans could live for months off the sale of one ball dress.

But Ingrid showed no signs of pretentiousness. Disapproval, assuredly, but he'd run into that too many times to care. One could win approval. One could not fix ostentation.

After indulging in several delicious sandwiches, he retrieved a cup of lemonade to wash it all down. He sipped slowly, enjoying the fancy drink he didn't often have the privilege of imbibing. He moved back into the ballroom area, carefully avoiding being jostled by passerby.

Suddenly, the ballroom as a whole stilled into a hushed silence. The orchestra quieted.

Gideon scanned the room, searching until he found the

subject of everyone's focus. Dark hair gleamed beneath flickering candlelight. The alluring Ingrid, whose odd behavior had lured him to dally at a ball, sat in poised elegance at a huge grand piano.

He could not take his gaze from the riveting woman and her exquisite expression. She was trouble. He felt the certainty of that deep within, just as he knew he would speak with her more.

After all, he had never been the kind of man to avoid danger.

Smiling with anticipation, he edged the crowd, drawing closer to the piano. He ignored the curious looks women gave him and the frowns from men who recognized the less-than-stellar cut of his clothes.

Ingrid's fingers descended upon the keys. A high note sounded, crisp and clear, jettisoning before a triad of other chords, and then they all blended together, creating a melody so light and flawless that Gideon felt the beauty of her playing to the marrow of his bones. He found himself studying the feminine planes of her features and the quirks of her mannerisms. He moved closer, slipping between silks and trousers, ignoring the odor of talcum, which women used to powder their skin.

Would Ingrid, with her flushed cheeks and slightly parted lips, smell like talcum powder? She looked as bright and clean as sunrays slicing through morning mist. His instincts insisted she'd always smell like jasmine. His gut tightened, and his jaw clenched. He should not be thinking of her so much. This was no place for a man like him. But he stayed.

For the music, he told himself.

Ingrid's enthusiasm for piano resonated. Like the ballroom audience, he was enthralled, taken aback not only by the synchrony of her song, but also by the abandon with which she played. Head back, lips parted. Gaze half-mast and unfocused. As though nothing else existed for her but the melodies flowing through the movements of her fingers. The harmonies filled him with the longing for something beautiful, something tender, something far beyond his reach.

Something forever lost to him.

Lady Ingrid Beauchamp, daughter to Lord and Lady Manning, was quite certain she could not wait for tomorrow's post to arrive. Her nerves positively itched to know if she'd be invited to interview as a teacher at the Conservatoire de Paris.

The elite school housed the venerable composer Francois-Joseph Gossec. The possibility of studying beneath his tutelage made all the years of suffering social calls, balls and the like, worthwhile. Her ultimate plan to be hired as a composer required that she mail a portfolio of the compositions she'd been working on for the past ten years to the school.

It had been over a month since she'd sent the compositions out. Now she waited.

Once the invitation to interview came, the Lord willing, she'd announce her plan to her parents. If they refused to help with costs, well, she'd saved a good deal of money herself. The trip across the channel cost a guinea alone. She'd also have to travel down to Dover and potentially need to stay at an inn until the weather permitted sailing.

How long she had prayed for this opportunity to follow her dreams, and she refused to let anything stand in her way. Least of all funding.

She played Lady Bunsworth's grand piano for as long as she dared without risking rudeness, and then she danced with the sweet and utterly boring Lord Frasier. His dull mop of hair swept across a prominent brow ridge. His conversation centered on himself, though in a self-deprecating way that she found almost amusing.

He'd do very well for Alice, she mused, for he wore the most fashionable of clothes. Hardly a crease to be seen in his starched pants, and nary a scuff on his shining Hessians. He'd tied his cravat in an unfathomable confection of knots. Indeed, her gaze kept straying to that dandified contortion. Her sister would admire such artistry.

Despite his pomp, the man danced in a thoughtful way. Not once did he step upon her toes, for which she was grateful. It had taken years to learn to dance again after the carriage accident. And while she'd finally mastered a modicum of grace, she could only dance a few sets before her hip protested.

Perhaps he exercised specific care, having heard of her weakness?

No matter the reasons for the young earl's carefulness, they finished the dance without incident. She bestowed upon him a bright smile to which he flushed and clumsily bowed, and then she threaded through the crowd to find the punch bowl.

Her throat was drier than Cook's English tarts. The room shrouded her: too tight, too warm. She fanned herself as she walked, making sure to avoid any eye contact with the guests. Lady Bunsworth's musicale had turned into quite the crush. Surely, the event had been meant to be a small affair, but the influx of people only corroborated the lady's popularity. Ingrid did not often attend social events. Besides what her father called an unnatural penchant toward snappishness, her physical limitations kept her from a good deal of rigorous activity.

Nevertheless, she had not been able to resist Lady Bunsworth's invitation to play the grand piano tonight. The newest model's keys had dipped beneath her fingertips effortlessly, the smooth ivory sensitive to the slightest pressure.

Playing had been a blissful break in an otherwise tedious night.

And she had managed to avoid her mother with great success. No doubt Mother would catch her soon enough, though. She sighed as she received a cup of punch from a maid. She sipped, trying to enjoy the pleasurable tang of lemon upon her tongue while watching dancers swing about the room.

Finding an empty space of wall to lean against, for her hip ached, she surveyed the surroundings. She caught sight of Alice speaking to a handsome blond dandy. Lord Merton. He wasn't Ingrid's type, but then again, none of them ever were. Her type spoke in notes and chords, harmonies and scales.

A few paces past Alice, their mother fit like a colorful puzzle piece into a little knot of similarly dressed ladies. Her lips moved rapidly, her perfectly coiffed hair bobbing up and down as she spoke.

Ingrid looked away. She hoped to leave for Paris in early fall, if that invitation arrived. Surely, she had saved enough of her ample pin money to afford the trip. If not, she felt her parents might assist her.

But before leaving England, perhaps she'd escape London for a time. Avoid the rest of the Season for the quiet comfort of the country. She owned a cozy little cottage bequeathed to her from a progressively minded-and music-loving great-uncle. The charming structure needed minor repairs, but was otherwise outfitted with every convenience.

Including a pleasant staff, outstanding gardens and a large conservatory that boasted an impressive pianoforte.

"Ingrid. We meet again." A full-bodied, masculine voice intruded.

Her hand tightened around her cup as she turned to face the disagreeable man who had so rudely spoken to her in the hallway earlier. His startling blue eyes sparkled like the Thames on a sunny day. He was taller than she, and broad about the shoulders. His jacket strained as though it had not been cut to the correct dimensions. His dark hair needed a trim, as well.

"Alas, I still do not know your name," she said, letting her bored expression state her lack of desire to learn it.

He chuckled, obviously ignoring her disapproval. "I see you have left the safety of the curtains."

"They are not the best hiding spot. One can hardly breathe without fear of getting caught." She sniffed, annoyed that he so easily engaged her in conversation. "How did you know I was hiding from my mother?"

"You bear a similarity in eye color. It was not a difficult guess."

"You are observant." She eyed his slightly out of style coat and clean trousers before letting her gaze rest on his face. A handsome face, no doubt used to getting its way on things. He resonated with a sort of confident air that smacked of conceit.

And then there was his impressive hair.

Dark and delightfully tousled. Most likely on purpose. Probably another fortune hunter who'd heard she was an heiress. He looked as though he'd fallen on hard times. Well, she'd been fending off the likes of men like him for seven Seasons now. He was not the first greedy hunter to be turned away, and he would not be the last.

"I shall remember not to hide behind curtains, then, if they are so suffocating," he said, continuing the conversation with a mischievous smile in his eyes. A dimple dented his right cheek. Ingrid was irritated that she noticed.

She turned her attention to the ballroom floor. The symphony started a waltz.

The man moved closer to her, bringing a whiff of fresh soap. At least he smelled clean.

"Will you dance with me, Ingrid?"

"Your conduct is atrocious." She shifted, for her hip was beginning to pain her horribly. Sharp muscle spasms rippled down her leg and she struggled not to wince. Oh, why had she left her cane at home? "I certainly will not dance with you. You don't belong here, and you know it. You are not a peer."

"Tsk, lady. Your manners leave much in the way of attraction."

"Attraction? I still don't even know your name. We should not even be conversing. It is the height of impropriety on your end." She would need to go home soon. The pain reverberated up her spine.

"My apologies." The man tipped his head, though she saw not an ounce of contrition in his eyes. "Mr. Gideon West."

"There you are." Mother swooped in just then, her smile loving and her gaze calculating. She skimmed a curious glance over Mr. West before giving him her back and focusing on Ingrid. "I've been looking all over for you. I want to introduce you to Lord Harting's second son. Wipe the frown from your face, dearest, before wrinkles etch themselves upon your skin."

Ingrid worked to smooth her features without scowling. Who cared if she developed lines? She held no hidden desire for courtship or marriage. Neither did she entertain any dreams of such. Why should she? She'd floated through her first Season without a single man catching her interest. The second Season proved even worse, though by that time she had garnered a reputation for piano playing and so passed the time in musical bliss. The third, the same.

Season after Season, and she still had not one single intention of fostering any kind of courtship. Especially now with her plans to go to Paris.

And a husband, after all, deserved children.

Ingrid shifted a tad to the right, just enough to block Mr. West from her view and relieve pressure from her hip. "Is Lord Harting's son looking for a wife?"

"They all are, dearest. But he seems as though he might also be looking for love."

"You are incorrigible."

"I want you as happy as your father and I have been."

Ingrid leaned into the side hug her mother offered, knowing it was true. But love didn't interest her. Music did, and her parents refused to understand that. "I need to go home, Mother."

"Are you in pain?" Concern knit her mother's brow. "Did you forget your cane?"

"Yes and yes."

"Very well." Her mother produced a folded sheet of paper from her reticule. "This is a list your father and I wrote up earlier this evening. Several *very* eligible men are on it. Study it, please." She nodded in a knowing way, her smile hopeful.

Ingrid took the paper, tamping down impatience. "I'll take my maid and head home, then send the carriage back for you, Father and Alice."

"Perfect. Oh, I see Lady Wells. I must speak with her regarding our poetry convention. Feel better, darling." Mother whisked an airy kiss near her cheek and then disappeared into the crowd.

"Lovely lady," came Mr. West's husky voice.

"She certainly is." Ingrid opened the paper, scanning the names. Mr. West leaned near, and she snatched the paper out of his line of view. "You truly have zero refinement."

He shrugged, deep, rumbling laughter tumbling out of him. "I'm not the type to need refinement. Now, that list, it's for eligible men?"

She huffed out a breath, glaring at him. "I suppose you find it funny to have others planning your future. Oh, wait, you wouldn't know about such an intrusion. Because you're a man."

"I am a man. Thank you for noticing." He winked at her, atrocious flirt that he was. "I'm a Bow Street Runner and you're right. I create my own future."

"It's certainly clear that you listen to no one." She pressed her lips together, trying to ignore the streaks of pain radiating from her hip. "And a runner? How very interesting."

"Not so much. I encounter the basest elements of human nature. My job tends to dampen one's belief in the goodness of humanity."

She'd heard, of course, of the runners, but from her understanding, they were not always men of stellar reputation. "What exactly do you do?"

"Investigations. Policing. I'm here tonight due to business." The corners of his eyes crinkled. "But I stayed to dance with you."

She waved off the silly comment as a different kind of interest flared. Was there more to this uncouth commoner than she had presumed? An idea percolated. Had Providence brought this stranger to her for a reason? She silently thanked God as her idea grew more clear. Her body might be weak but her will had never been stronger. She would play piano in Paris. Without a husband.

"Mr. West." She flashed him a bright smile that made his eyes widen. "I have a proposition for you."

"That sounds on the verge of inappropriate, Ingrid."

"You may call me Lady Ingrid Beauchamp." She gave him a firm look. "I want to hire you."

His dark brows rose. "For?"

She dangled the list in front of him. "I am in a marital bind, if you will. My parents believe these men to be potential candidates for marriage. My parents are fanciful people, though. They are choosing men based not on their merit, financials, or title, but on my ability to fall in love with them."

He plucked the list from her and scanned over the names. "I fail to understand what my job in this is."

"What do you see on there?"

He frowned, the skin of his forehead puckering into three wavy lines. "Names. Though I'd recommend removing Mr. Scotto. He's been known to skulk about the seedier sides of London. Not husband material."

Satisfaction swooped through Ingrid. She held out her hand for the paper, and he placed it in hers, his thumb skimming the surface of her glove. It was such a strange little touch but it elicited a not altogether unpleasant nervousness. She brought the paper back to herself.

"Your card, sir. I shall be calling on you to discuss services as soon as possible."

"Now, wait one minute." He stepped back, taking a full look at her, his thumbs hooked into the pockets of his rather shabby coat. "Women of your station don't hire runners."

"Men of your station do not sneak into balls and attempt to dance with unmarried ladies," she countered. "We are both out of our elements, and we are both determined to navigate our own futures."

"You know nothing about me."

"I know that you are bold and that you do not care what people think."

He eyed her, the dimple noticeably absent. "What do you want from me?"

"Simply to do what your profession calls for. Investigate these men and find the flaw in each and every one."

His gaze darted around her, to the people dancing, all unconcerned over their long conversation. A benefit of being in her seventh Season and somewhat plain. No one usually noticed to whom she spoke. Her heart thumped in her chest as he inspected the room. Surely, he wouldn't turn her down. This was a brilliant idea, a veritable answer to years of prayer. If she proved no suitable candidate graced the list, she could most assuredly be in Paris by the fall.

There were other runners, certainly, but Mr. Gideon West impressed her. Even his annoying use of charm to get his way somehow endeared him to her. She had the feeling he would do the job, and do it well.

Well enough that she could follow her dreams. *At last.*

He took too long to answer, though. His study of the room irritated her. What could he possibly be searching for?

"I shall pay you handsomely," she blurted, panic loosening her tongue.

His brow lifted. He reached out, palm up. A very nice hand, she couldn't help but notice. Clean nails. Strong fingers. Calluses. This was no dandy gentleman.

"Give me the paper," he said. "I'm hired."

Chapter Two

Persistence took one quite far in life.

Even far enough to disqualify an entire list of potential suitors. Satisfaction at how last night had turned out swelled through Ingrid, almost making her forget how much her body hurt. She shifted on her feet, using her cane to balance.

Her little sister had talked her into shopping. She quite regretted the trip already.

She studied the street and, seeing a break in traffic, used her cane to navigate a crossing. On her left a large, horrifyingly unkempt dog yipped and darted into the road. The poor thing barely missed getting run over by a carriage. Staring in horror, Ingrid froze.

A little boy chased the mutt, his bright red hair standing out against the sooty smudges on his cheeks. The dog bounded over to Ingrid, sniffing at her toes, his filthy fur rubbing up against her skirts. The boy reached her, grabbing the pup by the scruff of the neck.

"Pardon, m'lady," he said in a high voice. His thick accent indicated he'd been raised in the East End. Cockney.

Ingrid placed her palm against her heart, which pumped

hard in uneven, frightened beats. "You should never run out in the streets. A carriage could run you over."

He flashed her a toothless smile. "I be fast."

"Not faster than a carriage." She beckoned him to the side of the street and surprisingly, the bright-eyed urchin dragged the pup over to her. "What is your name?"

"Petey. Do ye have change to spare for a poor, defenseless mite as myself?" Big brown eyes begged at her. The dog continued sniffing her feet, as though sensing she carried a purse that might buy him sausages. Petey let go of him, but the pet sat at his heels.

"When I was a young girl, a boy ran into the road," she said, ignoring his question.

"Did 'e die?" Petey held out his hand, expecting coin.

"No, but my carriage tipped, and I was hurt very badly. I have a limp now." And the inner trauma had been worse, though she tried very hard to never think of *that*. "You may be fast, but your actions could harm someone else. Promise me you will not run out into the road anymore."

He cocked his head. "But what if Sir Beasley runs on? I can't let 'im be trampled."

A good point. She opened her purse and removed some coin. "Buy him a collar and a leash. Then you will both be safe. Use the extra for food." It would be better to buy the items herself, but Alice waited. Besides, this little boy didn't look as though he lacked for meals. His tummy strained against the ragged shirt he wore. And his shoes looked properly fitted. "Do you have a family?"

He grinned up at her, swiped the money from her palm and disappeared into the crowded sidewalks. Sir Beasley nipped at his heels.

An unexpected pang of longing shot through Ingrid. She did not like to remember her accident. It hadn't affected her ability to play piano, and music made her happy.

There was no use dwelling on what might have been if she hadn't been so gravely injured that day. A life lived in regret was no life at all.

And the accident had inspired a faith that had not existed before. Such a change could never be regretted.

Her sister marched over. "I cannot believe you gave that little thief money."

"He's just a little boy."

"A boy with sticky fingers, no doubt." Alice sniffed. "And look at your skirts. Jane will have a fit removing those stains. The road is clear now."

"I'm going." Ingrid crossed the street, shading her face with her parasol. The road was indeed clear, but she remained shaken. That horrible day years ago when the family carriage had flipped over... Almost as a response to the memory, the muscles in her thigh crimped, causing her to lose her footing. Her favorite cane, made of rosewood, helped her quickly rebalance. With great care, she finished crossing the street.

Most of the time her shoes, which held specially crafted inserts, allowed her to walk without a noticeable limp, and sometimes even dance. But every so often she moved the wrong way, as she had yesterday, and it could be weeks before the discomfort eased.

If she wasn't supremely cautious, she might even fall.

She often brought her cane when she went out. It came in handy.

She usually didn't care to be walking about anyhow. She belonged on a piano bench. Sitting for hours and hours, absorbing music. Reveling in harmonies.

Alice fluttered beside her, a beatific smile upon her face. "Wasn't last night ever so lovely? I danced every set, Ingrid. Every single one. I could not imagine a more perfect way to start the Season. And when you played, why, every eye was upon you. I daresay the room did not breathe during your song."

"That is quite a fanciful sentiment, even for you." But Ingrid could not restrain her own happy sigh as they entered a popular modiste shop. How lovely those piano keys had felt beneath her fingers, each perfect note slipping into melodious sound. And how wonderful that Alice had invited her shopping. Their relationship had improved ever so much in recent years. "Any new interests?"

Alice fingered a bolt of richly hued material. Her dark locks, as black as Ingrid's, fanned across her shoulders. "Sir Everett is rather handsome and cultured. He's been around the world, you see. He completed a tour and served our country. And there's some money to him as well."

"Hasn't he called on you several times?" Ingrid shifted slightly, hoping to ease the ever-present ache.

"Yes, and we danced two sets last night. I expect a proposal soon. Being in love is divine."

"Love is not for me," Ingrid said. But her sister's words, said in a lilting way, brought a flush to Ingrid's throat, for immediately Mr. West's teasing smile, aquiline nose and overly long hair flashed into memory.

"I daresay you'd marry a piano if you could."

"I would certainly never tire of the piano. Every day would hold the promise of a new song to enjoy, and not the monotonous melody most men sing."

"What a dreary outlook. Why, I want to fall in love and live forever on the wings of joy that love brings."

"Have you been reading Lord Byron's poetry again?"

Alice wandered to the next bolt of cloth. "And if I have?"

"Does Mother know?"

She rolled her eyes. "She is the one who bought the book for me. All our parents want is for you to be in love, sister dearest. To experience what they have enjoyed. Not everyone in the *ton* can say they have known love. It is a gift."

"A gift you can keep, sister sweet. I am called to other pursuits. A husband has no part in my plans." Ingrid played a simple Bach against the bodice of her dress. She wanted to leave London so very badly. To escape a world she would never fit within.

Gideon crumpled the missive he'd just received and threw it into the fire. His father, if the man could be called that, just wouldn't accept Gideon's refusal to see him. This had been the third time the man reached out. But Gideon wanted nothing to do with the immoral earl who'd abandoned his mistress and his son years ago.

Lips flattening, Gideon stood and stretched. He had spent the morning wrapping up an investigation for a local constable. Then he'd gone food shopping. The street urchins who slept at his lodging were like feral cats who showed up for hot meals and little else.

He looked around his rectangle of rooms, noting the blankets and pillows strewn in odd places. There were two rooms on the bottom floor, and one upstairs. They were tiny, barely big enough to store a table, oven and beds. Soon, he'd run out of space, but he couldn't turn a child away.

The tiny townhome located near Bow Street was not made for a large family, or even a small one with servants. It was just a box of rooms next to other boxes of rooms, clogging the city streets in one long, line of brick buildings.

"You be fine, Mr. Gideon?" Sarah peered up at him from her place on a cot near the wall. She hadn't been feeling well lately and he'd convinced her to stay home and rest. The orphans were an untamed lot: they ran around London, doing what they wanted, and though he tried to give them a safe haven, he knew the streets as well as they did. London was no place for an orphan.

He needed to get them away from here.

Swiping his hand through his hair, he offered the little girl an affirming smile. "All's well. Just a long day at work. What say I play with Gus for a bit?"

She nodded eagerly, her blond curls matted and dirty. Gideon hated that he could not care for the children better. The burden weighed as heavy as a boulder on his shoulders. He wanted more for them than what he experienced in childhood. If he could get them to the country, out of London, their chances of growing to adulthood were so much better.

He picked up Gus, the feel of his sturdy violin soothing the torment within. He may not be a musician in the same category as Ingrid, but he did find peace in song. As he played for Sarah, his mind went back to the lady. What was it he found so attractive about her? So engaging? Her raven hair? Her almost-acetic personality? There was a focus to her gaze, as though she did not care to play the games of her society, as though she did not play any games at all. Perhaps due to the pain she seemed to be in? He had caught only a little of the conversation with her mother, but it seemed to have something to do with her hip. Even if the lady had an injury of sorts, he did not think she was one to flirt, though he had enjoyed flirting with her immensely. Perhaps he would teach her the art of flirtation.

The thought drew him up short.

He would *not* teach her anything. She was of a different world. She lived a life that he would never be comfortable living.

He'd stay away from her.

After taking her money, of course. Falling in love, or even into attraction, was foolish. Look at his mother. So in love with a man that she threw away her reputation to be his mistress. And then when she'd become pregnant, the earl dismissed her. They'd moved to the slums, and she had died when Gideon was ten.

Died still in love with the man who'd abandoned them. Still believing he'd show up to rescue them.

Of course he hadn't. No one had, not even the God his mother began to pray to toward the end of her days.

Gideon frowned, drawing the bow sharply against the strings, letting his anger translate into music. Sarah watched, eyes wide, smiling.

He finished, the strings quivering from the bow's sudden departure.

"That was lovely. Like a storm," said Sarah.

"Thank you." He set the violin in its stand. Sarah burrowed under her covers, as if hiding. He didn't blame her. Orphans went missing so often, stolen for workhouses and worse.

He slept deeply that night. The next day he met a fellow runner, Michael, and together they tracked down a suspect who'd stolen from a local merchant. The afternoon found Gideon swiping his sweaty, bloodstained hands against the towel Michael gave him. The blood had dried, though, and his hands remained soiled. His muscles quivered with exertion and his lungs still burned after the chase their criminal prey had given them through the streets of London.

But they'd caught the man, cornering him in an alley. Trotted him over to the constabulary, and now he was safely off to Newgate. The man's dagger had done some damage, though more to the wielder than anyone else.

"I've never seen someone dodge a knife the way you did." Michael's tone held respect.

"Been dodging blades since I was a naughty lad." Gideon grinned. "Now I'm on the right side of the law."

"It may be the right side, but it's definitely not the lucrative side." Michael frowned down at the payment in his hand.

"Pays the rent." Gideon walked to Michael's dresser and dipped his hands in the warm water of the washbasin. His friend rented rooms not far from Bow Street, and conveniently close to the prison. After getting the rest of the blood off his fingers, he wiped them on a clean towel. "Now I go home and rest. Tomorrow we hopefully see less action."

Michael smirked. "I'm sleuthing for Lord Ludwig. He thinks his cook might be nabbing extra food, and mayhap a wine bottle or two."

"Peerage problems," said Gideon, and both men laughed.

By the time Gideon was almost home, his pulse had slowed and he'd had some time to think about the very interesting Ingrid Beauchamp. The lady looked like your normal society flower: proper, well-dressed and sedate.

But she was far from that. She actually wanted to hire him to discredit potential suitors. *Before* she'd even met them. He shook his head, incredulous at the idea, and yet admiring her for it.

He supposed he should start his investigations for her soon. But not until he received payment. He was too busy to work for nothing.

He spotted his lodgings ahead. He was thankful to have a place so near Bow Street. The long line of well-kept buildings posed like a walled sentry over the narrow street. Good, working class families lived here, and crime had been kept to a minimum. The rent, however, had been steadily increasing in the ten years he'd lived here, and it was getting harder to both make ends meet and feed the ragamuffins who showed up at his door.

They were like wild creatures. Different children at different times. None of them wanted to settle down in one place, with the exception of Sarah, and that was only because she didn't feel well at the moment. He trudged toward his door, contemplating how he could possibly get them to stay for more than a safe night's sleep.

The sound of a pianoforte reached his ears as he jiggled his key in the lock. But the door was unlocked. An orphan must have entered using the secret key he left tucked into a hole in the wall.

The orphans were smart, with a strong sense of survival. As far as he could tell, no one knew about the key's hiding place but those they deemed safe enough. Thus, his home had remained relatively protected from thieves and saboteurs.

He put away his own key and pushed the door open. He had told Sarah to stay put, but would the girl listen to him? She had only trusted him enough to tell him her name a fortnight ago.

The room looked the same as when he had left at dawn, with one exception. He smelled the sweet scent of perfume. He went all the way in and shut the door behind him.

"Mr. Gideon!" Sarah popped out from the covers on her cot.

"I say, she's a good 'un." Petey's voice pulled Gideon's attention to where he sat next to the pianoforte. And to Ingrid, who perched on the bench, beaming. There was no other word for the self-satisfaction upon her face. Her dress looked like the sea today, and it billowed over the bench in silky green folds of lace and fabric. A maid sat on a chair in the corner of the room, knitting, while a little girl with eyes the color of ebony sat at her feet.

Word of mouth brought children to his door, though the same child rarely came more than once.

A new mouth to feed; another soul to worry over.

The sick king and his regent certainly didn't care, and the wealthy only did so much for the defenseless.

The day crashed down on him, and fatigue subdued his smile. He walked to the little chair near the furnace and sat. "You let yourself in?"

Ingrid swiveled awkwardly on the piano bench to face him. "Sarah let me in."

"Mr. Gideon, she said she wasn't going to leave until you answered the door. So's I told 'er you wasn't 'ere."

Ingrid's generous mouth stretched upward. He rather liked that feature of hers. "I noticed Sarah's matted hair and I thought maybe I could comb it for her."

"Then I came back and I knew 'er," put in Petey.

"You know Lady Ingrid?"

"Oh, so now you use my proper name." Her eyes crinkled in an attractive way.

"Aye, she gave me money the other day."

"A carriage almost ran him over," she said. "He had Sir Beasley with him and asked for money. I had extra coins."

The mutt's head popped up, and his tongue lolled.

Gideon rested his elbows on his knees. "Why are you here?"

"Might I speak with you quietly?" Ingrid rose from her seat, coming toward him with a determined stride that dipped strangely as she walked. A limp, he realized, well disguised. Perhaps the source of her hip pain at the ball?

"I suppose." It was a tad overwhelming to have this beautiful woman in his house.

"I shall increase your payment if you will prioritize my case. I assume you still have the list." She cast a suspicious look about the tiny, disorganized room.

"Yes," he said curtly.

"Excellent. I am here with part of your money. I really must disqualify these men before I leave."

"Leave?"

"Oh, I do not think I told you. I plan to go to Paris to teach piano. I am awaiting an audition invitation."

He rubbed his neck. "You begin to make sense."

"Of course I do." Smugness entered her tone. She pulled out a bag of coin and tossed it to him. He caught it with a startled *oomph*. "There is extra in there. I want an update at least every other day. A missive shall do. Questions?"

He was too tired to think of any. "Anyone ever tell you no?"

"Not that I recall. Jane," she called, summoning her maid. "We are taking our leave."

"No, no." Petey came running over, voice pleading. "We want you to play more."

Gideon saw the hesitation on her face, and it warmed him. All business but then turned to putty by a child. He completely understood.

"Please." He gestured to the piano. "If I cannot get a dance out of you, perhaps I may obtain a song."

"Always flirting," she said, but she did not sound displeased.

The children surrounded her, chanting the word *please*. The new little girl looked to be about the age of Petey. She went to the pianoforte and began plucking keys. "Can you teach me?" she asked.

Ingrid's dusky violet eyes widened, obviously surprised. "I have never thought of teaching small children." She turned to Gideon, contemplative. He wasn't sure he liked that look on her face. He folded his arms across his chest.

"How many children do you house?" she asked.

"Whoever shows up."

"Really?" She walked to the pianoforte and carefully

sat. Her fingers, long and slender, splayed across the keys. "I often get bored of silly parties and teas. Perhaps helping children learn music would fill some of my days."

An uncomfortable sensation began spreading across his chest. This woman, in his house, again? There was something very homey about how she sat in her spot, three little children clustered around her, begging her to play. If their childhood resembled his, there had been no music but what spilled out from bawdy houses into the streets.

They looked at him then: Sarah, with circles beneath her eyes and hope on her face. Petey grinning his gap-toothed smile. And the new child, a wisp of a girl whose face told stories that one could not read without tears.

"I can teach them for free." Ingrid met his gaze. "Your pianoforte needs more playing."

He wanted to say no. Because the feeling he'd had the first time he saw her persisted. She was still trouble. A raven-haired, violet-eyed, silken-skirted mass of trouble. The more she inserted herself into his life, the more trouble he felt coming. It seemed as his entire life had been spent courting trouble.

But… He wasn't one to back down. Not from trouble. Not from challenge.

Not from a woman whose purse strings held the future of these children.

"For how long?" he asked, and the children cheered.

Chapter Three

Patience had never been Ingrid's strong suit.

After sifting through the mail on Father's desk one final time, she huffed with annoyance and left the office. Still no invitation from the conservatoire, and no missive from Mr. West, either. It had been two days since she'd promised his little sprites that she'd teach them music. She'd expected some sort of communication from Mr. West since then.

And yet…nothing.

Surely, he was not so enmeshed with his life that he could not even update her with the progress he'd made on her case. They also needed to set a time for the children's piano lessons. Perhaps the man was simply too busy to be bothered.

She frowned and slowly made her way to the parlor, to her beloved piano. Shouldn't he at least keep in touch? He was, after all, an employee. Short-term. She could not afford him for long, not if she wanted to have enough money to pay for niceties when she stayed in Paris.

The invitation to audition would arrive soon. There were, of course, other places to study. They would perhaps accept a woman of superior talent. But did she qualify?

Her mind somersaulted with too many thoughts.

Feeling a scowl tugging at her face, Ingrid went to the drawing room. Her mother sat on the couch, sewing. The scent of her perfume filled the room with a comfort that revived childhood sentiments.

"Wrinkles, darling. Wrinkles." Mother tilted her head, hardly looking up from her pile of cloths.

"What are you working on?" Ingrid asked as she settled herself at the piano. What to play? Something violent, perhaps, to release the pent-up irritation crawling beneath her skin.

"I've been helping with The Society for the Friends of Underprivileged Children," her mother replied. "We are providing clothing for the poor dears. It is heartbreaking. One wishes one could do more."

"Very practical," murmured Ingrid, thinking of Petey's tattered clothes. How had he even come to stay with Mr. West? It was an odd situation, to be sure. Shaking her head as if it could remove the curiosity distracting her thoughts, she thumbed through her music books, and stopped at a lively Bach concerto. As she played, her fingers warmed up, gliding across the keys, and she wiped all musings away and simply felt the music.

She played several more pieces and would have kept going had their butler not entered the room with a vigorous throat clear. She stopped playing, the last trill of B minor reverberating through her in a pleasurable wave.

Coggins waited patiently. He knew she did not like being rushed after finishing a piece. It was like taking the final bite of a French confection. One must enjoy the sweet aftertaste as much as the consumption. At last, she beckoned him over, realizing her mother had left the room at some point and she was alone.

She had not even noticed, so consumed in her music had she been.

"My lady Ingrid, a missive for you." Coggins held out a paper.

"Thank you." She took it slowly, not wanting to appear too eager, and gave him a dismissive nod. Once he'd gone, she scanned the contents.

Mr. West requested her presence on the morrow after teatime. Smiling, she tucked the note into her pocket. Excellent. She must find her maid and hasten to his home today to tune his pianoforte. The children could not learn if the pianoforte was not in tip-top shape.

Gathering her skirts, she called for Jane.

By the time they arrived at Mr. West's threadbare rooms, Ingrid could hardly contain her enthusiasm. Instead of a boring afternoon listening to gossip and prattle, tomorrow she would be plunking out chords with enthusiastic souls.

Certainly a better way to pass her time.

She instructed their carriage driver to come back in an hour.

"My lady, do you think this is wise?" Jane looked in a furtive fashion to her right and then to her left.

"We are near Bow Street. Of course it is safe. I also have my cane." Ingrid twirled it through the air in a relaxed fashion. "I shall stab anyone in the eye who dares accost us."

"But what of your reputation?"

"That is why I have you."

Jane nodded, though Ingrid did not think she had convinced the timid servant.

"Come now. We shall ascertain the condition of the pianoforte. I will need your skills."

A smile edged Jane's pretty features. Feeling triumphant already, Ingrid marched as well as she was able to Mr. West's door and rapped on it with short, sharp clacks.

The door opened quickly enough, but only a crack.

"Who is it?" The gravelly voice sounded like Mr. West, but Ingrid really couldn't be certain.

"It is I, Lady Ingrid Beauchamp."

"Ingrid." The voice did not sound happy.

"Lady Ingrid," she corrected him crisply. "We are here to service the pianoforte."

The door swung wide open, and Ingrid stepped back as Mr. West came into view. Behind her, Jane let out a little squeak. His hair lay rumpled in cacophonic curls, dark and thick. A shadow covered his chin and traveled up his impressive cheekbones. Worst of all, the man wore only breeches and a loose, cambric shirt.

And he was barefoot.

And there was dark hair marching across the tops of his feet.

Of all the shocking things! A hot blush burned Ingrid's face as her eyes quickly averted from his form. She did not think she had ever seen a man's bared feet before. They certainly did not look like hers.

"Could you not dress before you opened that door?" The words stumbled from her stiff lips. She kept her eyes fastened to a nasty spot to the right of his door frame. Dirt? Old food?

"I haven't slept in more than twenty-four hours. So no. What do you want?"

She made a delicate throat clear, unsure where to place her gaze. "We must ascertain the condition of your piano. It was a bit off-key the other day, and that must be remedied."

He made a noise that almost sounded like a laugh. She still couldn't bring herself to look at him.

"This visit edges on inappropriate, don't you think?" Now his tone held tease, and no doubt his ridiculous dimple made a debut.

"Do not be silly," she said in a firm tone. "Go and get dressed. We've work to do."

She gave herself leave to take the tiniest, most minuscule peek at Mr. West. She hoped to get a look at his toes again, just because they were so very different than anything she'd expected, but he'd moved behind his door.

Bother it all.

She buried the traitorous disappointment spiraling through her. It was for the best that he respected propriety. Feeling a bit more stout now that she knew he'd covered himself, albeit with a door, she faced him. Yes, his dimple cut a groove into his cheek, and his eyes flirted.

His arm snuck out and he leaned against the door frame, the door itself still tucked between him and her.

"You're used to giving orders," he said. "I like it."

"Do not try your playful little smile on me. I'm not susceptible to men like you." For good measure, she swept a contemptuous look over him. "You are wasting your superficial charm. I am, however, susceptible to those children. They have a need for music in their lives, and I find that I am the perfect person to fulfill that need."

Mr. West shook his head, his blue eyes lively despite the dark shadows beneath. "Bossy and confident. Not the most complementary duo."

Ingrid forced her teeth to stop clenching and slapped a hand onto her hip. "You're wasting my time."

He laughed then, a deep and melodic sound that trickled through her in much the same way a perfect high note excited her senses. She swallowed hard, wondering at the feeling his laugh engendered, the visceral pleasure it induced.

"Lady, all you have is time. What do you people do all day? Shop? Gossip? Dance?" Censure gilded his amusement.

"I'll have you know that my mother spent her morning sewing clothing for children in need."

"While drinking her expensive tea, and sitting in her clean and comfortable drawing room, no doubt."

Ingrid shifted on her feet, suddenly uncomfortable. He was not wrong. "If you have such a concern with people who have money, then why work with us? Surely, you have better things to do with your time, as it is so much better spent than mine."

Once again, she eyed his clothes, knowing she spoke caustically, but caring little. The man had prodded her too far.

"I'll let you explain to your children why there will be no piano lessons," she continued. "Let them know you've a bitter boulder residing upon your shoulder."

"Melodrama, Lady Ingrid? I'd think you'd find that beneath you."

"Please, dress yourself and let us in to look at the piano."

"Very well. This will not bode well for your reputation."

"No one saw us and Jane shall not speak of it." She glanced at her maid, who gave her a reassuring nod. "We are progressive women."

He released what sounded near a snort. "Give me ten minutes."

Gideon crossed his arms, watching with a great deal of suspicion as Ingrid and her lady's maid sauntered into his lodgings. They brought immediately the perfume of flowery blooms that accompanied women of upper classes.

Ingrid did not even spare him a glance but marched in her curious gait to the pianoforte. "Jane, just look at this." Her fingertip tapped the top of his piano, then she lifted it and stared as though it had grown mold. "Does this man never clean?"

Jane, to be fair, shot him a sympathetic look.

"This man," he drawled, "works for a living. Unlike some people, I can't afford to hire a housekeeper"

Ingrid grimaced as though she had not thought of such a thing. She said nothing more on the matter but proceeded to examine parts of the piano he had not even known existed. Her maid appeared equally involved.

Their whispered exclamations irritated him. Or perhaps it was the lack of sleep. Either way, he rubbed the back of his neck and watched for several long moments before picking his way over to the small settee he owned. Sinking down, exhaustion rushed through every part of him. He had worked all night tracking a swindler.

He could nap now. The backs of his eyelids burned, gritty with tiredness. He had just drifted off to sleep when a loud gong burst through the haze of dreams cloaking him. He bolted up, his hand automatically reaching for the dagger stowed in a strap at his ankle.

The women muttered to themselves, tinkering with something inside the body of the piano. What a strange lot: Ingrid in her fancy dress, her dark hair pulled back into a regal chignon, and the maid, a pretty girl with sharp eyes who wielded tools with determined movements that bespoke knowledge.

He shook his head again, trying to clear the fog. He had planned to sleep today. Already, Ingrid was interfering in his life. He never should have accepted this position.

A loud knock at the front door interrupted his musings.

He got up and went to the door. To be cautious, he shouted, "Who is it?"

"Your rent is past due."

The landlord. Frowning, Gideon opened the door a crack. It wouldn't do for the nosy landlord to see two women inside. He'd never believe the innocence of the situation.

"What can I do for you, Mr. Crabtree?"

The man scrunched his mustache, his eyes beady behind thick-rimmed glasses. "Rent was due last week."

Gideon swallowed the irritation that rose within. He had the money, barely. If he used some of the coin Ingrid had already paid him. "Give me a moment." He shut the door in his landlord's face, gently, of course, and then turned to survey the women.

The maid had taken a seat, her face respectfully impassive. Ingrid was another matter. Her eyes burned bright and curious and she leaned forward on her cane, watching. One brow arched in a fine, aristocratic sweep.

If Gideon had been irritated before, he was doubly so now. Everything within yearned to sweep the imperious, beautiful lady out his door and never see her again. But he found himself in a bind, and she had swooped in at a most opportune time.

"Aren't you happy now that I've money to hire you?" A magnificent smugness pasted itself to her face.

A random urge to kiss that wide and smirky mouth dared tickle his thoughts, but he pushed the impulse away.

Ignoring the smile she gave him, a strange upturn to her lips that he hadn't seen often thus far, he trudged to the washbasin at the far end of the room. Dirty and empty. He'd have to fix that later. Sighing, he bent and reached behind it, his arm snug between the basin and the wall. It didn't take long for his fingers to hook the small burlap bag containing the bulk of his savings.

After the women left, he'd find another hiding spot.

The door shook again, his landlord's fists leaving a pounding echo. He snagged the bag and pulled it out. Darting a glance at the women, he noticed the maid's gaze averted but Ingrid pinned him with a knowing look.

He loped to the door. He dug into the bag, pulled out the rent he owed and opened the door a sliver.

"Here." He thrust the payment through the crack.

Mr. Crabtree sniffed, snatching the money from Gideon's hand. "And take this." He stuffed a paper into Gideon's palm.

"What's this?"

"Eviction notice." The brows on Mr. Crabtree's face knit together for the briefest moment, distracting Gideon from the sudden pit widening in his stomach. "I hate to do it. You've been a good tenant, but those kids of yours caused a ruckus the other day while you were out."

Gideon's displeasure deepened. Forcing an impassive expression, he leaned against the door frame. "What did they do?"

"Stole food. Broke pottery. I didn't get a good look, but one for certain had hair like carrot sticks."

Petey.

Firming his jaw, Gideon gave his landlord a hard stare. "There's nothing I can do to stay? I've been here for years."

"I know, West, I know." His landlord scratched his whiskers with a sorrowful air. "I'm right sorry but there's another couple looking to rent for a higher price, and this is a nice property for the area."

"How much time?" asked Gideon, his tired brain whirling.

"I can give you eight weeks. Maybe nine."

Gideon nodded and shut the door. He turned to face the women, who stood like quiet sentries by the broken piano. "Now I've really no choice but to work for you."

Ingrid stepped forward. "Was that in question?"

He gave her a rueful smile. "I had entertained thoughts of quitting should it become too irritating."

"Irritating?" Her brow rose. "I assure you, you shall not regret my case, Mr. West."

And though she was beautiful in her quietly direct way, and though she made his lodgings smell like a garden, he had the distinct impression that he would indeed regret working for the persistent lady.

Chapter Four

Mr. West clearly regretted their agreement.

Three separate piano lessons in the past week, and Ingrid still had not heard from him. When she'd arrived that very first day to give lessons, a trio of children awaited her. The children had been present, but not Mr. West.

For this fourth lesson, only one child awaited Ingrid. With a great deal of satisfaction, she surveyed the little girl who sat beside her on the piano bench, playing a simple tune. Jane sat on a chair knitting a baby blanket. She'd told Ingrid that her mother was pregnant again with the eighth child in the family.

Anna plunked through the song one more time and then beamed a bright smile at Ingrid. "I played it well, didn't I?"

"Yes, indeed you did." Ingrid touched the girl's hair, the texture far different than her own. Springy and black, the curls softly haloed her face. Today she smiled, for she had played her very first melody. A popular tune called "Mr. Beveridge's Maggot."

Warmth suffused Ingrid. At least Anna had come. It seemed the other children enjoyed listening rather than actually playing.

"I've brought treats," Ingrid said, leaving the piano bench for the basket she'd set on a small table near the stove.

"Oh, I lo'e treats." Anna popped up and trailed after Ingrid.

"You must tell the others that in order to have some, they will have to be here for lessons. Three o'clock on Wednesdays, Thursdays and Fridays. Is that clear?"

"Yes." Anna's nimble fingers swiped a tart from the basket.

The front door jolted open, letting in a bright swath of sunlight and a masculine silhouette.

"Why, Mr. West. Just the man I wanted to see."

"You're not the first woman to tell me that." He winked, looking so adorably handsome that Ingrid frowned.

"I haven't time for your nonsense," she said in a brisk tone. "Your method of sending a note and then not being here when I arrive has been most irritating."

"Are you here to play for children or for me? I am working, my lady, if you will recall."

"We have a deal and you have not been keeping to your side of it."

One of his brows rose, and with aplomb. She truly did not know how he managed to look offended and amused at the same time. "A most grave accusation, and yet unfounded. I have, amidst my other responsibilities, put out inquiries."

She studied him, not quite believing him, but then gestured to Anna.

"Anna has a natural ear for tune. Show Mr. West what you have learned."

The little girl brushed crumbs off her hands and then settled back at the pianoforte.

"This is three lessons' worth," Ingrid added, listening as Anna launched into her tune. The girl played flawlessly. With time, she could have a true skill.

Anna finished and then darting up, grabbed another tart before scooting out the front door.

How very different these children seemed from those in her own youth. Wild and ill-mannered, yet still retaining the charming innocence and generosity native to all children.

"Is she the only one who came?" Mr. West moved farther into the room, positioned in such a way that his blue eyes seemed to glow like her mother's sapphires beneath sunlight.

"There were more last week," answered Ingrid, feeling unaccountably defensive. Not only that, but she felt suddenly very aware of Mr. West. His tall stature, his broad shoulders and that flirtatious smile that always seemed to be bandying about his lips.

Firming her shoulders, she gestured to the table. "I brought treats for the children, whenever they deign to arrive. I also found clothing that may fit some of them. Petey seems in need of new shirts."

Gideon tilted his head. "That's thoughtful of you."

"Yes, well, the children have an unbathed smell and it is difficult to concentrate on their lesson when there are holes in their apparel." She crossed her arms, lifting her chin. "Where are their parents?"

Gideon's mouth lost its smile. Ingrid swallowed, meeting the detective's suddenly stern eyes with an unwavering expression.

"Their parents?" He laughed, but it sounded coarse and without mirth. "Lady, these are street urchins. Most of them named themselves, or they go by whatever name the first adult they remember called them."

"Thank you for the clothes," he said in a more gentle tone, "but perhaps next time it's best to leave your snobbery at the door." He bent toward her, too close for comfort, and she cast a panicked gaze at Jane and the manservant they'd brought for protection, but they did as all good servants do and pretended not to see a thing.

Heart skipping in an unnatural way, she met his eyes. "You're welcome." Her voice came out smaller than expected, a peculiar annoyance as she no doubt sounded dutibly chastened.

A little sigh escaped without permission. "I had great hopes more children would want to play."

"I commend your heart, Lady Ingrid, but these children, they're used to doing whatever they want. You'll not be able to rein them in with a spot of music."

She nodded, feeling a great well of disappointment caving her insides. "I can well understand, which is why we shall move on from those important matters to other important ones. Namely, when will you finish discrediting my mother's list of suitors?"

"Soon. But before you leave, I have a favor to ask of you."

Gideon suppressed a smile as he took in the lady's disappointment. The children had told him at different, individual times how much they enjoyed her company.

He had begun working on her list of suitors. They needed culling, certainly, and it amused him that he'd never heard of a woman so bent on ridding herself of suitors rather than obtaining them.

He'd been tempted to attend the piano lessons, but the fact of the matter was that this lady had kissable lips and a tender heart.

Best he stayed away.

The future did not include any woman, but especially one of the peerage. The very idea of a lady of the *ton* consorting with a man of the working class was untenable. They lived in different worlds.

He'd come home specifically today, however, in order to ask her help.

"A favor?" she asked now.

"I'm assisting a nearby parsonage to raise funds for orphans. I'd like you to play for the attendees."

"Oh." Her wide mouth pursed into a pretty pucker.

Once again, Gideon's traitorous brain shot straight to kissing. He averted his eyes before the two servants caught on to his less than gentlemanly thoughts. He had no intention of causing harm to Ingrid's reputation.

She eyed him, her shoulders impossibly straight. "Very well. I am not averse to performing charitable deeds. I shall play, though it is a bit unorthodox," she said at last. "When is this to happen?"

"In two days." He paused. "There is something else."

"More? I know you've no respect for my time, being a lady of leisure and all that, but I do assure you that I have responsibilities to attend to. I am a busy woman."

He couldn't stop his grin. "No doubt your hours of piano practice factor into your version of busy. Let us not forget your teas and your promenades."

"Do I look as though I promenade? Whatever happened to make you so biased?"

Behind her he caught the servants exchanging glances. How naive this lady was. How naive all ladies of her station were.

"This isn't bias, but let us move on from that. I shall be playing the violin and I'd like to perform a duet with you."

"You play?" Perhaps for the first time, a different sort of interest flashed across her features.

To his dismay, pride swelled within. He didn't care what she thought of him. But her beaming face kindled his ego. "Yes," he said shortly.

"Wonderful. We shall practice. How about now?"

"Does your schedule not beg you to return home? I would not wish to impede your busy life." He couldn't stop a wry tone from shaping his words. Perhaps she'd invite a few of her wealthy friends with money to spare for the orphans.

"Nonsense." She waved a hand airily. "We must sound our best. That requires practice. I will need to hear you play, though. Are you an amateur?"

"I am not an amateur, but neither am I a professional." He just wanted money to buy a little cottage in the country where the children could grow up safely, in happiness.

Nothing more, nothing less.

It grated that Ingrid knew he needed money. Her kind were all the same, including his sire, who not only kept sending notes, but also had attempted to waylay him at Bow Street earlier this very day. He hated that a part of him wanted to take his father's money. The submission would make life easier, but then he'd have to find a way to get along with the man who broke his family into pieces. Perhaps he'd even have to forgive him, and that was something he could never do.

Ever.

He went to the kitchen and tugged out bread and a hunk of cheese for Jane and the manservant standing near the wall. He put the food on a plate for them.

He smiled at them, noting that Ingrid watched them crossly. Did the lady ever not look cross? His smile deepened at the thought.

He returned to the pianoforte, plucking Gus from his perch near the wall.

"Now," Ingrid said in a voice so prim and starched that it could rival the queen, "whatever are we to play?"

He pulled a chair near the piano bench and propped

the violin into its proper position. "Are you familiar with Mozart's sonatas?"

"But yes." She swiveled to him, her eyes clear and direct. "He is my favorite composer."

"I suggest we tweak two or three compositions to suit our duet. Are you up for the challenge?"

Her mouth parted and the barest hint of a smile crept across her face. "Indeed, I am."

And so forth they engaged in spirited banter as how best to play the songs. He pulled his bow across the strings, eliciting the smooth, harmonic sound that never ceased to still his breath and enchant his heart. They warmed their fingers on their instruments and then determined what each must play, where they'd solo, where they'd harmonize.

He tried to contain his fervent admiration, but it proved difficult as Ingrid plunged into her music like a woman starved. Her fingers flew across the keys, limber and strident, saying with notes what perhaps she could not say with words.

A pink flush suffused her cheeks, and her lips plumed to rose as she played. He dragged his gaze from the enigmatic lady beside him.

It had been smart to invite her to duo, despite the churning feelings she provoked within him. Her presence might bring wealthier guests to the event, and perhaps having a lady in the midst might bump up donations.

He drew his bow quickly, strongly, relishing the feel of its warmth in his hand, the stability of his chin in the rest, creating and honing as they played Mozart together.

Had he expected to produce music with her? Had he secretly hoped for such a thing from the moment he'd first heard her play?

After a childhood of poverty and grief, he had fashioned a life for himself that consisted of song and contentment.

He'd grown weary of the superficiality of cheap relationships, and never had he found a woman to love.

Then the children came into his life. First Petey, unexpectedly and not necessarily welcome. But now, two years later, Gideon could not imagine a life without their wild little footsteps, their dirty fingers snagging plums and tarts from his kitchen cupboards.

He had not even known that anything was missing from his life until they arrived.

That was the strangeness of it all. Since his father had begun to reestablish contact, Gideon had discovered that an angry, bitter part of him resided within. Covered for years, perhaps, with pride and perhaps even a cocky sort of confidence. His father's newfound presence in his life opened old wounds. He'd realized that there were hollow, lonely places within his soul.

As his violin fought to keep pace with Ingrid's piano, he was reminded again of those places.

Playing with her warmed a part of himself that had been so cold, so unalive, that he had not even noticed the deadness. Not until the joy of companionship and belonging touched him, warming his soul like frozen toes thawing before a fire. He pulled his bow faster, his fingers moving in scheduled abandon across the strings, harmonizing with Ingrid until in one final sweep, they reached crescendo.

The music reverberated to a slow stop as their eyes met. She sighed deeply, her mouth a rosy bow, her eyes sparkling, and that frosty place within him began to thaw in earnest.

If he was not careful, the trouble he'd sensed her to be would be far more dangerous than any he'd ever encountered.

She was the kind of trouble, he suddenly realized, that could utterly and ruthlessly destroy a man.

Chapter Five

"Are you trying to destroy my reputation?" Alice barged into the library, interrupting Ingrid's practice.

She stopped playing immediately, eyeing her sister's flushed cheeks and snapping temper. This interruption was most inopportune as the charity event started in a little over three hours. She'd managed to practice with Gideon once more yesterday, but today he'd had to work, he told her, so they must make do with what they'd already practiced.

Now she watched Alice and her frenetic pacing.

"You—" Alice stopped to point her finger in a condescending way "—have been playing fast and loose with your reputation."

"I beg pardon?" Ingrid rose, clutching her skirts and rounding the piano.

"Yes. My maid has warned me of talk amongst the servants." Alice's hands cupped her cheeks. "Do you not know what shall happen to me?"

"Can I first answer the accusation you have made? Come, sit." Ingrid guided her sister to the couch and rang for tea. "I would never wish to harm you."

Alice shuddered, sitting down in a defeated way. "I

do not think you do so purposefully. It is simply that you have been away from society far too often, and you have not been a debutante in years. You forget that your actions reflect on me, and as this is my first Season, I am more heavily scrutinized."

"I see." Ingrid sat quietly for a moment, digesting her sister's words. What could she have done that was so harmful? She cast through her previous days' activities. "It is true that I made a quick trip to Lacking and Square's The Temple of the Muses. I heard they had a bit of sheet music I wanted, and for the cheapest price."

Her purse was much lighter now, and she must be careful not to overspend. But how easily news of cheap sheet music lured her.

A maid brought in their tea, and Ingrid poured her sister a cup, which Alice accepted.

"I should have brought a maid, I know, but I really just wanted to dodge in and out," she continued. "Also, there was Gunter's yesterday. I had such a sweet tooth, and Father offered to buy us both a treat."

"Oh, Ingrid. You really are a ninny." Alice sighed deeply, her pretty features scrunching into a frown. "I am disheartened that you are running about London without a chaperone, but those excursions are not to which I refer."

"I see." Though she did not, not really.

"It is Bow Street." Alice set her cup down and cast a look about the room. "Bow Street, sister? Truly? You've been reported to have had little in the way of chaperonage. It's an alarming tattle."

"Oh, my." Ingrid wet her lips. What to say? How to say it? Conveniently for her, though, Alice continued speaking, saving her the need to come up with a ready explanation.

"Now, my maid assures me that nothing untoward has happened and the story has not left the house. But it will, you know. And how shall that make me look? I *like* Sir Everett. I feel certain he shall be proposing soon. Should my reputation even have the slightest of smear to it…well, he may not make an offer."

"Based on your dowry, I think not."

"Sir Everett has his own money. He does not need mine."

Ingrid tapped the chair, studying her sister's fine-boned features. "Are you certain of that? Have you two discussed financials?"

"I should think not." Alice frowned. "Whatever has gotten into you? To discuss money is unladylike."

"But you shall be the one running the household," Ingrid pointed out. "Will you not need to know the budget?"

Alice tilted her head. "Why do you worry? My point is that I am going to need you to stop running around willy-nilly doing who knows what until after I am good and married."

"I can assure you there is nothing beyond the pale in what I am doing. And I have made a commitment." Ingrid stared at her tea. Alice made valid points. Shame on Ingrid for not realizing how meeting at Gideon's little house could affect her sister. In the country, one maid sufficed as chaperone.

Ingrid sighed, thinking of her little cottage. She would not have to prance about with a maid if she lived there. Her every move would not be speculated upon. But of course, her activities here only mattered because of Alice.

What would life be like for Alice if Ingrid were accepted into the Paris conservatory? She had not told them she was female. This small detail should be of no consequence, she told herself fiercely, although perhaps it would yet prove to be of some importance.

An unfair world.

They all lived in such an unfair world.

Which circled her thoughts back to tonight's event. How did it feel to be an orphan? To have perhaps one set of ragged clothes, and one pair of shoes? Discomfort twisted within her. She looked at her sister anew, at the opulent room in which they sat. Her glistening piano, well loved and shining to perfection.

"Would you like to come with me tonight?" she asked Alice suddenly, the idea appearing as quickly as a bolt of lightning. "And you should bring a group of friends. Sir Everett included."

Alice set her teacup down. "To Bow Street?"

"No, a few streets over. I am playing for a charity event at a local parish. For orphans," she added, seeing the doubt on her sister's face. "Really, I think we should gather a group of friends." They would be Alice's friends, of course. Ingrid did not have time nor energy to chitchat with people. She had one very dear friend whom she had not seen in ages, though they exchanged letters often.

"I hardly think my friends would be interested."

"Tell them it is for the good of little orphan children. Only an hour or so of your time…and think how awed everyone will be to have the titled in their midst. Tell your friends to fill their purses."

"I don't know…" An uncertain expression flashed across Alice's face.

"You do not know?" demanded Ingrid. "Nonsense. Send a quick note and tell them you'll pick them up in our barouche. Or they can bring their own carriages, though I daresay the streets will be narrow and filled with pickpockets. Best they are dropped by hackney, now that I think of it."

"Pickpockets?" Alice's hand went to her collar.

"Oh, come now. You are no wilting flower. Let us help

the children and do good. Surely, Sir Everett, with his kind and generous heart, will jump at the chance to help those less fortunate."

"He certainly will."

"It is settled, then." Ingrid stood. "I shall see you all tonight."

Gideon did not expect the wealthy.

They filed in, a group of six, with their fancy hair-pieces and silken skirts. A collective silence descended upon the small church as heads dipped in acknowledgment of their social betters. Even the children stilled, for they did not often see such lavishness in their midst. The orphans watched with wide eyes as the group walked the center aisle toward the front of the church. The stone walls closed in the small building, but the bell tower above the altar area allowed natural light to flow into the tiny parish. The newcomers filed into an empty row.

He recognized some. He had learned that Ingrid was the daughter of Lord and Lady Manning, a well-known couple in the ton. A girl who resembled Ingrid enough to be her sister strode next to Lady Manning. Then there was Sir Everett, richly clad and wearing boredom like a cape, and beside him another man Gideon did not recognize. Two more ladies accompanied the group, looking as young as Ingrid's sister and clearly nervous.

His gaze skittered across the rest of the room, taking in several local store owners and a few landowners. It was a good turnout, overall, and the children of the orphanage would have a ready audience for the songs they had prepared. A few brave children were to share their life experiences.

Though Gideon did not like using their personal pain to gain funds, this was not his charity to run and he trusted

Mr. McCallister, the current vicar, to keep their best interests at the forefront.

Though faith did not influence his life, he'd met McCallister through a job and held much respect for the man. The vicar often told Gideon he was praying for him, which left Gideon with an unsettled feeling, as if losing something of great import and yet unsure of how to find it.

Ingrid flowed into the church next, her uneven gait an elegant component to her stride. She found a seat in the back. The program began. After the children sang songs, the personal testimonies began.

Gideon's gaze kept straying back to the plucky Ingrid. She'd invited her family and he'd like to believe it had been for the benefit of the orphans.

What had she said? That she was planning to go to Paris? He squinted, studying her until her gaze flitted toward him. He looked away to the pew where her family and friends sat. Ingrid's mother lifted a lace kerchief to her face, dabbing at her cheeks as though the current child's plight hurt to hear.

As it should.

He well recalled the finery of the upper classes, the peerage, when he was a child. While his mother withered away in the tiny room they rented above the butcher's shop, the rich lived in blissful ignorance. Even now, years later, the memory of the ache of his empty stomach haunted him.

He held back his frown, forcing memories from his mind, focusing instead on the people in the church. People who cared enough to give of their time and purse for a good cause. Sir Everett and his male companion displayed an air of disdainful ennui, which did not surprise Gideon in the slightest.

They were young, still in that selfish, adventurous stage of life in which the entire world revolved about themselves.

The door to the church opened. He stood straighter, crossing his arms, as his father entered the little building. The child at the altar did not cease speaking, despite the newcomer.

No doubt the orphans wished to make this as successful an event as possible. He'd heard a few speaking in hushed voices earlier, hoping for new shoes, warmer coats and perhaps even a book to read.

His father stopped to speak to Ingrid, and Gideon's breath sucked in quickly, so quickly it knifed his lungs. Ingrid gestured to the piano near the child, and then to him. She acted as though she knew Lord Hawking.

His *sire*.

The man did not deserve the title of *father*. Throat closing, he refused to look any longer at the earl and instead listened as the final child, a skinny little girl with straggly hair and big brown eyes, pleaded her case. She cited abandonment, hunger and finally this place, a safe haven.

He hoped her story dug holes in his father's conscience. He hoped his father bled.

Then the girl finished and Mr. McCallister came up, thanked everyone for attending and reminded them that there'd be food and drinks after the next performance.

His and Ingrid's performance.

He caught her eye as she moved to the front of the church. She stayed near the wall, unobtrusive, a serious look about her face. Her sister winked at her as she went up, but Ingrid merely offered a sober nod in return.

He met her at the pianoforte, crossing the aged floor in quick strides. His pulse thrummed in his throat. The stained-glass window behind the piano seat splayed rainbow hues across her form in dusky reds and greens. She sat at the bench as though it were an expression of herself, her long-fingered hands resting lightly at the edges of the keys.

He felt her gaze on him as he retrieved his violin. He joined her at the pianoforte, noting the heightened color in her cheeks, the sparkle in her eyes.

The attendees murmured quietly, patiently awaiting their musical entertainment. And in that audience, his sire resided. His gut twisted and when he pulled his bow across the strings to check the sound, his hand shook and a discordant note shrieked from Gus. The metallic ring sounded much as his emotions felt: hard and cold and bordering on dangerous.

"One moment, if you will," Ingrid said in an authoritative tone to their watchers. "We must convene."

She turned to him, looking up with rounded eyes. "Are you well enough to do this?" she asked quietly.

"Yes."

"You seem..." She paused. "Uneasy. Have you never played for a group?"

In fact, he had not, and though it would be easy to blame his nerves on the earl standing near the doors, he suddenly realized that he was indeed all too aware of the people watching him. His palm felt slick. He dared not drop his violin.

Ingrid's eyes flickered. "You shall be competent, I assure you. Gideon, you are an accomplished violinist and though your hand may at first be unsteady, as you play, you will recover. Do you believe me?"

How could he not? She spoke with conviction. Frankly and firmly. Hadn't he liked that quality from the first? But his tongue scraped for words, and his mouth had dried as though in drought. Despite her assurance, his throat worked to swallow and his heart beat unnaturally fast.

She chuckled then, a surprising sound as she did not laugh often. "The great detective, afraid? Come now. Put your violin beneath your chin and play a few chords."

He did not know why or how, but his body obeyed. He lifted the violin, still facing her, feeling the people's stares burning into his profile.

"We shall play," she said in a low voice, her fingers poised above the keys. "And we shall be magnificent."

She tapped a key, then another, and when it was his turn, he felt something loosen within. The tight band crimping his stomach eased. The worries he felt about his father, the anger, flowed away in a synchrony of sound that washed over him in melodious, harmonizing waves.

They played and they played, and for once, Gideon did not feel like a man overcome with worries, but rather a musician in control of this moment. Alive and free and filled with power.

He lost himself in the songs, at times following Ingrid's lead; at others, leading her. Their music undulated throughout the church. Not a sound could be heard and even the orphans did not fidget.

When they had finished the last song, their eyes met, and then Ingrid's mouth stretched into a smile that pummeled him with its beauty.

Perhaps she might be trouble, but at this very moment trouble seemed to be just the thing he needed.

Chapter Six

Trouble was definitely the last thing he wanted in his life.

Gideon arrived home from a long day trailing a thief to a fight in the main room. Just what he needed. Not only did his stomach growl with hunger, but he had not been able to finish investigating Lady Ingrid's list of potential grooms, either. A day had passed since the charity event and no doubt she'd be pounding on his door if she did not hear from him soon.

But at this moment he had to break up a ruckus. Petey and another boy he did not recognize had squared off in the living area. Their grimy fists were risen in front of their faces, and Petey's normally jolly eyes squinted at his opponent with a surprising level of severity.

About ten children circled the budding pugilists. He'd heard their shouts from outside, and once in the house, the noise deafened him.

Gideon slammed the door shut. As one, the children turned toward him, though Petey did not lower his fists.

"What's going on here?" He raised a brow, crossed his arms.

A mix of guilt and anger crossed the fighters' faces. The other children scurried to their places of sleep, which happened to be haphazard piles of clothing. None dared to escape through the front door, which Gideon blocked.

"He snatched my bread." Petey's face scrunched in anger. Sir Beasley yipped excitedly, but a little girl held him back from presumably eating the other child involved in the fight.

"Is that true?" Gideon looked at the other boy, a taller version of Petey.

"I's 'ungry and 'e 'ad 'is already." The boy's English was thick with East End Cockney.

An angry knock thumped the door. *Great.* Sighing, Gideon pointed a finger at the boys. "Be still." He opened the door a crack.

"What's all this noise I hear?" His landlord stood on the step, another angry face to add to the mix.

Gideon forced a smile. "Mr. Crabtree, what can I help you with?"

"That racket." The short, squat man tried to peer past Gideon, but he shifted his body to block the view. The children remained silent, attuned to danger and freezing in response to Crabtree's tone. "I've had enough, West. You've got to go."

His stomach cramped. "So you've said."

"Comings and goings, all hours of the night. Kids everywhere. You've been a good tenant until the last year or so. The wife can't handle it anymore. My other tenants complain."

"You said eight to nine weeks. Only two have elapsed." Gideon lifted an eyebrow.

Crabtree flushed. "I'll keep my word. I know you're doing a good thing, but the children should have beds. Schooling. The missus doesn't approve of them scurrying around like rats in the night."

Rats. A terrible comparison. He controlled the spurt of anger that darted through him.

"Get rid of those street urchins. There's workhouses and orphanages all around London." The man's brow crinkled, as if utterly confused that Gideon wouldn't dump them in one of those.

"Anything else, Mr. Crabtree?" He kept his voice level.

"Six more weeks, West." The man pivoted and Gideon shut the door.

He faced the children. "Do you have anything to say for yourselves?"

The new boy, the one who'd taken Petey's bread, shuffled his feet. "Eh, can I go now?"

"Don't come back unless you intend to treat others fairly," Gideon told him firmly. The boy nodded, and Gideon moved out of the way. Five children trailed after the boy, leaving Petey and a few others. His regulars, as he thought of them. "How do you all feel about a nice cottage in the country?"

The little girl who had played piano with Ingrid smiled so brightly the room lit with her joy.

Petey scratched his head. "Can I bring Sir Beasley?"

The dog, hearing his name, yipped.

"Yes." Gideon flopped into a chair, feeling the day crashing upon him. "No more fighting. I've got to finish some jobs and look for a home for you all."

Gideon couldn't bring himself to turn the kids over to the authorities. The orphanages he knew of were already bursting at the seams with children. He still had some of the money Ingrid had paid him. Once he finished that list of hers, she'd pay him the remainder due.

But then he'd need to find employment somewhere. Unless he found a cottage near enough London that he could go into the city to work. He scratched his head, his worries so heavy he thought they might implode his brain.

"Oh, Mr. Gideon." Anna hopped over, her eyes gleaming. "You've a note. Someone dropped it off this morning."

"We didn't answer the door," piped up Petey from where he sat in the corner petting Sir Beasley. "They slipped it under the crack. We was quiet."

"Hadn't started fighting yet, eh?" He took the note from Anna and opened it. A quick scan and he fought the urge to growl. It was unlike him, yet Lady Ingrid seemed to bring out the worst in him.

And the best, his traitorous mind whispered. For how could he forget the sight of her magnificent playing? The flushed rhapsody upon her features as their instruments blended in natural harmony? Her kind encouragement had bolstered him, giving him confidence in his instrument.

But there was more than just her talent that impressed him. After their performance, while he rounded the room and finagled donations, she had played with the children. It had been surprising to see her expression relaxed into laugh lines. He knew she did not enjoy society and he had assumed that she did not like people in general.

She liked children, though. And what did that say about her?

He glanced at the note again, observing the slanted, firm lines of her handwriting. A woman who knew her own mind, and bold as well. It was not quite proper for an unmarried woman to send a note to a man. Smiling, he folded the paper and slipped it into his coat pocket.

"I've a bit more work to do." He patted Anna on the head. She stood near, her brow wrinkled as though she'd been trying to read Ingrid's words. "Have you all enough food to last?"

"I brought home mutton from that butcher on the corner. 'E's a good chap." Petey grinned.

Sarah popped up from a cot at the far end of the room. "I've some bread."

"You children behave yourselves. I've got to go out for a bit, and we don't want Mr. Crabtree nor his wife calling the constable on you while I'm gone."

Petey paled. His freckles popped to attention. "Quiet as mice, we'll be."

"Good." Gideon scratched his chin. "Can any of you read?"

Anna raised her hand.

"I've a few books near my bed. Teach Sarah and Petey their letters," he told her, then winked at them all. That should keep them busy for a while.

He, on the other hand, had a business meeting. He'd need more time to go through the list, but the sooner he got his money, the better off his children would be. He went to leave but paused long enough for a surprise hug from Sarah. He patted her head, his heart constricting.

As he made his way outside, his mind raced with thoughts and memories. He had not seen the earl since the charity event. Feeling unnaturally grim, he changed his mind about hiring a hackney and set out on foot toward Berkeley Square.

Ingrid wished him to meet her near Gunter's at three o'clock, if available. That gave him thirty minutes of walking. Despite his internal stress, he inhaled the afternoon air with a modicum of pleasure. Even the odor of soot riding the breeze could not hide the scent of spring. Carriages clattered past him, and the streets teemed with children dodging about while flower sellers, bakers and craftsmen hawked their wares. As he left Bow Street, the streets became cleaner, the populations more mannerly and the carriages shinier.

Though London could not claim any type of regular fresh air, it did seem that as he neared Berkeley Square, the wind's clear crispness increased. He trekked toward Gunter's.

He scanned the sunlit grass, noting the emerald beauty of London's popular square. The fine weather inspired the peerage to venture out for ices from Gunter's. Employees scurried to the restaurant's patrons, delivering orders and retrieving trash.

Ingrid had written that she'd be wearing a peach-color dress and sporting an ivory parasol trimmed in blue. He continued his perusal, finally spotting her sitting in a sunny spot upon a colorful blanket. He made his way over, noting she'd brought two maids as chaperones.

She saw him and waved. "You made it. Please, sit." She gestured to a small blanket set a few feet away from her. Far enough to discourage any talk of impropriety, yet close enough to converse. Smart lady.

He lowered his body, situating himself so that he could see her without sunshine blinding him. She looked far too pretty today. A faint blush stained her skin, brought about by the sun, no doubt. Relaxation softened her features and when she met his gaze, the brightness of the day made her lavender eyes sparkle.

"Would you care for a lemon ice?" she asked.

He shook his head.

"Perhaps another flavor?"

His gaze cut to the two maids seated behind her. They chatted quietly together, one knitting and the other holding her own ice.

"I'm not thirsty," he said, though he became aware in

that moment of his parched throat. Nevertheless, he did not intend to allow her to buy him things.

"The charity went well, did it not?" She fingered the folds of her dress.

"You need not use niceties with me," he told her in a kind voice. She could not help, after all, the station she'd been born to nor the narrowness of her experiences. She did not see the incongruity of her lounging on a blanket whilst children went hungry. "Yes, it sufficed. The children may have nice clothing and warm food for at least a year, if McCallister can stretch the funds that long."

"Is it really so difficult to care for them?"

"You've no idea," he said, knowing she truly did not and could not imagine the poverty they experienced.

Ingrid pressed her lips, wanting to ask more but somehow afraid. She did not think she'd ever had a hungry moment in her life that was not quickly remedied.

She glanced at Gideon. How strong and tall he appeared as he had walked to her. His eyes fairly gleamed in the afternoon brightness. She knew others considered him handsome, but it still surprised her when she noticed. She felt…restless?

Perhaps it was nerves.

She was rattled. Who would not be? She intended to escape the net her parents sought to trap her within. Any true lady knew the risks involved with doing so. Perhaps some ladies might even faint at the thought of Ingrid's plans. Her lips curled as the idea inspired amusement. She, of course, had never fainted. The very idea curdled her ego.

"For what have I been summoned?" asked Gideon.

"Have you evening plans, Mr. West?"

Surprise flit across his face. It was then she noticed a

type of tiredness near the corners of his eyes. He looked far more serious than she supposed he liked to be.

"I do not," he said slowly. Perhaps dreading her next words?

"I've hatched a plan of action regarding your investigations."

"I can assure you that I can handle my own investigations."

"Yes, but I am on a tight schedule. As soon as I hear from the conservatoire, I intend to leave for Paris." She plucked at a blade of grass, marveling at its verdant hue. "I still must speak to my parents about the suitors they've picked for me. The more quickly I can accomplish this, the better."

Gideon absorbed her words, his expression thoughtful. He reclined onto his elbows, and once again, his tall frame struck her as unbearably attractive. She looked away, tossing the blade of grass to the side.

He flipped onto his back, his hands behind his head as he stared upward toward the heavens. "You are risking much by following your own path."

"It is the only path for me."

"An odd path for a lady."

What other path, for one such as she? But, of course, that was not his business. She frowned. "I did not bring you here to discuss my life choices. Have you the list?"

He dug into his pocket, raising up on his elbows as he did so. She noted the scuffed appearance of his shoes, and once again, her mind wandered to the children. Did they have enough to eat? Were they eagerly awaiting another lesson? Had anyone brushed Sarah's hair?

"In all, there are ten names remaining after the one I crossed off."

"You have not discovered anything else in these two weeks?"

"I've been busy, Lady Ingrid. However, I do have out a few feelers and should receive information soon."

"Very well." She sighed. "Your reason for ridding the list of that name will suffice for my parents. But as for the others, at first glance, have you any objections?"

"No. I would have told you immediately. There's nothing that stands out as unacceptable."

"Then we shall move to the next step of the process."

His brow crinkled. "You are more precise and detailed than I expected."

"Because I am a musician and you expect someone artistically inclined to be disorganized?"

"I don't know," he said in a thoughtful tone.

A butterfly flitted between them, its pale yellow wings gilded with golden luminescence. The insect paused, suspended over the grass, hovering in contemplation until fluttering to Ingrid's dress and landing on her knee. She held her breath, entranced for the moment.

The butterfly's wings slowed to a stop until it realized that her dress was not a flower. Then it popped upward, zigzagging away from them in a delightful pattern. If only she could be a butterfly. Free to roam, to be herself.

As she had felt the other night at the church. How lovely the children had been, gathered around her, chitter chattering with the abandon to which children were prone. She had noticed Gideon greeting those who attended, mingling with that easy charm he possessed. She herself had not mingled with the adults in the church, choosing instead to show the children the keys on the piano, and the sounds each press could elicit. There had been a sense of rightness to the busyness, and she had not even minded that they kept touching her hair and clothing.

She had not been alone.

She reminded herself firmly that she liked being alone. It was her preference. How beloved, how precious, music was to her.

She had played for herself for so long, and she had thought it enough.

But the past weeks had taught her several lessons. Painful ones, at that.

For one, music was so much sweeter when shared. An image of Gideon with his violin invaded her thoughts.

How dulcet the notes. How quick his bow. And the look upon his features as he played. She recalled the concentration of his brow, the way his hair fell over it in a happy way, the concentrated purse of his lips.

Thinking about his lips had a strange effect on her, for his were full and almost always smiling, and she knew people often kissed each other on the lips. She'd caught her own parents doing so, and then there was all that poetry Alice indulged in.

Kissing seemed an essential component to romance.

She touched her own lips, wondering suddenly if they were kissable. Had any man ever thought about kissing her? She did not think so, though she had not had a particular shortage of suitors. Perhaps her dowry and inheritance proved far more attractive than the pinkish feature located between her nose and her chin.

She shook her head. Utterly ridiculous thoughts. Kissing. *Pfft.*

"You enjoy the outdoors," said Gideon, breaking into her thoughts. Her cheeks burned. Thankfully, he could not know the exact nature of those thoughts.

She returned her attention to him. "I am not on that list. Cease your investigation of my character."

"Said with such censure."

"The reason I am detailed is because I was raised to be so."

"I'd hazard a guess it's in your nature."

Shrugging, she met his grinning gaze. "Who can know? I am the eldest daughter of an earl. No doubt they'd expected me to be running my own household by now. Which brings me back to the list."

"I don't need your help."

"But you do, for you will not be looking into the ordinary things with these men. Rather, you shall ascertain their individual personalities to determine their compatibility with mine."

He laughed, though she could not tell whether it was with amusement or disbelief.

"I have been thinking, and we must figure out a way," she continued firmly, "for you to accompany me or be nearby when I speak with these men. Note their flaws, their incompatibilities. My parents want me to marry for love."

His head tilted. "But you do not wish to do so?"

A tiny cinch tugged beneath her breastbone, but she ignored it. "I'm inclined toward monogamy, and the piano stole my heart long ago."

"Stolen hearts, unsuitable beaus. I find myself in agreement with you. Love is far too overrated. All right, my lady." He pushed to his feet. "Send a missive with the time and day that I am to rescue you from your parents' nefarious plans."

He winked before strolling off, and once again, Ingrid's breath shallowed and her heart raced.

Anticipation, that was what she felt.

Pure anticipation.

Chapter Seven

Three days later Gideon arrived at Covent Gardens precisely ten minutes before instructed. He looked about, admiring the bustle of people. Busyness surrounded him. Fruit stands lined the area, interspersed with herb stalls and vegetable stands. People meandered everywhere, filling the air with the odor of dirt, sweat and various scents from roasted meats. From this vantage point, he counted three taverns alone.

Why had Ingrid suggested this place? Her note had not contained a multitude of details. Only that he should wait near the Piazza and she would find him. He didn't visit Covent Gardens often and it took a bit of reorientation and a question to a stranger to find the place.

As he neared the crowded coffeehouse next to the Piazza, his stomach growled. Frowning, he walked to a corner of the theater building, placed his back against the wall and studied the crowds. A good mix this afternoon of the middle and upper classes. The occasional beggar threaded through the throngs.

He scratched his jaw, his stomach reminding him again that he'd missed luncheon. Perhaps Ingrid was going to the theater next door? But what did that have to do with him? He crossed his arms and waited.

"Here you are." Ingrid came to his side, about a foot away. He glanced over and saw that she'd brought Jane as her chaperone. "You are on time."

"What plan is afoot?"

She flashed him a look he couldn't read. Surprise? Amusement? Then she sniffed in that haughty way of hers. "I am meeting Mr. Barton and a group of his friends at the theater to take in a performance. My sister is here as well, but she darted into the coffeehouse to procure libation. This is our moment to speak."

She adjusted her hat, a rather large and silly-looking creation. Quite unlike the woman he was beginning to know to wear such a monstrosity.

"Nice hat," he said, testing the waters, so to speak.

For that, he earned a scowl. A pretty scowl, yet a scowl nonetheless.

"Though I do not believe Mr. Barton will like me, I am determined to discourage any possibility. He is first on your list, by the way."

"Yes, a solid and rich gentleman who spends his leisure time attending poetry readings and cultural events."

"I'm sure you can see immediately that he and I would not suit."

"I've been told he's a good-looking chap. Well liked by those who know him."

Her eyes widened. "You've investigated him already? I am impressed."

A tiny swell of pride lit within, and he tamped it down. "I need to get paid."

Sighing, she put a hand on one hip and fluttered her fan with the other hand. "I'd like you to attend the play. Sit near us. Not close enough that anyone would notice, but perhaps close enough to see that Mr. Barton is lacking whatever quality my parents think he possesses to deserve a place on that list."

"A play?" Not his favorite form of entertainment. Now, pugilism…that was something else entirely.

"Yes. And at intermissions, should he get up, I'd like you to make conversation with him. Follow him. Get the feel of his character."

Gideon grinned. "Anything else, boss?"

"I was probably meant to be a man." She spoke in such a resigned voice that a pinch of empathy struck him.

"But you make a beautiful woman." The moment the words left his mouth, he wondered if he should regret them. But he could not bring himself to do so. Had anyone ever told her such a thing? Her flushing cheeks and quickening fan told him likely not.

"I am happy with myself," she said, not meeting his gaze. "I chafe at the restrictions placed upon women. I suppose it's rather odd that I have such a domineering nature."

"I don't find it odd at all. A domineering nature is quite common to women. Beyond that, you are a fascinating, complex lady with a rare talent."

Charm came naturally to him. He enjoyed giving people, especially women, compliments, but he realized that he meant exactly what he had said. More than a flirtation, it was a corroboration. She blinked slowly, her profile still to him, her cheek a deep pink.

"I told you that I am immune to your flirtations. You are silly to even try." Yet, a corner of her lip trembled, as though she tried very hard to contain her smile.

"Shame on me for even trying." He smiled back at her. "I shall spy on your Mr. Barton. Do you want me to send my thoughts by post or shall we meet?"

She peeped at something over his right shoulder.

"My sister returns. Meet me after the play in this very spot."

"Yes, my lady," he said, allowing his smile to widen even more.

Casting him what he supposed must be a disapproving glare, she tossed her head and walked past him.

"Jane," he said, sweeping his hat off for the maid as she followed her employer. The girl just shook her head at him. Such a serious lot. If he had the amount of money they did, he'd be dancing his way through life.

"Mr. West." A voice called to him from the crowd.

A frisson of frustration shuddered through him as recognition dawned. Slowly, he swiveled to meet the eyes of the man who had abandoned his mother. Abandoned *him.* His heart became a cold and heavy rock within his chest. Hands fisted at his sides, he let his gaze rove over Lord Hawking.

White strands interspersed with his brown hair, and blue eyes the shade of Gideon's regarded him with an annoying tenderness. Though a little taller than the man, at the moment, all Gideon could remember was being small and hungry on Lord Hawking's doorstep, begging for help.

And the icy freeze of Hawking's demeanor as he turned him away.

Though it had been over fifteen years ago, the moment burned in his mind, searing the edges of his emotions and stiffening his spine.

When he thought of God, he saw his father's cold eyes.

"Bold of you to approach me again."

Lord Hawking's mouth, lined from the years, drooped. He carried a ruby-encrusted cane and looked more frail than at the charity event.

"We must speak." His voice even sounded thinner.

Gideon's eyes narrowed. "I have nothing to say to you."

He pivoted, intending to leave his father standing in the proverbial dust.

"Please, son."

Gideon stumbled to a stop, his shoulders weighted with a fiery anger he didn't care to defuse. Slowly, he turned, eyeing the man whose riches cloaked his deceit and inhumanity. "You have no leave to call me that."

"But I do." Lord Hawking drew closer, almost stumbling as a child dodged past him. "I've read the letters your mother wrote me. I hired a detective. The time frame fits. You must be him."

"Did you not say your son was named Wesley?"

The earl's wrinkled, purple-veined lids fluttered. "His first name. Perhaps your mother changed it. Why are you denying this? You came to me—"

"An action I deeply regret." Gideon glanced about and noticed Ingrid at the entrance to the theater, watching him. "I've a job to do and you're a distraction. No doubt you've other more important matters to attend to."

The man's throat visibly bobbed. Even the veins in his neck looked fragile, threads of blue and lavender that wove beneath his pale skin. But no, Gideon could not afford sympathy, nor did he intend to give credence to Lord Hawking's words. The truth of them no longer mattered and that sore, bruised place within him did not allow even the possibility that their relationship could be restored.

"Spare me an afternoon, please."

But Gideon pivoted, leaving the earl to trek toward the theater, ruthlessly shoving every frayed emotion down so that he could focus on the matter at hand: discrediting the handful of suitors on Ingrid's list so that she could go to Paris unencumbered by a husband.

And so that he could house the children, feed them, without receiving help from the earl.

Mouth tight, he paid to enter the crowded theater. He would bill Ingrid for the cost. The building's opulence pressed down upon him, a reminder of all that he lacked, all that Lord Hawking had kept from his mother. If the earl had really loved her, or even esteemed her as the mother of his child, he could have ensured that there had been food upon their table. Clean clothes in the dresser.

Medication for illness.

Swallowing, he entered the pit, the place that people like him stood to watch the play. On both sides the gallery and boxes rose in vertical stacks upon the wall. He had purchased gallery seating so that he might face Lady Ingrid's box. If he could find her. It was the height of the Season, after all. And though Covent Gardens may not be suitable for certain naive ingenues, a woman her age and status could attend without gossip. And so the peerage boxes were nearly filled, and the gallery bustled with those awaiting the show to start.

He threaded through other patrons, making his way to the edge of the gallery to find Ingrid's hat amongst the boxes rising above him. Perhaps that was why she had worn it? A grudging admiration swept through him. His search proved an exercise in futility, though. Too many people. And the distance…how was he expected to spy upon them?

He shook his head. This entire idea was ludicrous. He forged his way out of the theater. He'd buy a mutton chop for his growling stomach, maybe shop for the household, and in about two hours she should emerge. He'd watch her in the party then. He'd observe their interactions and any opinion he formed, though just an opinion, should be enough to cross Mr. Barton off her list.

Throughout the play, Ingrid looked in vain for Mr. West. She had seen him near Lord Hawking before she'd entered the theater. Did they know each other? Had they been speaking? She'd been too far away to be able to tell. Frustration sizzled just beneath her skin, quite like the electric shock she'd received at a rout in which the hosts decided to show off their friction machine.

It had been rather unpleasant, the way the crank turned fast enough to create a current, which then ran through the guests' joined hands, shocking them all. Most people had laughed but Ingrid had been irritated.

Rather how she felt now.

She had told Gideon to attend. He was in her employ. And he had not.

At last, the play ended.

She suffered through the tedious conversations required, proffering a strained smile when Alice nudged her forcefully, and followed the group out of the theater.

"A fine play, indeed." Mr. Barton stuffed his hands into the pockets of his coat and rocked back and forth upon his heels. His brown hair curled about his face in teased waves and his ruddy face cracked into a giant grin. "What next? A bite to eat? We could go round about Covent Gardens. I daresay there's a good deal of fun to be had."

Beside her, Alice clapped her hands. Her face flushed with excitement. "Oh, yes, that sounds marvelous. Can we, Ingrid?" A rosy blush stained her cheeks, and she looked so overwhelmingly lovely that Ingrid felt a fierce protectiveness rise within.

How could she tell her no? But she must. A tenderness had invaded her hip and she did not want to exacerbate it. Their group consisted of several men and women, including the widow Lady Asterly and her niece, one of Alice's friends. In her late thirties, Lady Asterly had an excellent reputation and could be trusted to chaperone.

"I am sorry to disappoint you but I don't think it would

be wise to do so much walking today," she said in a quiet voice to her sister. She turned and caught Lady Asterly's attention. "Are you planning to stay? Alice is in need of chaperonage."

Lady Asterly adjusted her ample, fashionable hat. "But yes, she is invited. We shall bring her home so that you need not worry about sending a carriage."

"Thank you." That had been easy enough, and a relief. "Alice, you shall enjoy yourself?"

"Yes." Her sister practically bounced in her slippers.

They exchanged hugs. She hugged her sister just a little longer than necessary, knowing their time together might be short. If she was accepted into the conservatoire, she might never return to England.

Ingrid waved goodbye to her sister as the group moved away from the theater and merged into the crowded streets. The afternoon held a warm breeze filled with the strong smells of food and people. It was not altogether unpleasant.

Sighing, she searched the periphery of the grounds for a glimpse of Gideon's tall silhouette. She had told him to meet her in the same place, but who knew if he'd follow directions? Why hadn't he stayed in the theater? Surely, he could have found a spot near Mr. Barton's box?

"Do you see Mr. West?" she asked Jane.

"No, but did you not say to meet in the same place? We should go there."

Ingrid clutched her skirts as she descended the theater's outer steps, and then crossed over to the side of the theater walls. She did not see her runner anywhere.

"Do you think this is a good idea, my lady?" Jane came to a stop beside her. Their backs were to the wall of the theater, giving them a good vantage point of the teeming masses of Londoners out for a nice day. The restaurant to the right emitted mouthwatering aromas.

"It is an excellent idea."

"Meeting a man with only me as chaperone? Engaging the services of a detective?"

"You are being abnormally outspoken today." Ingrid eyed her maid, annoyed yet also refreshed by her straight-forwardness. Jane's gaze skittered downward, and her shoulders looked stiff. Ingrid sighed. "Is it a good idea? Perhaps not. But I am in desperate straits. The money I have is not my own. It is what I've been given, and it can be taken from me at any time. I prefer to secure the future I want as soon as possible, and a husband is not necessary for such a future."

"Not necessary?" Gideon appeared, sidling over with a smirk upon his face. "As I recall, they only provide *everything* a woman needs for an enjoyable life."

"That is an exaggerated generality. Oftentimes they do not." She frowned at him. "Why do you smell like roasted fowl?"

"I was hungry." His dimple appeared. "Couldn't find you and so I thought I might take a repast while you enjoyed your show."

"That is not what I instructed you to do."

"And yet I did it anyhow. I think we may have a miscommunication, Lady Ingrid." He scratched his chin, eyeing her thoughtfully. She did not like that gleam in his eye. "You seem to think you own my time, when in fact, you don't."

"I'm paying you," she said stiffly.

"Indeed. As are multiple others, people who keep me on retainer. And then there is my work with the constabulary."

"What is your point?"

"Always direct. That's what I like about Lady Ingrid." He directed that last comment to Jane, winking at her as he did so. To Ingrid's dismay, the dratted man brought a blush to her maid's face.

"Speak to me, not my maid." She propped her hands on her hips, lifting her chin because her giant, irritating hat was beginning to shade her view due to the dropping sun.

"Very well." His brow lifted and she had the impression she'd annoyed him. "The rub of the matter is I've a bunch of children to feed and house. And so I've got to take this *job* of yours. The extra income is to be put toward a new home. At the same time I'm not your pet dog to be led about at will."

"Have I treated you so?"

"I think you might like to."

Heat licked through her blood, but she tamped it down. There had been many instances in her childhood and youth where she'd lost her temper. Over the years, she'd immersed herself in the Bible, in growing her faith, in attempting to be more pleasing to the God who'd forgiven her of so much. And she wanted to snap back at this infuriating man to do his job, and to do it more quickly.

But he felt that she'd mistreated him. A hard lump to swallow, certainly. Yet, she did, gulping back her pride though it frayed her ego on its way down.

"I apologize for making you feel that way," she said, knowing her voice sounded recalcitrant. "It was quite unchristian of me."

She did not miss the shocked lifting of Jane's forehead, nor the way Gideon's arms folded across his chest and how his eyes narrowed. She became aware of his height, of his legs planted apart. Everything about him bespoke confidence. She wet her lips, forcing herself to meet his steady eyes.

"As we've already discussed," she continued, "I've a bossy nature and I am actively pursuing important goals.

Nevertheless, I do not mean to ride roughshod over your feelings."

He barked out a laugh then, his arms lowering to his stomach as he bent at the waist. She shifted on her feet, that electric current beneath her skin resuming course. Was he laughing at her?

"Oh." He swiped at his eyes and straightened. "You are concerned for my feelings, you say?" He laughed again, lower this time, a pleasant depth reminiscent of a double bass that shivered through her bones and warmed her stomach.

She glanced at Jane, who made a face as if to say she was as boggled as Ingrid.

"My dear Lady Ingrid, my feelings are perfectly intact. You need not concern yourself over them. I simply demand that you allow me to do what you hired me for without dictating my every move."

"I have done no such thing." And feeling very snappish indeed, she added, "And if your feelings have not been harmed, then perhaps it is simply your massive conceit making you lash out at me."

He did not laugh this time. Had she gone too far? She planted her hands on her hips, little caring. If she had to swallow her pride, then he could at least have his ego taken down a rung or two.

He looked as if he wanted to step toward her, though she did not think he was angry. His brows pulled together, and he studied her silently, his full lips twitching at the corners.

"Well?" She had little patience for his pique or tantrum or whatever it was that a man did when his ego received a trampling. "What are your thoughts on Lord Barton? What shall I tell my parents regarding him? Jane, be so good as to write this down. I've a pencil and paper in my reticule."

Now Gideon's lips twitched so fiercely they appeared

to be seizing. "Though there is nothing in his background to disallow him as a husband, your interactions with each other are not noteworthy. He is prone to giggling."

She had not noticed Barton's laugh. Beside her, Jane scribbled the details. "And so I shall tell my parents I cannot marry him because he giggles?"

"No." Gideon's mouth finally surrendered to a smile. "You shall tell them that he bores you. And you will never fall in love with someone who cannot invigorate your mind nor allure your interest. You need not write this. I will prepare a report."

An immense satisfaction swelled within Ingrid. "Excellent observation. I believe that shall work. Now about tomorrow—"

"Wait." He held up a hand, and she couldn't help but notice how large and capable his palms looked. Not soft or white, but tanned and hardened. A man who worked for a living. Who did dangerous things of which she did not even dare to imagine.

Suddenly, she realized that she nurtured a terrible fascination for Gideon West. Perhaps because he was so different from the men in her world? Or was it that he was not afraid to counter her directness? She must derail this curiosity at once. He was a runner, for goodness' sake. A man who lived on the edge. He was also poor. She could not forget that fact.

Summoning a will to ignore his charms, she squared her shoulders.

"Send me a copy of your schedule for next week. I have the list of remaining suitors. I will update you as I go," he said before she could speak.

"But I—"

"But nothing, Lady Ingrid. I am not yours to command. Trust me when I tell you that I am very efficient, and very good, at what I do. You shall have your freedom, and I hope sincerely, your Paris conservatory."

She nodded, but for a very tiny moment, a very tiny moment indeed, Paris did not seem half as exciting as the look in Mr. West's eyes when he smiled at her.

Chapter Eight

Nothing in the mail. Again.

Ingrid ruminated about the lack of correspondence as she sat on a chair near a potted plant in Lady Sanderson's ballroom. Music swelled around her. Alice passed by, a wide smile about her face as Sir Everett swung her in a vigorous minuet.

She folded her hands on her lap, absently noting that her teal-colored dress somewhat resembled Gideon's eyes. Though it had been nearly a week since she'd seen him, she kept thinking about him.

About his eyes. About the children who had food and new shoes because she'd brought them some a few days ago. They spoke highly of him, even in his absence.

It was beyond maddening.

But not as exasperating as having to entertain suitors this week. Since her parents were making her attend balls, several poor sops who had heard about her dowry but not her personality had shown up at the doorstep with harebrained aspirations. She was not allowed to refuse their visits and so she discouraged them with her expressions.

And sometimes a biting sentence or two.

Through it all, Gideon remained in her thoughts. She

had hoped to see him when she taught the children piano, but he remained absent. Anna continued to learn and even Petey attempted a few songs. A new child had also shown up at the last lesson. Small and frail, a boy with missing teeth and sooty hands. Ingrid had made sure to bring pastries one day. The next visit she brought a bag of clothing she'd pilfered from her mother's stash of charitable goods.

Surely, the beneficiaries of The Society for the Friends of Underprivileged Children could part with a few clothes.

Mother appeared from a throng of people, her friend Lady Danvers at her side. They came to sit next to Ingrid.

"Have you noticed anyone of interest here?" asked Mother, her eyes alight with what Ingrid felt certain was mischief.

"Not a single person."

Lady Danvers chuckled. "You'll never catch a beau with that mindset."

Ingrid remained silent. The lady had known her since childhood, was kind, and Ingrid had no wish to hurt her feelings by replying with what could only be a tart response.

"I have heard you involved yourself in a benefit for orphans." Lady Danvers smoothed her dress. "Your mother told me all about it. Long have I thought it might be a good idea to offer those less fortunate music lessons. There is a certain comfort in having artistic skills."

Ingrid's head snapped up. Were they trying to trap her into betraying her most recent activities? But no, guilelessness filled Lady Danvers's warm brown eyes, and her mother was busy scanning the room.

Most likely for potential beaus.

"That seems a sweet idea," murmured Ingrid carefully.

"My husband's steward is working with our solicitor to craft a charity. My dear, would you like to be involved?"

"How so?" But inwardly, Ingrid quaked. She could not commit to anything, not when she planned to live in Paris. She studied the dancers lining up for a hearty reel. Alice among them, Sir Everett at her side.

"By teaching, of course. We'd set up a little school somewhere. Well, the details are not clear as of yet. I felt so inspired by your mother's recounting of your playing a duet with that man. Who is he again, Maude?"

"He introduced himself as a Mr. West. He's so familiar I feel that I've met him before."

She had, but Ingrid was not about to remind her mother how.

"He is not titled?" Lady Danvers's already wrinkled brow multiplied into more crinkled ridges. "However did Lady Ingrid encounter him?"

Mother shrugged. "No title that I know of. Perhaps he is a gentleman of leisure. Darling, how did it come about that you participated in that charity event?"

Both ladies looked at her with questioning gazes, and Ingrid once again had the suspicion that they were up to no good. Though she could not fathom their intentions, she must choose her answer wisely so as not to invite more questions. Yet, as words formulated on her lips, she paused, because to her right was the subject of their conversation. Dressed as a gentleman, cravat and all, and dancing with people who were not his peers.

Quickly, she darted her gaze back to the ladies beside her. Would they see him? Why was he at a ball? What would happen if Lady Sanderson discovered his infiltration? The thrum of nervousness vibrated through her, and she thought surely they could hear the pounding of her heart.

"Mr. West heard me play at a previous ball and asked

for my help." The simple and true answer. "If you both will excuse me, I am positively parched."

They nodded, though Ingrid did not care for their expressions. Studious. Inquisitive. She hoped her mother was not mentally expanding the suitor list. Frowning, Ingrid skirted the edges of the ballroom, keeping an eye on Gideon as she did so. He looked too handsome and jaunty. How did he conduct himself so easily among the peerage? How had he gotten in? Was he here because of her?

Frowning, she retreated to another room where refreshments had been set up. She accepted a cup of lemonade from a servant and sipped it while she found a corner to wait in.

The music faded to an end. A moment later Mr. Gideon West sauntered into the refreshment room as if he had every right to be there. As if he had wealth and a title and the connections required. A quick glance, and he then he saw her. Giving his cravat a hasty tug, he made right for her.

"Not hiding behind a curtain this time, I see." The barest hint of peppermint brushed her senses as he spoke, and Ingrid's heart flipped about beneath her sternum.

The intrepid Lady Ingrid looked surprised to see Gideon. Two identical flushes of color tiptoed across her cheeks as her eyes lifted to his. Her dress, like the color of the ocean, seemed to change in shade with her movements. Shimmering and delicate, hugging her figure as only a well-made ball gown could.

"What are you doing here?" Her gaze darted about, as though afraid the constabulary might come in and haul him out.

"It is not illegal for me to be here, Lady Ingrid. I had a desire to dance."

Her mouth skewed in a disbelieving look. "I hardly believe that. Are you working? Because it looks to me as though you're playing, and what could you possibly be telling people in your introductions?"

"I tell them I am Mr. West, a gentleman."

"Gentlemen usually have funds attached to their name."

She sounded so disapproving that Gideon chuckled. What was it about her that amused him? Her cranky, sour disposition could not possibly be likeable, and yet he did like her. Oftentimes it seemed that she was not aware of how she sounded, which made her all the more interesting in his book. She was unaware, completely focused on her thoughts and opinions and goals to the exclusion of all else.

Including artifice and superficiality.

How he enjoyed that.

She sipped her lemonade, brows narrowed at him. They were as black as her hair, which she'd pulled into some sort of curling concoction at the top of her head. Several curls trailed down her delicate neck to rest upon her silk-clad shoulders. Dark as a raven's breast, and glossy. So soft that if he touched her hair, he felt certain it would be silk sliding between his fingers.

She cleared her throat. "Well? It seems disingenuous to waltz in here, pardon the pun, pretending to be someone you're not."

"I bear good news." Why did he long to touch her hair? How could he possibly be attracted to this woman? He curled his fingers into his palms. "I have eliminated three more men from your list due to unacceptable vices. Mistresses, debts and other serious flaws in character that your parents would not approve of in a love match."

Her scowling, disbelieving expression lightened with what appeared to be relief. Silly as it was, his conscience still twinged at her censure.

"I do not pretend to be anyone other than who I am," he amended, moving closer to Ingrid as a trio of ladies passed. "Is it my fault if they assume my station? And should I be relegated to some sort of inferior status simply because society says so?"

Fortunately for him, she'd pressed herself against the wall, leaving no room for escape.

"There are no curtains here, and you cannot hide." He wanted to reach over and touch her cheek. Her skin looked ever so soft, and clean, and yes, even if he did not want to let society dictate his actions, it nevertheless held true that she lived in the upper echelons of London. If he made one wrong move, even one unacceptable look, he could destroy her reputation.

And that of her sister.

The thought quelled any more thoughts of touching her without good reason. He straightened, realizing belatedly that he'd been leaning toward her like a besotted fool. A waltz started, the strains reaching their room.

And that waltz could very well be his good reason.

"Shouldn't you go and find a dance partner?" Her tone held a snooty appeal that unaccountably made him smile. Did her eyes flash beneath the flickering lights, or was that his imagination? Making a sudden decision, he stepped closer to her, so close that it was almost something for gossips to remark on.

If they cared.

Thankfully, Lady Ingrid was closer to being on the shelf than to being the subject of the gossipy *ton*.

"May I?" he asked, holding out his hand for her cup of lemonade.

Eyeing him with a definitively suspicious arc to her brow, she handed it to him. He immediately turned and deposited it upon a nearby servant's tray. "Thank you, my good man."

The servant looked surprised but quickly covered with a tip of the head.

"Now, Lady Ingrid, that waltz you mentioned." He held out his hand again, but for an altogether different reason. Would she place that elegant palm of hers within his own? Would she step outside the box society had placed her in? Dance with a *commoner*?

If she said no, she protected them all but lived a boring life. If she said yes, she would remind him of the woman he had first met, the one who hid in a stranger's office and eschewed polite conversation for words with meaning. He waited, suddenly aware that his blood pumped through him in furious beats, that his mouth felt dry, and his hand a trifle sweaty.

She said neither yes nor no, but held his gaze very carefully, looking up at him with a serious cast to her pretty lips. "I do not like to dance."

"Why?" He moved again, closer because those not waltzing had decided to crowd the refreshment room. And perhaps because he liked the way she smelled. Jasmine again, and something else he couldn't define.

"I just do not."

"Because of your limp?" He flattened his back against the wall, making room for those wandering into the room. It was the first time he'd mentioned the disability.

"Yes and no."

"Were you born with it?"

"I'd prefer not to speak of this."

"Very well." He'd find out later what had happened, and why she hid in corners and behind curtains instead of dancing. "I noticed you've specially crafted shoes. Can you dance tonight?"

"I am not in pain, if that's what you mean." She stared ahead, her profile to him. Their position allowed for a half view of the ballroom through the open double doors. Other attendees, mainly the younger set, swirled about the floor, enjoying what had been lauded as a most indecent dance only a few years prior.

"Then dance with me. Enjoy the night. No one shall remark upon a gentleman dancing one dance with the eldest daughter of an earl who has been out six Seasons."

"Seven, actually." A pensive twist to her lips accompanied that remark.

"Exactly. I am not an unattentive dancer."

A soft sound, much like a chuckle, puffed from her. "Is that your way of assuring me that you shall not stomp on my toes?"

"It is."

"You are as humble as to be expected. I do not wish to dance. It is a precarious situation, you see. One wrong twist, and I am in pain for days. Sometimes weeks." Her head pivoted to him. "I do not wish to injure myself before Paris."

"And what if someone asks you to dance while there? It is my expert opinion that you should practice." It was also his expert opinion that he wanted to put his hands upon her waist, to draw her close. Could he be blamed? She, a beautiful woman with a heart for children. "The song shall be over soon. It might even be called half a dance. A partial waltz, if you will."

Her gaze flickered. "My turn to ask why."

"First—" he let his head tilt toward her ever so slightly "—if you had no limp, would you like dancing?"

She blinked and managed to move slightly away. Though should she slide any farther, she'd encounter a wall. The thought brought a traitorous laugh to his throat, which he promptly hid with a cough.

"Perhaps if I danced with the same person every time. But as it is, having to switch between different people, touching their hands that have touched others…" She shuddered. "There is something entirely unappealing to me about dancing with strangers."

"One man, then. Your future husband. Had you no limp, would you like dancing with him?"

Her eyes widened as if she contemplated the question deeply. Not that he wanted her to think too deeply about it all. She'd claimed monogamy to her piano, hadn't she? He just wanted a small dance with her. He had from the moment he'd met her, and this seemed as good a time as any. As fun as it had been to sneak into this ball, he didn't plan to attend many others.

He had information to impart to her, which had been partially why he'd chosen to attend tonight. Also, to spy upon two more men on her list.

"I think I would," she answered in a soft tone. Tenderness crossed her face as her arms folded against herself protectively. "Yes, if there were one man for me, I would dance with him every night."

Gideon swallowed, his throat suddenly tight at the look on her face. It was unlike Ingrid to look so vulnerable, so wistful. An odd little skip thumped in his chest. His heart? He cleared his throat, wiped his palms against his slacks.

"I shall wipe my hands clean just for you." He withdrew a handkerchief and made a show of swiping every crevice. "Spare this poor commoner a few minutes of your time. Dance with me and leave me with a happy memory of a life I shall never live. In return, I shall give you more information."

"Information I paid for?" Her mouth scrunched, though

he did not think angrily. "Very well. Let us find a quiet area of the floor. I cannot be swept about too much, and we shall have to take small turns."

She did not wait for his lead, but swished ahead of him with all the determination of her nature. And yet, as he followed, he couldn't but help note the flushed skin upon the back of her neck.

He must be very careful indeed. A dance. An exchange of information. He had come here for the latter, but he could enjoy the former.

Carefully. Very carefully, indeed.

Chapter Nine

Ingrid walked to a corner of the ballroom mostly absent of whirling couples. Perhaps due to less lamplight? Whatever the reason, it appeared the best place to waltz. She keenly felt Gideon's presence behind her. His watching eyes, the uninterrupted attention that he focused squarely on her.

Then there was the music vibrating around her. Each instrument thrummed with its own beauty and melded with the others in a glorious symphony of sound. She recognized the Sussex waltz, the piano's strong clear notes, the violin appearing in the background and gradually gaining strength. The song was almost over, but her ears strained to catch each note and the lovely cadence of their harmonies.

She stopped at the wall, turned, and there stood Gideon. His cravat white and crisp against his dark blue tailcoat. His eyes intense and such a deep blue, the blue of a midnight sky lit with moonlight.

Her heart moved into her throat as he stepped closer to her. She could scarcely breathe as his right hand cupped her own, his touch warm and exciting and ever so different.

She had been right about his hands. They were not smooth nor soft but callused and firm. Their strength translated to his grip and she tried to swallow, really she did, but her dreadful heart was still in the way. Blocking her airways.

She could not pass out. She must breathe. Why was it so hard? She forced a deep breath, and with the influx of oxygen, all the trembling and nerves moved to her stomach and her knees trembled.

"Are you ready?" he murmured.

She nodded because her mouth felt frozen, much like when she ate two Gunter's ices in a row. Unladylike to be sure, yet she had done it more often than she'd ever admit to anyone.

He gently swirled her on the floor, making the requisite waltz moves in a slower, modified fashion. At this close range she realized his eyes held specks of light blue within the darker irises. How very attractive.

Which was to be expected, she reminded herself forcefully. She could not allow herself to forget that he was an outrageous and accomplished flirt who seemingly snuck into balls often and easily. Who cared that he had pleasing eyes?

And so what if his palm fit perfectly against the small of her back? If his hand curled around hers ever so gently, and his thumb caressed her skin in a way surely a true gentleman wouldn't dare.

He was not her peer. He was a detective, a man not even on the perimeter of her circle of acquaintances. Thank goodness she'd be leaving soon. Any day the invitation should arrive.

But as they circled the floor in slower, circumspect steps, her mind clouded with his presence.

Why did he not speak? He should say something. Anything to get her mind off his squared jawline. How had she never noticed how perfectly well his head situated upon his neck? Such a silly, inane thought, but that was what waltzing was doing to her.

Forcing her to notice the oddest features.

"You frown." His own mouth mimicked hers. "Is your leg in pain?"

"I am well," she said a little breathlessly. His hand tightened, pulling her a little closer. Almost indecently close. She had danced the waltz before. Not a lot, but often enough to know there were multiple ways to skirt convention if one wished. Many a couple had contrived intimacies that would never be tolerated in any other dance.

That was what was happening now. She felt closer to Gideon than she'd ever felt to another dance partner. She found that her gaze was on his lips again, and so forced her attention upward to his eyes. She searched them.

"You are holding me rather tightly, Mr. West."

"To keep you from stumbling, my dear lady."

"I am not your dear anything." She put a smidge of distance between them but that did little to stop the excitement humming through her.

"I daresay you are no one's dear, but why?" He turned her gently, and she followed his movements. "You are highly accomplished. I understand that you do not wish to marry for love, but what of security? What of children?"

"I did not think you so audacious as to ask questions of such a personal nature." She nibbled her lip, suddenly saddened by his inquiry. The music stopped and Gideon led her to an alcove with a settee. They were in full view of the room, but if he stayed near her much longer, the gossips would notice.

It was one thing to waltz. Quite another to keep company with each other for an extended period of time.

"You cannot speak to me much longer," she told him, swishing her skirts away from his legs and checking to see that a large swath of settee fabric remained between them. "Though I couldn't care a fig for what anyone might say about me, there is Alice to consider. Her reputation must remain intact."

She glanced over at him. Irritation spiked through her at his attractiveness. How could he sit there and look so charming and handsome when he had no business even being here? "You do not even care that you were not invited to this ball. Why are you here?"

"Back to this again." His brow rose in a most annoying manner. "How do you know I wasn't invited?"

"I know," she replied in a voice more scathing than she probably should allow.

It was just all too much. This ballroom, that dance, those questions. She wanted to escape to her home, curl up in her bedroom, but she was afraid if she did so, she'd find herself daydreaming about the way his hand held hers as they waltzed. About the gentleness in his eyes.

She clenched her fingers together.

"Very well." Gideon's voice took on a softer tone. "I am here to spy upon two of your parents' choices. Lord Whaley and Mr. Rathbone. I also completed my investigations of all the other men on your list but one. I know you said your parents are more concerned with a love match, but I took it upon myself to make inquiries into both their personal lives and financial statuses. I shall be compiling a report for you."

His professionalism soothed Ingrid. Better to see this man as a detective than a man. She had thought herself immune to his charms, but she was far more vain than she'd realized, and his attentions disarmed her more thoroughly than expected.

He could never know that.

She gave him a cool look, sure her thoughts remained

shuttered from his view. "Excellent news. When shall I expect it?"

"Soon. I will leave now. I believe we have been spotted by your mother, and she is headed this way."

Ingrid stifled a groan.

"When do you teach the children again?"

"Tomorrow," she said, watching her mother weave through the ballroom. Thankfully, her friends kept stopping her. Ingrid looked to her right. Toward a doorway. She could escape easily. Collect Jane from the servants' quarters. Send word that she'd gone home with a megrim.

Not a total untruth, as the thoughts pounding through her skull were all a bit uncomfortable.

"I shall see you tomorrow then, dear lady."

She scrunched her nose at him but rose to her feet. This was no time to argue about his choice of words. She had a mother to avoid.

A short bow, and Gideon left.

Breaths a tad too shallow, she watched his broad back as he disappeared into the crowd. As soon as she received the report from him, she would tell her parents of her opportunity, present her case against those suitors and be free to move on with her life as she saw fit.

"A certain lady known for her sour disposition was spotted waltzing with a mysterious dark-haired man. They appeared utterly enchanted with each other." Alice dropped the paper to the kitchen table the next morning, her mouth agape. "Do you hear this?"

Dappled morning sunlight spilled into the room from large windows beside their table. Alice glowed with vibrant health and happy spirit and entirely too much interest in the gossip columns of the morning paper.

Ingrid did her best to ignore her sister by focusing on

the book she'd plucked from the library at four this morning. Even though she'd finagled an early exit from the ball, she hadn't been able to sleep for thoughts of Gideon circling her brain.

Her mood was not the best today. So much so that she had considered canceling the afternoon piano lesson with the children. They needed their music. A strong part of her longed to see the children today. She liked them, somehow.

"Well, keep going," said Mother from the other side of the table. "What else does it say?"

"Drivel," muttered Father from beside Mother. "What of the latest *on dits* about Byron? Is he still in London? We've missed a poetry reading or two."

Ingrid trained her eyes on her book but she couldn't read a thing. She snuck a look at her sister and found her staring at her as if trying to read her mind.

"A lady known for her sour disposition. Surely, you all know who that is?" Alice's gaze popped from person to person. "Dancing with a man."

"You do not mean to say you think it's Ingrid?" Mother laughed and plucked a bacon from her breakfast plate. "I would not call her disposition sour. Perhaps intense. Artistic. Besides, no one notices her."

"Now, darling, that's not true," Father gently admonished. He looked polished this morning, his light brown hair combed back and his whiskers neatly trimmed. "Ingrid is distinguished."

"Oh, you know what I mean." Mother waved her hand, bacon and all, through the air. She had come to the table in a peach day dress that gave a youthful flush to her skin. "She is not the topic of conversation, and she prefers it that way. Don't you, dear heart?"

Ingrid offered a firm nod. Why was everyone so dressed up? She touched her hair, which she had quickly tied back with little thought for neatness. Her family must have morning plans. She should excuse herself now but food still remained upon her plate and she was quite famished.

Alice folded her hands. "This is most certainly about Ingrid. So, sister, who is this mysterious dark-haired man who has so enraptured you?" Her eyes gleamed with merriment. Or was it maliciousness? Ingrid could never be sure despite the great strides she'd made in restoring their relationship.

"Oh!" Mother made an excited sound in her throat. "What of that Mr. West with whom you played music? He was at the ball last night."

Teeth clenched, Ingrid nodded. She would not stoop so low as to lie, but this conversation was veering into territory better left undiscussed. If she even tried to speak of Gideon, she was certain to blush and that would intrigue her romantic family more than a silly gossip column. The last thing she needed was her parents paying attention to her comings and goings.

She did not know how they'd feel about her teaching music to street children by herself, and she did not want to find out. She scooped a forkful of eggs into her mouth.

"Mr. West is utterly charming," her mother continued, seemingly satisfied with Ingrid's terse nod. Or perhaps expecting nothing more. "I had the opportunity to speak with him at a charity event. A well-spoken man with both wit and intellect."

"But why would the gossips be remarking upon Ingrid?" asked Alice. "There has never been any interest in her except for that time in her first Season when she stomped out of the ballroom. How I wish I could have seen that. Oh, and did she not cause Mr. Handley to cry in her second Season?"

Ingrid cut a glance at her father, hoping he was not taking heed to the table talk, but no, he watched her with a strange light to his eyes. A *curious* light. She swallowed the food that had unexpectedly gotten stuck in her throat.

"Firstly, I stomped out because that pompous Sir Crosby implied that with my personality, I should be thankful to have a fortune because that was the only way I'd ever catch a husband. And when I told him that it was too bad he had neither personality nor fortune, he dared insult my skills at the pianoforte." She let her fork clatter to her plate. "He did not deserve to dance with me. As for Mr. Handley, how was I to know that he'd been nervous about his dancing skills? That it was his first ball? He was older than me and he trod upon my toes not once, not twice, but four times. I limped for a week."

Mother made a small humming noise and Alice's lips twitched.

"Which brings us back to the man." Alice cleared her throat. "Mr. West, is it? How were his dancing skills?"

"Perfect," Ingrid replied testily.

"Ha." Her sister's mouth widened into a triumphant grin. "You did dance with him."

Cheeks burning, Ingrid grabbed for a slice of plum cake. Duped! And now the entire table stared at her.

"Ingrid?" Father watched her much too closely for comfort. "Do you like Mr. West?"

Mother grinned. "Shall we add him to the list? Lord Manning, take note."

"No." The cake lodged in her throat, creating a coughing fit. She grabbed for her orange juice and swished it down. Her eyes watered. "Do not add anyone else to the list."

"What list?" Alice looked back and forth between her parents and Ingrid.

Something like a rock sank to Ingrid's stomach. She

was not one to easily feel humiliated, but at the moment she did rather wish to disappear. Just poof into thin air.

"Your father and I are helping Ingrid find a husband," her mother said in a much too perky voice.

"I did not ask for help," she pointed out.

"Of course you did not," said Alice. "Why am I not involved? I could find Ingrid the perfect man."

"We didn't want to infringe on your first Season, dear heart. This is simply to get Ingrid settled before you. Did you know I was an endless mass of nerves when your father courted me?" Mother clutched her hands in a swoony embrace against her heart and fluttered her lashes at Father. "He took a month to propose, even though we'd snuck a few kisses. Chaste kisses, of course. Which I do not recommend you ever allow a suitor. But I knew he was the one for me and that we would forever love each other."

Her parents made moon eyes at each other and Alice giggled.

Ingrid wanted to gag. Her throat fairly convulsed with the need. Sentiment clouded the room, but at least they were off the topic of Gideon West and his dark locks.

Alice continued to ask her parents about their romance, but Ingrid returned to her novel and focused on finishing her breakfast. Just as she drank the last of her juice, Rutgers entered.

The servant, who had been with Father since before his marriage, made a creaky bow. Then he straightened. "Callers have been leaving their cards this morning."

"For Alice?" Mother winked at Ingrid's little sister, and her cheeks pinkened.

"And also for Lady Ingrid."

She groaned. Please, no.

"There is a post for Lady Ingrid as well," Rutgers added, giving her a little nod. He knew, of course, of her hopes.

One did not normally share confidences with servants but Rutgers had been with them for so long that he felt more like a grandfather.

She bolted up and a hot arc of pain shot through her hip. Grimacing, she hobbled out of her chair. "Where is it?"

"I have it here, miss." He held out a small, cream-colored vellum that had been folded and sealed with wax.

Her mouth grew suddenly dry as she reached for the missive.

Chapter Ten

"Hello, ladies." Gideon swept a gallant bow as he passed a group of young women dressed for a day of shopping. The sun beat upon his head as he traipsed Bond Street, Ingrid's report clenched in his right hand, a walking stick in his left. Within the stick hid a blade. It had been a long morning, but he'd finally apprehended a man who'd stolen from a mother of five. The walking stick proved an effective tool in convincing the man to hand over the money and submit to Gideon's arrest.

The mother had come to him in tears earlier this morning, unable to pay but a scant amount for Gideon's retrieval of her funds. Her purse, it turned out, had contained this month's rent. Thankfully, the thief had been too stupid to cover his face when he stole it and the woman recognized him.

Which handily enabled Gideon to track the thief down.

He whistled a happy tune as he maneuvered the busy streets. Though the woman had tried to pay him from her rent money, he couldn't bring himself to accept the offer. Her children had stared at him with wide, scared eyes. The youngest was just a babe on her hip.

No. He had not thought it right to allow her to pay.

After all, he'd have coin soon enough, as soon as he handed this husband report over.

He dodged a carriage and crossed to the other side of Bond Street. Busy day for shoppers. He'd popped over to meet a fellow runner because he'd picked up a lead on a crime that had happened a month ago and it was faster to meet the man than to pen a note and pay someone to deliver it.

The busyness of the day had been a great boon, for his sleep had been restless.

Memories of dancing with Ingrid last night plagued him. The scent of her, the feel of her frame encircled within his. And to be so close to look into her beautiful eyes… their depths pulled at him no matter how hard he resisted.

She was a conundrum.

And the way she had stared back, not blushing, not demure, but forthright and curious. A woman unlike any he'd ever known.

He shook his head as if that would clear his thoughts. This had to end.

He stopped whistling as he flagged a hackney to take him over to Bow Street. She was to be there an hour from now. He'd allow one last lesson but then he must never see her again.

The woman impeded his plans. She bothered him, and a man trying to care for so many children could not afford an infatuation for a lady so far outside his own world.

He stepped up into the hackney, paid the driver and told him where to go, then settled against the squabs and heaved a giant sigh. Long day. His muscles relaxed but his mind raced. In a few minutes he would see Ingrid. Unbidden, an image of her came to mind. Violet eyes. Capable fingers as she created art on the pianoforte.

And that stubborn lift to her chin.

His body gave in to his tiredness and he let his eyes drift shut. This report was her key to freedom. And the bag of coin she'd give him in return was his key to stability.

He didn't know how many kids would leave London with him. He'd take as many as he could. On his next slow day of work, he'd ride into the country and search for a cottage in a village where the children could learn trades. Where food was abundant and crime scarce. He'd find a tutor as well, or perhaps strike a bargain with someone to teach the kids in exchange for… Well, he hadn't worked that part of the plan out yet.

Surely, to rent a cottage would prove cheaper than renting these lodgings, especially now that rates had risen. Crabtree was kicking him out anyway. Tension coiled in his forehead and he rubbed the left side as if he could massage away his worries.

He didn't blame Crabtree's wife for wanting them gone. Bow Street was already dangerous enough. Add in boisterous children, most who picked a pocket quicker than a man could blink, and anyone might feel unsafe in their own home.

The hackney rolled to a stop. Gideon exited, only to see Lord Hawking lounging upon his stoop. Did the man not understand plain English? Sighing, Gideon approached with heavy steps.

"You are persistent." He reached around Lord Hawking and turned the knob to his home. The door swung open, revealing an empty room. No children today. He ignored the earl and went inside, closing the door behind him.

Ingrid would be disappointed if no one showed. Might be a bitter lesson on the ephemeral nature of street urchins.

The door creaked, opening. Gideon pivoted, his jaw dropping as Hawking let himself into the place. The impertinent man closed the door behind him, leaving them both in a darkened room.

He shut his mouth, a tic tugging in his jaw as he crossed to the kitchen area and lit a lamp. After moving about the room and lighting more candles, enough light splayed about for him to notice the annoying jut to the earl's chin. The man stood silently observing, his mouth twitching every so often and his hand fiddling with a gold watch fob.

Gideon sat on a chair near the oven, stretching his legs out and lacing his hands behind his head. Beneath hooded lids, he peered at the man who'd abandoned him. "State your reason for letting yourself into my home uninvited."

The earl shuffled his feet. He glanced about the place, perhaps judging its shabbiness, perhaps searching for a chair since he looked frail enough to fall over. "You're doing a good thing with the children."

Gideon raised his brows and waited.

"I've a proposition. Your mother's letters."

"What of them?"

"I will let you have them in exchange for something."

Gideon straightened. "There is nothing I want from you."

"Even letters your mother penned? She wrote of you often, with pride."

"And what did you think when the letters ceased arriving?" He plunged upward, his stomach sour, his temples pulsing. The man wanted something from him. The audacity. He didn't want anything to do with Lord Hawking or his fortune.

Indeed, the very thought sparked loathing.

"I thought she'd continued on with her life. Perhaps married," the earl said in a subdued voice.

"And you thought nothing for your son? To discover his whereabouts or to even inquire of his health?" Gideon pinned a glare on the man so pointed and angry that the earl could not hold his gaze.

"I had a family." The old man's voice cracked as he stared at the vicinity of Gideon's chest.

"Yes, and where are they now? This family you loved so much that you could not even care for a helpless little boy and his mother?"

Lord Hawking's gaze flicked to the ground, then up to Gideon. The lamplight highlighted the startling blue of that gaze. "I have recently had a conversion, of sorts. I have realized the depths of my depravities and in repentance to my Savior, I beg your forgiveness." "You shall never have it." Gideon delivered the words with no small amount of venom, but within, his gut ached. Savior? Was he crediting God with his change of heart?

"Perhaps not." His sire gave a short nod. "Nevertheless, I shall not cease begging for it until I die."

"As my mother begged and yet received no mercy?"

The earl reached into his tailcoat and withdrew a packet of letters, yellowed and faded, strung together by an old string. "These are yours."

"For a price."

"Yes." The old man nodded slowly, and his eyes shone with moisture. "My nephew will get my title and estates. He is a wastrel who will not care for your sisters. He will turn them out. I have other properties, though, that are unentailed. I have left them in my will to you. There are renters on my estate needing a reliable and honest landowner. I'd like my daughters to have Seasons and to be cared for with these funds."

Gideon was already shaking his head, his heart a cold lump in his chest. "I've enough to deal with. And I know nothing of farming. Give someone else your money. Why not leave it to your daughters? Shouldn't they have married by now?"

"They are stubborn girls." A rueful smile crossed Lord Hawking's face. "They shall have generous settlements, but I want your word that you will make sure they are cared for and protected."

"By your illegitimate son? Surely, there is someone else." He didn't want to have this conversation, but best to get answers now, satisfy the earl and then send him on his way with a solid no.

Lord Hawking's cheeks drooped. The hand holding the letters plummeted to his side. "There is no one."

Gideon's jaw clamped. How tempting to peek at those words, to read his mother's thoughts, to know her feelings. She'd been gone a long time now, and he'd lived his life without her, but her absence had carved a hollow within him that could never be filled.

And her death had been this man's fault.

"I don't want your money or your property. Leave it to someone else." Gideon swung the door open, the knob cold in his palm. "You have said your piece. Now, leave."

Lord Hawking moved as if to do so, but stopped suddenly.

"Why, Lord Hawking, whatever are you doing here?"

Ingrid's voice spiraled panic within Gideon. She was early. The last thing he wanted was word of his association with the earl being bandied about. Illegitimate, and other worse names might follow, affecting his ability to move unnoticed within society.

Ingrid, dressed in a pale blue dress and carrying an armful of what looked to be pastries, barged in. Behind her, Jane carried in full burlap bags. Ingrid's gaze moved from Lord Hawking to him, her expression curious.

"Lady Ingrid." Lord Hawking offered a gentlemanly

bow, impressive for a man who appeared ill. Perhaps his grieving had aged him. Gideon ruthlessly shoved any compassion he felt to the side. "I was discussing a business matter with Mr. West. And you? Practicing for more charitable causes?"

"You could say so." Ingrid swept in, dipping her chin to the items in her arms. "I shall set these upon the table. Where are the children?"

"I will take my leave," said Lord Hawking, his expression inscrutable. "You should think upon my offer."

"Are you engaging Mr. West's services?" Ingrid set her goods down and swiped her palms against her dress. "I have it on good authority that he is most efficient."

Suddenly, Gideon felt unsure. Not a normal feeling for him, and he frowned. The earl had moved closer, his gaze skewered upon Gideon's face, and for a moment he felt like a child again. Looking into those eyes so like his own, wanting acceptance, receiving rejection. The past intertwined with the present.

He felt the focus of Ingrid's perusal as well as amused censure. He, of course, had been the authority who bragged upon his own efficiency only days ago. She enjoyed tossing that boast in his face.

"So I have heard," murmured Lord Hawking, his eyes still arrested upon Gideon. "I am in search of a boy named Wesley. A brave and bold person who disappeared, and I am praying one day he will be found again."

Ingrid looked between the two men. Gideon's stance, feet planted apart, arms crossed, appeared stiff and angry. Lord Hawking on the other hand looked sad.

What had she unwittingly stepped into? She shared a look with Jane, who only lifted her shoulders as if to wonder the exact thing.

"Mr. West is certainly the man to accomplish such a task," Ingrid put in, tone brisk. "If Wesley is to be found, Mr. West can do it." She shifted as her hip had retained the minor ache from earlier. Poor Gideon. Not a dimple to be seen at the moment. Did he dislike Lord Hawking so?

The earl's estate neighbored her cottage. She'd grown up visiting his home. Indeed, Alice and his eldest daughter were great friends. If only she had paid more attention to society dealings and gossip. She had not interacted often with Hawking himself.

He had lost his son recently. She knew that much. And his wife had died a few years back. She studied the elderly gentleman. He had the look of a grieving man. So why did Gideon glare at him so crossly? Could he not spare an ounce of sympathy for the earl?

She crossed the room. "I've no doubt Mr. West shall ease your concerns in any way he can."

Lord Hawking tipped his head to her, giving her shoulder a fatherly squeeze before releasing it.

"I shall not." Gideon's jaw jutted in a most stubborn way, certainly far more stubbornly than Ingrid had ever seen employed. "Lord Hawking, take your leave."

Ingrid gaped, then snapped her mouth closed. "How severely you speak. Lord Hawking, take no heed to Mr. West. He is clearly hungry and not in his right mind."

Was it her place to interfere? No. And though she preferred to ignore people in general, in this circumstance, with the frailty of Lord Hawking's visage and the sorrow in his eyes, she felt a strange need to protect the man.

She narrowed her gaze at Gideon. "Do you not care about this Wesley? That he is found? After all your work with the orphans—"

"Wesley is dead," Gideon said in such a tightly strung

voice that Ingrid felt cut by his tone. "And Lord Hawking knows that it is his fault."

Oh, she had definitely stepped into something far deeper than she'd anticipated. Squaring her shoulders, she said, "Nevertheless, the man is bent in sorrow. Have mercy, Gideon."

"I shall not." The vehement statement rippled through the room.

"You are familiar with Mr. West," Lord Hawking said in a thoughtful way.

Gracious, she'd misspoken. She'd used his first name. Clearing her throat, she met the earl's curious look with a nonchalant response. "He has done some work for my family and as you know, we've played music together. It seems silly to not use his Christian name at times."

"Indeed."

She did not like the speculative crease to the corners of Hawking's eyes. Casting her a faint smile, he bowed and then straightened. "I shall go now. Consider my offer," he said to Gideon before walking out.

"Well." Ingrid walked to the pianoforte and lowered herself to the bench. The change in posture offered relief to the persistent ache. "That was awkward."

Gideon shoved a hand through his hair. He pivoted and paced to the other end of the small room. "It's not proper for you to stay here. There are no children today. Here is your report. Take it and I do not wish to see you again."

Ingrid blinked as his words found their mark and stabbed far more fiercely than she'd expected. On her way over she'd been so excited to tell him her news. But now he was distracted. Angry. Not the carefree man from last night's waltz.

He carried too much on his shoulders. Maybe the stress of caring for the children had finally worn him down. In that case, she would pay him his due and perhaps relieve some of his worry.

After retrieving the bag of coin from her reticule, which she'd plopped beside her on the bench, she held it up. The velvet blue bag hung by two strings looped around the tip of her finger.

Gideon advanced, a packet of paper in his own hand. His full mouth flattened into a firm line and his eyes lacked humor. She pressed her own mouth together, feeling the way her lips moistened. She rubbed them together. She had thought often of Gideon's mouth and how it might feel upon hers.

It was rather shocking, she supposed, and if anyone knew, they'd be appalled by her unladylike thoughts. But if she didn't marry, she'd never kiss anyone. Which had never bothered her in the least.

So why this dreadful curiosity besetting her? Why this terrible need to discover the mystery behind a kiss?

He handed her the papers. She took them and gave him his bag of coin.

"Our agreement has ended," he said tersely.

"It has," she agreed, but she made no move to rise. She might never see him again. The notion made her feel slightly ill. An ache started in her stomach and it traveled upward to where her heart beat in unsteady rhythm. "Do you dislike Lord Hawking?"

His brows rose. "That is not your business."

No, but if she could not finagle a kiss—and oh, where had that horrid thought come from?—perhaps she could offer advice born from her own experiences.

"You hold unforgiveness toward him," she said.

Gideon's gaze flickered. His face took on a raw and vulnerable cast that carved his cheekbones into sharp blades and darkened his eyes. "What is it to you?"

"Nothing at all. I have my own life and care little for what you do…but there is still that little bit of care, and I quite miss your dimple at the moment." She paused, eyeing him. "I have had my own battles with unforgiveness. My hip, you see."

His arms crossed, as if warding off her words. "This is not the time for confessions, lady. Lord Hawking could be at White's this very moment, speaking of your untimely arrival and creating speculation as to your character. If you care about your sister, you may want to staunch the flow of gossip."

"I do not take the earl for an idle gossiper."

"I suppose you do not consider him a murderer, either?"

Chapter Eleven

Ingrid's skin prickled at Gideon's words. "That is a serious accusation, Mr. West."

He towered above her, masculine and angry, and she longed to hug him.

But no, Jane hovered nearby, a paltry chaperone but one nonetheless. Even more, Ingrid did not imagine Gideon welcoming affection in this moment.

"Very well," Gideon continued, "perhaps not an outright murderer, but one who has murdered through his neglect."

"Perhaps you should sit?" Ingrid patted the bench, her heart hurting for him. "This seems to be a story best told while seated."

Gideon shook his head but then surprisingly came to sit beside her. Her reticule rested between them, a tiny reminder of propriety. Ingrid shifted, too aware of his presence.

Whatever was wrong with her?

She must be sick. She'd caught something, something terrible, and she blamed her mother and father and sister. They and their poetry readings and their nonsensical Byronese spoutings.

Inhaling a cleansing, decidedly nonromantic breath, she

faced him. Back to the matter at hand. "Unforgiveness will destroy you. Have you faith, Gideon?"

"Why should I?" He chuckled without humor. "Lord Hawking claims to have had a conversion experience. He claims that God has changed him."

"You do not believe him."

"It matters not what he says. He knew my mother. She lay half-starved and dying, and so I went to him and he refused to help, despite their acquaintance. Her death is on his hands."

The monologue, delivered in a low, flat voice, almost shredded Ingrid's resolve to offer advice. His mother had died. Information she had not known, and her mouth felt dry with shock. But she had never been one to let obstacles keep her from her intended goal, and she was not about to start now. Even if his loss brought sorrow to her soul.

"I am sorry to hear about your mother," she said quietly. "No child deserves such a situation. Nevertheless, holding on to destructive feelings will only serve to harm you."

He eyed her. "Don't tell me you've had one of these conversions, too."

She shrugged. "It is more that I came to realize the truth of the parable. He who has been forgiven much, loves much."

"That makes no sense." He squinted at her, a lock of his hair falling in an adorable way over his brow.

"I held my injury over my sister's head." She touched her hip, remembered the rocking of the carriage, the sudden skid and then flying through the air, only to crash to the ground, her bones crumpling, pain hazing through her lower body in blazing streaks of agony. Swallowing hard, she continued. "Alice took my seat in the front. I was to sit next to Father. I had said so, but she skipped ahead of me. We were always vying for his attention. When a child ran in front of us, the horses startled and tipped the carriage. Father managed to grab Alice, but I went flying out."

"You blamed Alice."

She leveled a look on him. "But of course. Had she not stolen my seat, I would not be maimed." Both externally and internally. She would not share *that* with him, though. How could she? Such an intimate detail. Such a devastating blow.

"I understand the comparison you are attempting to draw, but I can't bring myself to forgive that man," replied Gideon. "He ruined my mother's life."

She nodded slowly, forcing her attention back to the hurt that plagued Gideon. "It is not the circumstances, but the emotions, which are similar between us. My faith in a heavenly father, has deeply changed me."

"Father," scoffed Gideon, something inscrutable in his eyes.

"Yes, Father." She lifted her chin. "Here is the rub of it, Mr. West. If you do not forgive, you will be miserable the rest of your life."

Gideon, in a surprising change of expression, grinned, his dimple appearing like a beacon of light. "This from the lady known for her biting responses and surly demeanor."

Ingrid raised a brow. "I'd hardly use the term *surly*. I prefer *aloof*."

"Why prefer *aloof* at all? Why hide behind your music and your acerbic nature?"

Her back stiffened. "I do not hide."

"Don't you?"

Was it her imagination, or did he lean forward, his eyes alight with a mischief she could not decipher. She cast a glance at Jane, but her maid had taken a seat and studiously avoided looking at them. She had brought along more knitting, perhaps for the new sibling she'd said was on the way.

Once again, a familiar sadness engulfed Ingrid, a tender ache behind her ribs. She would never hold her own baby. She moved her hand to her abdomen, to the womb the doctors claimed damaged beyond all repair.

Suddenly, she became aware of Gideon's staring. He waited for her answer.

"I don't hide," she insisted, dropping her hand. "My parents despaired of my irascibility, as my father puts it, when I was but a girl. My governess insisted I read happy poems in an attempt to introduce me to the jovial side of life."

"Were you so unhappy then?" Gideon leaned back, putting a little space between them. Just as well, since Ingrid's thinking felt frumpled like a day dress worn too long in a carriage.

"No. Not at all." Indeed, she often felt content with her day-to-day life. "She assumed me to be malcontent due to my preoccupation with music and my less than stellar interest in the normal activities of young ladies of leisure."

"Such as sewing and gossiping?" Gideon's handsome mouth quirked upward.

What a strange conversation for them to be having. A Bow Street detective and a woman who'd rather be a pianist than a lady.

She met his grin with an answering smile. "It is true. I didn't fit the mold. My family, beyond being respectably eccentric, also holds a fondness for the works of Lord Byron, Donne and Wordsworth."

"I've heard of Byron. Who are the others?"

"Poets." She grimaced. "Romantic poets. But we are not speaking of my propensity for eschewing a social life in favor of my piano. We are speaking of your attitude toward Hawking."

"And yours toward your sister."

"Precisely." She gave a firm nod, though she had a

sinking feeling she'd lost his attention somehow. He really ought to stop staring at her so. As if there was a spot upon her face that he wished to wipe off. "I was filled with bitterness toward Alice and because of that, I did not love her, nor did I love the Lord."

"Let me guess. You forgave her and now you are the closest of friends."

He sounded bemused. She tilted her head, feeling the serious cast to her face. "No, I asked both her and God to forgive me. They did, and I love them the more for it."

"Surely, you weren't that horrible."

"Indeed I was," she answered severely.

Gideon's dimple deepened. "I suppose I can believe that."

"I'm simply concerned for you. I've never seen you look so angry. It cannot be good for your health."

"No, no, it cannot." But he looked entirely too disaffected by her words. His hand crept out and before she understood what he was about, he touched her hand, which rested on her lap. His forefinger traced a scintillating pattern from her wrist to the tip of her middle finger. "This is to be our last meeting. Our last conversation. You wish to ruin it with boring speeches about forgiveness and religion. This is unlike the Lady Ingrid I've come to know."

"You obviously do not know me as well as you think." She snatched her hand away, cheeks burning. "Do not take my advice, then. Wallow in the stink of own hatred. What do I care?" She whipped her reticule from its place between them.

Irritation sparked through her and she popped to her feet, a foolish move that strained her leg and sent a darting lick of fire through her hip. She gasped, bending in reaction.

"Lady Ingrid." Gideon was at her side, and through the muddle of pain, she heard his concern.

"It is nothing," she managed to say, but her breaths were short.

"I must get her home." Jane had come beside her. "My lady, can you walk?"

"Yes, yes." Oh, wasn't this rich. Even more humiliation. She could not even stride away with any sort of regal air. How she disliked her maimed body. How she wished that accident had never occurred. A terrible, oppressive weight settled upon her as she strained to breathe through the pain.

The fire was already ebbing away in slow, throbbing undulations. If only her sorrow would do the same.

Gideon desperately longed to scoop Ingrid up in his arms and take her to a doctor. To someone, anyone, who could relieve the pinched whiteness of her face. He had never seen her lips so pale nor her face so strained.

He glanced at Jane, noting the worried furrow to her brow.

"Are you sure you can walk?" he asked Ingrid in a low tone.

She nodded, straightening slowly. "Yes, the pain is already fading. Jane shall assist me."

"I did not realize your injury was so grievous." Gideon swallowed, his gut tense and his jaw tight.

"You thought my words an exaggeration?" She did not look at him, but a round emblem of color filled her cheek.

Well, yes, he had. He knew that she limped and sometimes felt pain. But now he reworked their conversation in his mind as he followed Ingrid and her maid to the door. They went slowly. He could offer an arm, but it seemed unwise. He had, after all, caressed her hand.

She had been trying to be serious. To give him advice, of all things. And he had brushed her off. He groaned.

Ingrid stopped to look at him. "Are you well?"

"Me?" He shook his head. "Do not worry about anyone else but yourself right now."

She chuckled, a low and pleasant sound that skittered awareness through his senses. "Mr. West, this is nothing. I can already tell that by tomorrow, as long as I care properly for myself today, I shall have but a twinge to deal with."

"You have been in pain at least twice since I've met you," he said. How often did this occur?

"It is due to the Season. When I am in the country, I am able to be much more careful with my steps and movements." She offered a conciliatory smile but to his mind, it still looked labored. Thankfully, color slowly invaded her lips.

He moved ahead to open the heavy wooden door. "Can I help you into your carriage?"

"I brought my coachmen. They are experienced in assisting me."

The two moved past him, Jane's arm expertly looped through Ingrid's in a steadying fashion. He followed. Ingrid's neck, long and elegant, still looked too pale and the hair at the base of her scalp clung to her skin in damp wisps. He recognized the effects of sudden pain. Whether at the pugilist's gym where he often trained to stay quick on his feet, or on the streets, where death occurred unexpectedly, he knew the signs.

She had been in so much pain that her body produced a cold sweat.

The realization sobered him. He should not have been so quick to dismiss her confession. To make light of her injury. And he should not have touched her. The combination had sparked a riotous red to her face and because of that, she had stood without caution.

Her carriage waited at the curb. The streets were busy today. Hackneys clattered in the road, and shouts filled the air as people hailed a ride or bought wares. The coachmen came around to help the women into their carriage. Gideon watched with a helpless, yawning emptiness in his chest. The maid entered first, and then the coachmen brought out a box for Ingrid to step on. They both assisted her. As her dress bunched, as she climbed in, he realized he would not see her again.

And how could he?

They lived in separate worlds.

Before he could stop himself, he rushed forward. The carriage had just started to move but he caught the driver. "A word, a moment, sir. Please."

From within the carriage, he heard Ingrid direct the driver to wait. Her face appeared in the window of the door. Her dark hair framed her face and only the slightest evidence of strain remained.

"Mr. West, did I forget something?" Oh, how prim she sounded. Distant and very much the lady. But he had seen the way she played piano. He had seen the tenderness when she spoke to children. He had seen her eyes alight with passion, tenacity.

"You forgot to say goodbye, my lady." He reached a hand up, hoping she'd give him hers in return.

"Indeed, I did." The corner of her mouth tilted. Her hand, delicate and slender-fingered, slipped out to meet his. "Goodbye."

"I wish you the best." He faltered, his flirtatious wit deserting him. Her palm was warm. He let go, reluctantly, without pressing a kiss upon the soft skin. "I hope you get into your conservatory."

Her lips parted into a wide smile, and finally, her gaze relaxed. "Oh, but I meant to tell you. The letter came today. I shall be going to Paris."

A great wave of happiness crashed over Gideon, followed immediately by the knowledge that this truly was the last time he'd speak to this spunky lady. "Excellent news. I am not surprised in the least."

"Thank you." Her lower lip tucked beneath her teeth for a brief moment in an oddly vulnerable way. "I shall pray that your heart softens, Mr. West. That you may be healed of your wounds so that you may properly care for the children."

Though her words could offend, he did not take them as anything but in the spirit she offered them: gently and kindly, with humility. A strange and beguiling facet to Lady Ingrid that surprised him.

So many facets, and it did not seem fair that just as he was beginning to know her, she must leave.

But such was the way of the world.

He gave her a sharp nod and stepped away from the carriage. She disappeared from view and the driver snapped the horses into movement. As he turned to go back home, he caught sight of Petey rushing toward him, mangy mongrel in tow.

"Be that the lady?" he asked, his little face red from exertion.

"She's gone."

"But today is piano."

Gideon rubbed the back of his neck. "She couldn't stay, Petey."

The little boy's shoulders dropped and the droop of his lips brought a lump to Gideon's throat.

"They never do," Petey muttered. There was a clogged quality to his voice, yet no tear slid down his cheek. Too many years on the streets, too many heartaches and disappointments that dried up emotion like a hot sun withering young grass.

Gideon swallowed his own disappointment and clapped the boy's shoulder. "Come, she brought treats. We shall eat and I will play the violin. We shall plan our move and talk about the kind of cottage we want."

Petey nodded but as they trudged into the house, Gideon could not shake the feeling that he had just lost someone priceless.

There was nothing he could do, he told himself. If he took Lord Hawking's offer, if he protected the man's daughters and provided them Seasons, he could move into the outer circles of the haut monde.

He could bring the children with him. There would be more than enough for all.

But he couldn't bring himself to squander his pride for the lure of security.

And forgiveness? What would that look like? How did one go about forgiving the egregious acts of Lord Hawking? He did not even know how to begin, nor did he want to.

With the money Ingrid had paid him, he could afford to begin looking at cottages. He could buy a run-down one. A little cottage that he could fix up. His work with Bow Street would cover some costs but he would also need to hire a nanny for when cases took him across England.

How much did a nanny cost?

He scratched his head, opening the lodging's door for Petey and following him in. He had no earthly idea. His expulsion loomed nearer and nearer, and as of yet, he did not know which children would come with him.

Petey, for certain. The boy was an orphan dodging the authorities. He'd already run away from two different orphanages and Gideon had no intention of putting him in another. The boy didn't even have a last name. He watched as Petey scrounged around the goodies Ingrid had brought, finally landing on a large, cream-colored dumpling topped with clotted cream. Beside the pile lay a piece of paper.

Frowning, Gideon moved toward the kitchen, picked up the sheet and read the first line. His frown deepened. He folded the paper without finishing, the words running through his mind in an endless script, and he stuffed it into his pocket.

Dearest Hawking, father of our child.

He marched to the corner of the room. He pulled out Gus, plucking the strings and tuning as needed, as his thoughts moved back to Ingrid.

He would miss the intrepid lady.

He would miss her more than he would ever admit.

Chapter Twelve

The time of reckoning had come.

Ingrid sat in her dressing room, staring at the paper inviting Mr. I. Beauchamp to audition for the Paris conservatoire as a potential professor. She propped her hand on a fist and eyed her reflection in the looking glass.

They thought her a male. She had not signed her application with a mister, but she had not given her first name, either. When they saw her, they would know immediately their incorrect assumption. Overly wide mouth, pointy chin, eyes too big and skin too pale. Then there was the matter of her form. She had not the beauty of Alice, and though she was tall, she was not slender nor willowy. It would be impossible to hide her curves and there would be no way to pass as a man. She'd have to win the directors of the conservatoire over with her musical skills.

She was just too womanly.

Had she ever really felt womanly, though? Gaze unwavering, she nodded to herself. Yes, when Gideon looked at her, she felt different. Admired or pretty or some unnamed feminine emotion. A pleasant feeling she hadn't realized could exist within herself until she'd met him.

A long month had passed since she'd received the interview invitation, since she'd said goodbye to Mr. West and received her reports. It was all for the best, she told herself firmly. She hardly missed the dimpled detective who surprisingly held a grudge more tightly than a dog guarded a bone.

She was far too busy dealing with the soirees, poetry readings and balls her mother insisted she attend to think of him.

Sighing heavily, she pushed back from the dressing room vanity and went to the dresser in her bedroom where she kept her pin money. Paying Gideon had used more of her resources than she'd anticipated. Mathematics had never been her strong suit, much as it irked. Alice was the one with a head for numbers. She thumbed through the coins, wishing more would magically appear.

They didn't, though.

She planned to speak to her parents today. She had taken time to gather her courage. She'd hidden the report and the invitation at the back of her armoire. She was forcing herself to plead her case this afternoon. The case of nerves had been unexpected. She did not normally retreat in the face of conflict, but every time she'd tried to gather the boldness to approach her parents, her spine went as weak as a string of yarn.

But tonight the family planned to spend their evening playing whist, even though Alice had protested. If it was up to her sister, she'd go out every day and every night. But their parents, eccentric as they were, subscribed to the notion that families should spend time together.

The *ton* treated her parents with amused respect. Ingrid had often overheard her peers discussing her parents' unusual approach to life with a sort of confused admiration. Ingrid herself was thankful for their laissez-faire approach to propriety. They were not so lax as to dismiss it altogether, but they had allowed Ingrid more freedoms than other women in her station.

She hoped their freethinking would extend to paying for her travel to the conservatoire. She did not have the means to bring Jane. She had no means at all, and it was a tad irritating. Someday she hoped to be paid for playing her music, but for now that would be entirely unheard of and potentially disastrous for her family's reputation in the peerage.

Even her parents would not allow their friends to pay Ingrid when she played. Making money? Only the certain sorts of individuals went into business. The gentlemen flitting about London's social circles were men of means, not titles. They were regarded cautiously by the haut monde, but the titled poor were not averse to marrying off a daughter to a wealthy gentleman if it meant securing their futures and keeping their estates.

She sighed again.

It was all so irritating.

All she wanted was to play the piano, to immerse herself in music for the rest of her life.

Unbidden, a memory of teaching the children popped into her mind. Were they safe? Petey's wildness brought worry. And what of the girls? It seemed so meaningless and silly to parade about society while they passed hungry days and dangerous nights.

She frowned and turned away from her dresser.

Nothing to be done, she supposed. She had helped where she could. Nevertheless, a nagging sense of guilt filled her while she allowed Jane to dress her for the day.

Gideon spent his funds on caring for children. His life consisted of ensuring they had a safe place to sleep.

Was it so wrong to dream, to hope, to pursue goals at the expense of other more worthy pursuits?

"My lady, if you frown any more deeply, your mother shall dismiss me for allowing your wrinkles to develop." Jane's voice held a teasing note. She snagged Ingrid's hair and wound it into a high chignon. She lifted a looking glass to Ingrid's face. "How is this for the day?"

"It feels terrible."

"Something more relaxed, perhaps?" Jane's face took on a thoughtful look.

"I do not care." Ingrid crossed her arms. "What do you know of the poor?"

Jane set the glass onto the dresser. "That they are always with us. Why?"

"The children. I wonder how they fare. If they are safe."

Jane patted Ingrid's shoulder in a motherly manner, which was a little odd as the woman was younger than she. "The world is a dangerous place. One cannot worry over things outside our control."

"My invitation to Paris came." Ingrid turned to meet her maid's eyes. "Will you travel with me? Or must I search for a new maid?"

Jane bit her lip, and Ingrid could see the confusion playing across her features. The maid was close to her family and often visited them on her days off. "I would love to see Paris. I truly would. But my mother is expecting another child, and I need to be here to help."

"Do you not think they'd wish you to go? You could learn French, a boon for any lady's maid." She hoped Jane agreed to the travel. She liked her and it was ever so hard to find a servant that did not gossip. Not only that, but Jane had a practical and efficient way about her that served Ingrid well.

"I do not wish to leave your employ." Jane hesitated, her fingers fluttering at her side. "You said that I could leave for a week to help my mother with her birthing time?"

"Yes." Jane had asked months ago, though Ingrid did not know what all that entailed. She had never seen an infant, let alone a birthing. "I shall not decrease your pay, either."

Jane laughed. "You needn't wrinkle your nose so."

"Our lives are very different."

"That they are, my lady. Count your blessings, for you know as well as I that there are so many less fortunate than us."

Jane's words echoed within Ingrid as she made her way to the parlor for her daily piano practice. Try as she might, she couldn't shake the notion that Jane's perspective held a good deal of merit. As she played, she prayed and thanked God for all she owned. She even thanked Him for her strange and eccentric family.

After two hours she slipped off the bench and made her way to the gardens to gather her peace before speaking to her parents. The invitation crinkled in her dress pocket, a reminder that she'd done it. She had procured an audition based on her compositions alone.

Surely, her family would be excited for her.

They did not understand her love for music. They thought it foolish. But even so, they had allowed her to play for friends rather than dance with suitors. They *must* allow her this.

It was the only pleasure in her life.

Not the only one, a voice whispered within. She paused on the path that wound through verdant plants and colorful flowers of the gardens. Spring brought a profusion of colors and scents. Gardeners kept the area neat and trim. The town homes shared the courtyard space but each home held its own private greenery, separated by tall hedgerows and short walls to give the illusion of privacy.

She bent to sniff a rose. The fragrant perfume filled her with a sense of peace. As she straightened, voices carried across the hedgerows. Masculine voices. She edged farther into the gardens, suddenly aware of the scuffling sound her slippers made against the stone.

Her father...and Gideon?

She tiptoed toward a large flower bush. They were behind it, perhaps sitting on the bench near the bird fountain. She paused before touching the bush. The thickness hid them from her view, but also her from theirs. Should she make herself known?

A sudden desire to see Gideon swept through her. She had fooled herself well in thinking she did not miss him. Her fingers twitched against her dress as she recalled the way they played music together. She debated her next move.

Gideon had said her father kept him on retainer, but as far as she knew, there had been no recent crimes committed in the *ton*. Let alone her household. She wet her lips and then rounded the bush.

Father looked up from where he sat on the bench, a packet of papers set upon his knees. His eyes widened. "Why, Ingrid, good morning."

She gave him a quick nod and then surrendered to the overwhelming urge to look at Gideon. He leaned against the opposite ivy-covered wall, his elbows balanced atop it and his ankles crossed. His wore gray trousers and a casual waistcoat over a cream-colored shirt. His hair flipped over his forehead in its usual charming way, and his eyes riveted upon her, sparkling like the Serpentine River on a sunny day.

Her throat closed and nerves beset her. Ridiculous. Yet, her gaze feasted upon him entirely too long.

"Can I help you with something, daughter?" Father broke into her unabashed staring.

Sucking in a strong lungful of air, she turned to him. "No, just out for a walk. What are you two discussing?"

"Business." Father set the papers on the desk, bending down to pick up a small stone to set upon them so that the wind did not blow them about. "Will you excuse us?"

No, she wanted to say. But she could not. For all Father's liberality, he'd not countenance blatant disobedience. Nor would it do for him to find out she'd hired Gideon to discredit potential suitors.

"Business in a garden?" she asked.

"It's a beautiful day." Her father's gaze shuttered.

"Indeed." So their business was to remain private. Very well. She inclined her head, peeking at Gideon once more. She could not decipher his expression, but it seemed his smile had dimmed.

"It is good to see you again, Lady Ingrid." He moved off the wall to offer her an impressive bow.

She responded with the slightly lopsided curtsy she'd perfected over time.

"You two are acquainted?" Father's eyes narrowed behind his spectacles.

"He is the Mr. West with whom I engaged in a charitable duet," said Ingrid, dismayed by how her words rushed out in a breathy manner quite unlike her normal speech pattern.

"I see." And then Father's mouth pursed in a way that suggested contemplation.

She cleared her throat, cutting a quick look to Gideon before aiming her attention back on her father. "Remember? Mother and Alice attended."

"He is the dark-haired man you danced with." Not a question, and she did not like how his eyes brightened.

"Briefly. Very briefly." She emphasized the word *very* with a firm nod.

"Interesting," Father murmured and now he looked at Gideon as though seeing him through a different lens than those resting upon his nose. "Were you there on business, West? And yet you finagled a waltz from my daughter?"

Was it her imagination or did Gideon's shoulders straighten?

"Yes, on business. I did indeed finagle a dance. An apt word, as Lady Ingrid claims to dislike dancing." Though he spoke with confidence, his foot tapped ever so slightly against the stones. "I hope I have not overstepped."

Father laughed, taking off his spectacles and wiping them against his tailcoat as if by cleaning them he might see Gideon more clearly. "Oh, my boy, you have indeed overstepped." He chuckled again. "But it seems that it was an overstep my daughter welcomed. Ingrid?" He peered at her.

"Mr. West is an accomplished dancer," she said formally, feeling a burn within her cheeks. He had been more than accomplished and remembering brought back the sensations of his hands upon her waist, how close they had been… Her pulse raced hard and fast, and she forced herself not to look at the subject of her thoughts. "It was a pleasant experience."

And wasn't that the grossest understatement she'd ever made? She clasped her hands in front of her, now fervently wishing to be dismissed.

"Well then, although you've overstepped, Mr. West, I trust my daughter's judgment in dancing partners. In fact, the other morning I was reminded of how adept my Ingrid is at dancing with whomever she pleases. And likewise, refusing to dance with those who displease her." He proffered her a smile of approval. "She is a woman of strong will and opinion."

Gideon inclined his head. "That she is. I daresay I have

never known a woman to be invited to teach at a musical conservatoire. You must be so proud."

Father had been in the process of readjusting his spectacles but now he paused, his hand midair and the spectacles dangling precariously from one finger. "What's that you say?"

Gideon winced. He'd surely stepped in it now. If Lord Manning's reaction wasn't enough to tell him that he'd goofed, then Ingrid's surely was. Her mouth gaped at his words, and he might have laughed if the tension in the air had not become suddenly palpable.

Jaw snapping shut, she leveled a vitriolic glare in his direction. He suddenly understood what she meant when she said she'd been horrible to her sister. That expression alone induced fear. He lifted his palms. "I apologize that I have spoiled the surprise."

"Surprise." Lord Manning's brows drew together. "If you want to call it that. What's this about a conservatoire, Ingrid? To what does he refer?"

Ingrid's tongue peeked out and wet her lips before disappearing. "I was planning to speak with you and Mother tonight, actually. Let us wait and discuss it later, in the presence of family and not some loose-lipped stranger."

Gideon held back his smile at the disdain loaded in that word *stranger*. Passion filled Ingrid, and most people didn't know because she bottled it within and released it with music. She was livid, no doubt, and it was his fault, innocent though his words had been.

"This stranger knows more about my daughter than I do." Lord Manning popped the spectacles back upon his face.

Ingrid frowned. "I mentioned the conservatory to him because it was relevant. Gid—er—Mr. West is a fellow musician who can appreciate the boon of acceptance. I have waited to involve you and Mother until I definitively knew my plans."

Lord Manning's expression took on an inscrutable look that caused Gideon his first concern. He hadn't thought of it, but this could go very badly indeed. He could be blackballed by the peerage if the earl grew angry enough with him.

"I know not of his musical skills, but he is a Bow Street Runner, first and foremost. A man not of your station and with whom you should not be sharing confidences." Lord Manning stared at his daughter, whose hands twisted in her skirts.

Gideon did not like the cowed look upon her face, nor had he ever expected to see it there, but with her conservatoire on the line, the fear made sense. That was her future. She did not plan on securing a husband, but rather a career.

"West, what have you to say for yourself?" Lord Manning turned on him.

"My lord, it is complicated."

"Well, we shall uncomplicate it, and quickly. Inside, the both of you." Ingrid's father gave Gideon a pointed look that stood the hairs on the back of his neck on end.

Chapter Thirteen

"**S**hould I be concerned for my career?"

Gideon's breath, quietly brushing against Ingrid's ear, struck a shiver down her spine. She followed her father at a distance, and Gideon followed her closely.

"Must you trod upon my heels?" she snapped, even as goose pimples rose on her arms.

He was so very close. She smelled his cologne.

He had ruined her plans, though. With his congratulations, of all things. His admiration had just put her careful waiting at risk.

"I would like to know if I should be worried," he said again, but with a little more distance between them.

"No," she said, softening the slightest at his vulnerability. "At worst for me, my father and mother will discuss the situation and deny me travel. At your worst, they shall release you from any business you have with them." She glanced beside her, for Gideon had lengthened his stride to parallel hers, and she noted the worried crease to his brow. "All shall be well, Mr. West. You may trust me on this."

He let out a rush of breath. "I would like to. My future hinges on it." He cut her a look. "It has been weeks, and yet you've not told your parents of your acceptance? Did they never even know that you applied?"

Ahead of her, Father marched into the house. A maid held the door for them as they followed.

"No," she said in a hushed tone. "I did not tell them for I wasn't certain they'd approve. Besides, it's not an acceptance. More of an audition. I've been going over the reports, by the way. And really, Mr. Wharton's hairstyle would be an impediment to our romance? Was that a serious accusation?"

"A small joke." Gideon flashed his dimple, which she ignored.

By all rights, she should be miffed with him for spilling her private business. But in truth, he had no idea she'd kept it a secret. Most ladies relied on permission for all of their activities. It probably had not occurred to him that she'd sneak behind her parents' backs.

She wrinkled her nose. Not that she had thought of it as sneaking. She was a grown woman, after all.

They marched down the hall after Father discovered from a footman that his wife was in her drawing room. Ingrid squelched a groan. Her very least favorite room in the house. When they reached it, she glanced at Gideon to see his reaction.

A visceral surprise crossed his face as they entered, and she tempered her resulting smile. The parlor could be a bit much, especially for one not within the daily realm of the ton's excessive tastes in design.

Directly across from the doorway, richly hued coral satin curtains waterfalled from tall windows overlooking the street. Mother had decorated during her Egyptian fascination, and so the furniture boasted intricate carvings of animals of the savanna. Lions were a special favorite of Mother's. She'd managed to procure several gilt-framed paintings of massively maned lions, and the paintings lined the walls, interspersed with sphinx-shaped candelabras.

The room always made Ingrid feel that she'd been sucked into a pink desert. Even worse, Mother did not allow any books except those that contained romantic themes. And no instruments at all, as they distracted her from romantic musings.

"Maude, we've a situation." Father stopped in the middle of the room, his hands on his hips. Mother looked up from where she reclined on a settee, knitting. Alice sat in a chair brocaded with golden elephant heads. She looked up when Father spoke, but Mother kept knitting.

"Can it not wait, Manning? I'm behind and the Society for the Education of Mothers is meeting this evening. I want to finish this so that I can gift it to Mrs. Longwood. She is ever so sweet. A rector's wife who is new to the area and knows little of necessary womanly skills. Her knitting is…" Mother trailed off, making a sound of disappointment in her throat.

"This is important." Father's consternation prompted Mother to lift her head.

As soon as she saw Ingrid and Gideon standing behind her husband, a speculative gleam lit her eyes. Ingrid suppressed a groan. Alice giggled.

"I see that indeed it is. Mr. West, how lovely to see you again." Mother set her knitting on the table beside her settee. She gestured to the couch opposite. "Please, sit. Alice, do ring for tea. Now, Manning, there's no need to look so concerned. Come, sit by me, husband." She patted the settee and gave him the kind of smile that Ingrid was sure she'd used more than twenty years ago to snag a proposal.

Father gave in now, just as he had then.

Pressing her lips together, Ingrid moved to the couch and carefully lowered herself. Gideon followed suit. Mother's mouth curved even more as she assessed them. A sinking feeling spread through Ingrid. Yes, she had not imagined that gleam in her mother's eye.

Something was amiss, but what?

"Have you been conducting business with Lord Manning, Mr. West?" asked her mother.

"That is my purpose here today." Gideon's voice sounded deeper than usual, and very serious. His gravelly, masculine tone scuttled awareness through Ingrid.

"I so enjoyed the duet you played with Ingrid. Would you be interested in participating in further charities? My dearest friend Lady Danvers is working on a new charity venture for children. We want to put music in their lives." She paused to take the tea tray from a maid. "Tea, Mr. West?"

"No, thank you." He pulled a pocket watch from his trousers. "I really must be going."

"Please, spare us a minute of your time, if you can." Mother flashed him a gentle smile. "Alice, darling. You may leave. Shut the door as you go."

Ingrid shut her eyes and inhaled deeply. She prayed for patience. As much as she loved her parents, they indulged a penchant for drama with an enthusiasm that far surpassed practicality. She opened her eyes to find both Mother and Father regarding her with concern.

She reached into her skirts and pulled out the invitation. "Before I discuss this with you, should we talk about the list of potential suitors you drew up for me?"

Her parents exchanged a glance, and then her mother clasped her hands together and squealed. "Have you decided, then? I have been trying so hard not to bother you with this. Ask your father. Manning—" she smacked the side of his arm "—isn't it true? Many a time your father has given me a stern look and told me to be patient. You took much longer than I expected. That is to be sure."

"Mother," Ingrid said in a serious tone, because she was certain her mother would not hear anything if she sounded triumphant in any way. "The men were unsuitable."

"But whatever do you mean? They are all very nice. Gentlemanly."

Father's brows squished together. "We handpicked them ourselves."

Excellent, she had efficiently rerouted their concerns. She cleared her throat, ignoring the incredulous look Gideon gave her. "And you did a masterful job with your choices. Positively impressive. Sadly, after much investigation, I have found numerous concerns."

Mother's eyes narrowed. "That cannot be possible."

"It is indeed, and I shall share them with you. In all, you provided eleven names. Four of which are men with secret vices such as mistresses and gambling debts. Surely, you do not want me to secure a love match with men of such low character?" She listed their names.

"I have heard nothing of the sort for any of those men." Mother nudged Father. "Have you, my love?"

"Indeed not." He scowled, which he did not normally do, and Ingrid felt a small twinge of guilt. She squelched it easily, reminding herself that her parents were attempting to force something that could not be forced. Love, for one.

And Ingrid, for another.

Biting back a smile at the sudden image of herself as an unmovable stone, she met her parents' concerned looks. "Now, on to the remainder of your choices." She cleared her throat. "Mr. Scotto skulks about the seedier sides of London."

Mother made the appropriate gasp.

"And Lord Whaley's hair is atrocious. Surely, I cannot

pledge my life to someone whose own styling is worse than mine? We shall be laughingstocks."

"But you care nothing of style."

"Exactly." Ingrid jabbed a finger in her parents' direction. "One should always find a spouse who makes them better, and not worse."

"Darling, that is so true." Her parents shared a mooneyed gaze with each other.

"Now, Mr. Barton is a jolly sort of fellow, but his humor escapes me. I tried to enjoy his company, truly I did, but alas, the man bored me."

"Ingrid." Father's voice held disapproval.

"No doubt I bored him as well, and so we are even," she assured him.

"Well, what of Lord Messner? He's a sparkling wit. Many a time I have seen him make women laugh." Mother tilted her head as if confused by her daughter.

Ingrid suppressed a grin. This was proving to be far easier than she'd anticipated, thanks to Gideon's fine investigative skills. "Oh, yes, he is quite a darling. In fact, I have been in his presence and found him to be terribly engaging. There is a flaw, however, and it is unfortunately fatal to any possibility of us forming a love connection."

"What is it?" asked Mother. She and Father leaned forward as though being told a story of horror.

"He is…" Ingrid paused for a lengthy moment, finding that she truly enjoyed thwarting her parents' matchmaking games. Indeed, triumph swelled so strongly within that she did not know how much longer she could hide her amusement. "That is to say…well, the poor man is veritably tone deaf."

Her parents looked at each other. Then back to Ingrid.

"And why is that a problem?" Father's nostrils flared.

"You would have me marry a man who could not appreciate my skills? A man oblivious to the beauty of my playing?" She pressed her hand against her heart. She was much better at drama than she had realized. Perhaps she was their daughter, after all. "I should not live a life chained to someone who cannot join me in the simplest of pleasures, that of musical indulgence."

Mother sighed heavily. "I did have high hopes for that one. Go on, what of the rest?"

Ingrid flipped through the last two, citing the shortness of one and how he would make her feel a giant, and then pointing out that the other man loved to attend society events. They would clash as she preferred to stay home.

"That is not such a bad thing. You might find that he complements your reserved nature." Mother nodded, obviously proud of her counterargument.

Ingrid pretended to seriously consider her words. "True. Perhaps I only need a lively companion such as he."

Out of the corner of her eye, she saw Gideon's face spasm. Laughing? Annoyed? She did not care to know. He had put her in this sudden situation, after all.

"There could be a small problem," she continued, ignoring the man beside her. "I have had conversations with Sir Dalton. And though he is an intelligent sort, I fear that his heavy consumption of garlic might interfere with any desire to indulge in kissing."

Father coughed, his hand flying to his throat. Mother's mouth formed a circle.

"Not that I have experience in that, but you and Father have often alluded to the fact that a kiss is a romance. Perhaps I am wrong, though," she said in an innocent voice, knowing she was not.

"No, no." Mother sighed. "You are not wrong. A kiss is very important to a love match. One should always enjoy kissing one's husband."

"And one's wife." Father recovered enough to give his wife an amorous look. Mother's face blossomed pink, and Ingrid rolled her eyes.

"So it is settled?" She interrupted their flirtations with a firm voice. "I am released from this list?"

Mother patted Father on the cheek in a decidedly loving way, and then focused on Ingrid. "We still need to discuss your situation. Then I must get back to knitting. I shall ask around. I will not give up on you, Ingrid. Ladies do not quit."

No, no, they did not. Though Mother might not like the philosophy reflected in her daughter's decisions.

"Our daughter," said Father, back to his irritation, "has been making plans for her future without our permission."

She resisted the urge to squirm beneath his disapproval. Mother's brows arched. "Plans? Do tell, dear heart."

Gideon watched with fascination as Ingrid's barely concealed smugness melted away. He did not think he'd ever seen such an amusing performance. And her parents had been enthralled. Entirely swayed by Ingrid's slightly superficial logics.

She pulled a rumpled piece of paper from her pocket and took care to smooth it upon her lap. "As you are all perfectly aware, I do not wish to marry. There are alternative ways to live, ones not dictated by society nor tradition."

The paper quivered in her hand as she picked it up and held it out to Lord Manning. "Last year I read of several schools in Europe where one can hone one's talents and even join an orchestra. Perhaps even teach. I mailed several compositions to them and I am working on a method book for curriculum."

Lady Manning visibly winced. Lord Manning scanned

the paper and wordlessly handed it over to his wife for her perusal.

Gideon almost felt bad for Ingrid. Granted, it was difficult to feel bad for a woman so rich she had never once had to worry about where her next meal might come from. When he had first entered the room, he'd had to work hard to tamp down resentment.

A character flaw he fought daily. It was hard to swallow that such diverse societies could coexist in one city, but they did, and while his younger years had been spent indulging in careless pleasures and resentments, he had eventually grown weary of it all.

Each life was different.

Which was why he did almost feel sorry for Ingrid. Perhaps her life was easier in some ways, but in others it was much more stringent and deprived of certain freedoms he and the lower classes enjoyed. What she had already done was far beyond the expectations of an earl's daughter. To hope for a career could be seen almost as profane by her peers. It could even bring shame to her family.

Her future probably hinged on this moment. He watched her face, the strain tightening her mouth, the way her fingers clasped so tightly her knuckles turned white. The thought of her having to marry some decrepit old man just because he needed heirs and she needed the security of a marriage soured his stomach.

"Well, dear heart," said Lady Manning, folding the paper and handing it back to Ingrid, "it seems you've been busy. Have you applied to teach anywhere else?"

Ingrid slipped the paper into a pocket in her dress and lifted her chin. "This is the one I wish to attend. If they will not have me, then I shall look elsewhere."

Lord Manning looked like a hunted man, such was the horror spreading across his face. Lady Manning took the information more calmly, her eyes hardly flickering. Gideon suppressed his smile.

He really should go. This wasn't his problem nor his business nor his family. But a part of him, the part that had played music with Ingrid, that had argued with her, had even liked her, felt he should be there to offer comfort when her parents denied her this dream.

Lady Manning folded her hands in her lap. "I am concerned for your health. Our family doctor is familiar with your condition. What do those Paris doctors know? Nothing. And what if something happens while you're on the continent? What if you need us but you are so far away?"

"It is unwise to overestimate your health, Ingrid," said Lord Manning. "There are many mornings you cannot even leave your room for the pain."

"Not many." Ingrid's chin took on a stubborn slant. "And I shall bring Jane, if you allow. She is a great help. Perhaps you could spare two footmen? This is an important feat, and should the conservatoire accept me, I must be fully prepared." She slanted him a look. "Is Mr. West's presence truly necessary?"

"Necessary, no." The barest hint of a smile flickered across Lady Manning's face.

What was she up to? Suddenly, it seemed he might be playing a game in which he had not willingly entered. He took the moment to really study Ingrid. How injured had she been? Was it unsafe for her to travel so far?

And to think if her sister had not taken her spot, she may never had been injured at all. Perhaps she had more reason to be angry than he had given credit for.

Still, it had not been her mother who died.

He had tried for many years to forget the sight of his mother wasting away on the dingy cot in the room they rented. The smell where she died had often lingered in his memory, bitter and pungent, until finally time clouded his memories. He had not been sad to let them go. He had been happy to forget.

But Ingrid could not forget. Every day she lived with a reminder that her life could have been different. Had these thoughts occurred to her? In her place, would he have been able to forgive a sister? And what of Providence? Fickle Providence who let life ebb and flow with no concern for the heartbreak involved.

Jaw tightening, he shoved the thoughts to the side to focus on the matter at hand. He wanted to leave, but he did not want to endanger any possible kind feelings Lord Manning might still have for him. Better not to offend the elite, he thought ruefully.

"I am perfectly fit to travel. Please do not say the only reason you would deny me this is my condition?"

"It is a valid concern," her mother said softly.

"No." Ingrid shook her head wildly. "It is not. My injuries are not grievous nor life threatening. You cannot keep me from harm. I am in the Lord's hands. Let me have this." Her hands clasped on her lap. "Please."

Not quite a beg, but respectfully asked for. Gideon kept his features impassive, but his gut ached for Ingrid. How well he knew the want for something more, the driving force to achieve.

Lady Manning's eyes were compassionate. "Darling, your faith is all well and good, but we still worry for you."

"Please, I do not need your worry. And if you are to keep me from pursuing this, I shall retire in the country, on my own land."

Ingrid owned property? He scratched his chin speculatively.

"At that wreck of a cottage?" Lord Manning laughed.

"Yes." A haughty tone swept along Ingrid's words. "It

needs but a bit of care and Uncle Lorax left it to me. I am weary of society. I do not belong."

Lady Manning's hand fluttered near her lips, and she looked close to tears. "I am heartbroken you feel that way."

"It is nothing to be heartbroken about. I have no desire to fit in. Therefore, it is not a loss." The coldness of Ingrid's answer stung her parents, evidenced by their stricken features.

His cue to leave, but Gideon did not want to draw an ounce of attention to himself in this family drama.

"Oh." Lady Manning's expression abruptly cleared to allow a radiant smile. "I've had a most excellent idea. Manning, come with me. I must consult."

She swept up and out, taking Lord Manning by the hand and tugging him up as she did so. "You two behave. I shall leave the door open and we are merely in the hall."

Gideon narrowed his gaze at her retreating figure. Behave? What was in the strange lady's mind?

Chapter Fourteen

❧

"Look what you have done." Ingrid slapped Gideon's thigh with a kerchief she'd pulled from her pocket.

"Ow." He rubbed the spot, but he was smiling. "You are altogether too violent for a lady."

"Oh, don't be infantile. That hardly hurt." She glared at him. "Do you see the situation you have put me in? I had a plan, Mr. West. A purposeful strategy for approaching my romance-addled parents, and you have jinxed it all. I am so thoroughly put out with you that I can hardly breathe."

Indeed, she wanted to pace the room. To pop up and expel this energy coursing through her. This wild anger that needed release. But of course she could not because her ridiculous body would not allow such movement.

"My lady, did you just growl?" Gideon laughed.

"I made a sound of supreme annoyance. You know not what you've done."

"No," he said, shaking his head slowly, his gaze introspective. "I do not, nor do I understand the necessity of my presence here."

"Trust me when I tell you there is a plan afoot. Did you see my mother? She should be upset, should she not? And yet, she was hardly surprised to see you here. There is some plan, some ulterior motive, but I know not what it may be."

"Your father is angry that I knew of your audition. He did not seem to care that we waltzed."

A spike of heat bloomed within her. They had waltzed and she had thought of kissing him and she had not stopped thinking of it. She had thought she'd never see Gideon again, yet here he sat beside her.

Perhaps this was her chance to indulge her curiosity. She studied his lips, noting the way they curved upward. He had a touch of shadow upon his face, as though he was too busy to shave like a gentleman. Her heart pitter-pattered against her sternum.

"You are staring very hard at me, my lady," those lips said softly.

She lifted her eyes to meet his.

"If I were a different man, I may not point out the obvious, but I am not a different man. I am not even a gentleman in your eyes, and so it seems I am in the clear to point out that you have a look upon your face."

"A look?"

"Yes, a look that makes it very clear that you would like to steal a kiss." His mischievous eyes twinkled but they did not let her gaze escape.

Oh, ruthless commoner. Uncouth man. A sound rejoinder should spring to her mouth, but alas, no, her brain betrayed her and she could only stare at him. Thinking of a kiss. Knowing he was right. The blush she'd felt earlier suffused her and it almost felt as if the roots of her hair were burning with embarrassment.

And perhaps something else.

A desire to rise to his challenge.

To answer his accusation.

"You own a cottage?" His question diverted her intent to do something completely impulsive.

Swallowing back her emotions, she nodded. "Yes, surprisingly. My father manages it but the property is in my name. It does not bring in any income."

"I have been looking for a cottage." Gideon eyed her. "How far is it from London?"

"Why?"

"What say you let it out to me?"

"We have come to a decision." Mother swept in at that moment, clapping her hands merrily, utterly oblivious to anything but her own cleverness. Father followed, hands behind his back and a serious air to his demeanor.

Ingrid straightened, realizing belatedly that she'd somehow moved closer to Gideon than she should have. So close, in fact, that her skirts fondled his shoes. She shifted quickly, hoping her parents had not noticed. Lease the cottage to him? The idea held a great deal of merit.

"Ingrid," said Father, "it is not safe for a young, unmarried woman to travel to the continent with a few staff in tow. We've no property near Paris, nor relatives for you to stay with."

"This is not medieval times. I'm sure I can rent a room from a proper place." There. That sounded strong and independent and not as though only moments before her mind had been wholly centered on kissing Gideon.

"Nevertheless," continued Father, "your mother and I would not be able to rest for fear of your safety and health."

"I am not a child." She crossed her arms. "Seven Seasons in and I've no prospects, no desire for one. Must I be firmly upon the shelf before you'll consent to allow me my desires?"

Father's brow lifted. "And you accuse us of dramatics."

"Facts." She plucked the list from her pocket and waved

it around. "These men are not attractive to me. Everyone who is participating in this year's Season has already arrived to London. Do you really think I shall find someone in the coming months? I am confident that not a single man shall stir my interest."

Excluding the unabashed charmer sitting next to her.

A man whose career and lifestyle was firmly enmeshed in London.

"That is why your mother and I have come to a sad conclusion."

Oh, dear. This could not be good.

Father cleared his throat. "We should sit, my darling." As one, her parents sank into their previous positions on the couch. "You will not like our decision, but please know that it comes from a place of love."

Beside her, Gideon made a sound and she glanced over at him. He looked sad, somehow, and a feeling of sympathy swept through her. His mother had died, but what of his father? Who had raised him? Suddenly, it occurred to her how little she knew of this man who'd meandered into her life.

"We still believe you must marry," said Mother, "but rather than marrying for love, you shall marry for protection."

"I beg your pardon?" Ingrid's chin dropped as she stared at her parents.

"It is not unheard of, though a bit archaic to our way of thinking."

Ingrid let out a sharp laugh. "Archaic? Is it not what every woman in the ton is seeking? A match that will protect her interests and provide security? You are relegating me to a loveless marriage."

"You could stay in London and search for love," her mother pointed out. "There is no need to travel abroad.

But if it is what you want, we insist you travel as a married woman with the blessing and protection of a husband."

"What man will wish to travel to Paris with me?"

"I'm sure you can find someone." Father looked altogether too satisfied, and Mother's mouth curved with pleasure.

Ingrid wanted to bury her head in her hands, scream with frustration. Instead, she took a steadying breath and sat up straighter. "Very well. The terms of this agreement?"

More of a never-ending dilemma that she'd thought she'd finally solved.

Alas, she had not.

"You shall marry and we will fund your travel. Your husband must promise to take care of you for however long you are there. That, plus the generous settlement we've placed upon you, should be enough to induce some impoverished titled man to marry you."

"The prize heifer," she muttered beneath her breath.

"We are perfectly content if you marry a baronet. Or perhaps even a second or third son of a titled family." Mother acted as though she had not heard Ingrid, her voice lilting with optimism. "It matters not so long as he is kind and will provide—"

"Protection," finished Ingrid sharply. "And how am I to find this paragon of virtue? Remember, he cannot want children."

"Why?" asked Gideon, breaking his silence in front of her parents.

"Because I am not having children. I have plans," she answered in a tight voice.

Thankfully, her parents did not reply, did not expose her greatest hurt. What man wanted a wife who could not carry on his name, his legacy?

"We've a proposition for Mr. West, if he is willing," said Father.

Out of the corner of her eye, she saw his head snap up.

Father scratched his chin. "Mr. West, would you consider a task? We shall pay you handsomely."

Ingrid's head felt as though it was spinning. She gripped the edge of the couch, eyeing her parents. They'd gone insane. Absolutely mad.

"I had a most genius flash of inspiration," gushed Mother. "I have been so impressed with Mr. West. The way you've helped those children, your musical talents and your conversation. Not to mention that you have been a perfect gentleman while Ingrid gave your orphans music lessons."

Ingrid stifled her gasp, but it was difficult. They knew? But how? Had her sister tattled? She frowned, crossing her arms again.

"Alice did not tell us," Mother said, anticipating Ingrid's suspicions. "Did you not think your father and I are aware of your comings and goings? Particularly as you tend to flaunt propriety. We could not have you endangering Alice's prospects." She folded her hands in a prim manner. "And so we had Bennett follow you."

"Bennett? Really." Ingrid rolled her eyes. The manservant had been with the family since her birth, almost as long as Rutgers. "That traitor."

"He is not on your payroll," her father reminded her, quite unnecessarily.

"As I am well aware." She scowled. Not only had her parents thwarted her, they had also made her plans even more challenging. How was she to find a husband who did not want children and would travel to Paris at summer's end? "You realize I shall have all the fortune hunters lining up at my door?"

Mother nodded much too vigorously. "Yes, that is where Mr. West comes in."

"Is it?" he asked faintly. He looked as flummoxed as Ingrid felt.

"We want you to accompany Ingrid on any outings with potential suitors. We want your presence during any calls." Father pushed his spectacles up his nose and leaned forward. "You've a keen sense of character. We will pay you to suss out the unfit, the unkind."

"My idea," said Mother with a triumphant finger in the air.

"This is not within propriety." Ingrid felt compelled to remind her parents, though they were essentially doing what she had, but in reversal.

"That is why you shall have a proper chaperone. I have already sent a missive to my sister." Father stood. "If you want to go to Paris, you will do as we say."

"But…" Ingrid sucked in a lungful of air. "Are you saying Aunt Mildred is to be my chaperone?"

The stricken expression upon Ingrid's pretty face gave Gideon pause. This entire scene was so implausible that he could hardly believe it had happened. His mind was still processing the Lord and Lady Mannings' decision.

"Yes. Millie will do nicely." Lord Manning stared at his daughter as if trying to corral her wild spirit.

Ingrid went to her feet slowly. "Aunt Mildred hates me. You know that."

"Pish posh." Lady Manning bopped up to give Ingrid a hug. "She is merely traditional."

"And she hates me." Ingrid's body looked as stiff as a corpse. Of which he'd seen plenty. Her arms did not move to hug her mother.

Gideon stood. "How much of my time will you need? I have other responsibilities."

"To my office and we shall come to an agreement." Lord Manning escaped from the room. After a quick glance at Ingrid, whose body had taken on the posture of one ready for a fight, Gideon decided he'd better follow the earl's lead.

They made their way up one level of stairs to the office Gideon had visited many times before. It was a wonder he'd never encountered Ingrid, even if she kept to herself.

"So you waltzed with my daughter." The earl walked into his office, shedding his topcoat on the chair behind his desk before seating himself.

Back to that. Gideon scratched the back of his neck, no good answer making itself known.

"It is curious that she allowed you the privilege. My wife—" Lord Manning eyed Gideon from the rims of his spectacles "—feels confident in her plans. I am not so certain life will go the way she is finagling, but I have agreed to support her for now. You had many an opportunity to take advantage of my foolish daughter. Besides the waltz, is there anything else I should be aware of?"

Gideon gulped painfully. He thought of the way he'd touched Ingrid's hand when she last visited. "No," he managed to say. "Nothing."

"Excellent indeed. My younger daughter has set her cap on Sir Everett. I'm pleased that your reports showed nothing of concern in way of his character and his circumstance."

A funny oddity of life. The day he'd given Ingrid her reports, her father had sent for him and asked him to look into Everett. The fellow was a snooty one, but Gideon had found nothing pertinent to disenroll him from the race to the altar. Which he'd told the earl today.

Lord Manning reached for his quill and they came to terms. The amount the earl was offering would go far in securing a cottage. His time was almost up, but if Ingrid's property was near enough to London…with this money… it seemed utterly providential.

"As usual, a pleasure doing business with you." Lord Manning held out a hand and Gideon shook it firmly, murmuring his response.

The earl seemed a little nicer than usual. There was a warmth to his gaze that caught Gideon off guard. His nerves fairly crackled with suspicion. He couldn't place why.

"My carriage shall take you home," the earl said.

"I can manage." Gideon shoved the contract into the inner pocket of his coat.

"Stuff and nonsense. Take my carriage. Save yourself the coin. You've all those mouths to feed."

Dumbfounded, Gideon could only nod. He found himself being escorted downstairs and out to the small stoop. Soon enough, the carriage rolled to a stop in front of him. Overly solicitous; that was what bothered him about the earl's behavior.

Not once had an earl ever sent Gideon home in his own carriage.

A droplet of rain splashed upon his nose just then, and he realized that while his mind had wandered, the wind had picked up and dark clouds thickened overhead. He hurried into the darkened carriage, closed the door and rapped the ceiling to let the driver know he was ready.

Sighing, he leaned back against the squabs and enjoyed the darkness of the cab.

The carriage rocked across the cobblestone streets, and the rain falling against the roof lulled him to even breathing.

"Certainly, after what just happened, you are not going to sleep?"

Ingrid's strident voice pried his eyes open. Alarm jolted through him and he bolted up, searching the interior for her. Movement across from him drew his gaze, and the faint outline of her silhouette appeared in the dimness.

"Do you always ride in a darkened carriage, Mr. West?"

He scrubbed his chin. The lady had crossed the line now. "I'm tired. What are you doing? If you want to ruin your sister, this is precisely the way to go about it."

"We are in a closed carriage and no one saw me leave. Besides, we are in dire straits."

"Dire?" He squeezed his eyes closed, pinched the bridge of his nose.

"I shall let you my cottage. When do you need it?"

"The sooner, the better." He should be elated, but if she was discovered here, he'd not only lose this job with Manning, but also the cottage. There was no way Manning would allow his daughter to let it out to him if he injured her reputation. "This job came at an opportune time for me. You're endangering everything at the moment."

"I have taken precautions." She lit the lamp hanging in the corner and the burnt orange firelight flickered across her features, illuminating the serious set of her lips. "Aunt Mildred is a positive horror, Gideon. You do not understand."

"Tell me why you're in my carriage late at night, alone. Tell me why you'll risk everything."

"Because—" she squared her shoulders and inched across the seat so that she was directly across from him "—if I marry, I will always wonder what it would be like to have a kiss."

"You'll kiss your husband," he said in a sour voice. His irritation scuttled through in prickly waves that grew by the moment. "I'm leaving the carriage."

"No." Alarmed, she threw off the black cape she wore. She carefully stood and, despite the rocking of the carriage, found her way to his seat. She sat beside him, jasmine and femininity surrounding her movements. Her dress splayed, shining.

The lamplight found her face, and that was when panic set in. The wild sort, where if he didn't throw himself from this carriage, he would do something highly regretful. Her lips, pinked in the soft glow; her cheeks looked as soft as velvet, and her eyes, earnest.

"Please stay, Mr. West." She reached and found his hand. "I am a woman who knows what I want. Should I marry, should the man actually allow me to travel to Paris and live the life I seek, then I will only have one regret."

He looked down at her, and his thumb rubbed across the top of her hand. So soft. So delicate. So perfect for his own. "And what is that?"

"That I have never kissed you."

Chapter Fifteen

Ingrid pressed her mouth against Gideon's, sure she was to do something more with them, but what? Sadly, she had not paid attention to all the silly poetry about kissing; nor had she listened to the gossip. Was she to continue leaning forward and keep her lips where they were? But for how long?

He did have a nice mouth. Warm and gentle. Feeling very pleased with herself, she made a small sound in the back of her throat. Gideon jerked away, breaking what she felt had been an acceptable kiss that should be allowed to continue a tad longer.

He grasped her shoulders and gently pushed her farther from him. "That is the kiss you would regret not experiencing?"

"My curiosity is satisfied," she said, even though she had anticipated something a little more deserving of poetry. After all the goings-on about kisses, and it was really just two mouths touching. "Now I need to orchestrate a way to return home undetected. I'm thinking of sleeping in the carriage and returning to my room in the early morning. If anyone sees me, they'll assume I went out for a morning stroll. In any case, you shall not be tied to me."

Gideon stared at her, his eyes darkened hollows in the lamplight. Silence followed her words as he stared at her.

She swallowed at the intensity of his gaze. "You are not upset, are you? That I kissed you? It has been a thought I felt prudent to research."

"You are an innocent," he said, his voice quiet gravel. Raspy, even.

He leaned forward, his eyes dark tidewater pools, searching her face. "It is audacious to confess to daydreaming about kisses."

"I did not say *a daydream*. I said *a thought*." She looked down and saw that she still held his hand in hers. Audacious, indeed. She looked up into Gideon's face.

"You have put yourself in a precarious position, my lady."

"I know." The sudden import of what she'd done crashed into her. What if Gideon was not the man she thought him to be? At this moment he seemed dangerous. Thrilling.

"What if I told you—" he paused, his breath a soft, peppermint-laced puff against her face "—that I have been thinking of kissing you as well?"

"You have?"

"To my consternation." He sighed deeply. "And I would kiss you far better than what just occurred. But I value you, Ingrid. Too much to endanger your reputation. You must find a way to get home without being seen."

"I shall," she assured him, though her mind kept returning to his claim that he would kiss her better. Her curiosity, it seemed, had not been satisfied but rather heightened. "This is your opportunity to kiss me."

The corner of his mouth cut down. "I cannot, Lady Ingrid. I will not."

"But why?" Her stomach plummeted as his rejection sliced her feelings.

"There are boundaries meant to be observed. And here, in this darkened carriage, alone, it is most unwise. Surely, you can see that."

She nodded, blinking hard.

"Ingrid... I find you greatly attractive." Gideon glanced down at their clasped hands. "Too much so. Please. Move away."

She released his hand, emotions warring within. She'd wildly overstepped propriety. Swallowing hard, for her throat felt clogged by the alarming presence of tears, she moved to the other side of the carriage.

Just in time, it seemed, as the vehicle came to a sudden stop. Gideon tossed her cloak to her.

"Quick, put it on." He cut a glance to the door, which would be opened at any moment by the tiger. "I'm going to get out on my own, but you should hide in the darkened corner."

The carriage rocked as the tiger jumped down. Panic rushed Ingrid as the full enormity of what she'd done hit her. She crept quickly to the dark area behind the door hinges. Gideon snuffed the lamplight and pushed the door open. He did not look at her, and shadows hugged his profile.

Without even a glance, he climbed out and shut the door, leaving her to darkness. She huddled in the corner as the carriage began its rumble home. The jostling matched the jumble of her thoughts. Perhaps even her feelings.

Eventually, the carriage jolted to a stop. Voices, dim and muted, carried across the night. She stayed where she was, praying no one decided to check the lamp oil or clean the interior.

After a very long time, perhaps even three quarters of an hour, she decided to venture out. Normally, someone helped her into and out of carriages, not as a necessity, but as a precaution. She had climbed in without incident, though. Surely, she could climb out.

Biting her lower lip, she eased the door open. A deep blackness pervaded the coach house but for a square of moonlight that splayed through a window across from the carriage. Careful, she told herself as she lowered her body to the ground. Her good leg's foot touched first, and bracing herself against the opening, she was able to gently place her other foot without pain. A small stretching tugged within her hip, but nothing to wince at.

Once both feet were solidly on the ground, she sighed with relief and tiptoed forward. An uneven tiptoe because she had worn slippers without their normal insert to even her gait. She'd forgotten her cane. It had been a wild, unexpected impulse to sneak into Gideon's carriage. She'd instructed Jane to tell anyone who asked that she was resting and not to be disturbed.

But she'd needed to see Gideon, somehow, some way.

Because there was a good chance she'd find a man desperate enough to meet her parents' stipulations in order to gain a small fortune. And she was sure she would not want to kiss that man.

She crossed the coach house to the door. The scattered moonlight was enough to allow her to see its position. Unfortunately, the coachmen's quarters were lit up. They obviously had not retired yet. She'd wait until their lights went out to sneak back into her house.

Foolish whim.

Stifling a groan, she peered out the window. Now she must pay for her impulsivity with a most boring wait. Time passed. Her mind wandered, replaying every second from the moment Gideon saw her to the moment the carriage stopped.

Finally, the servants' quarters lights dimmed.

She ventured out, sneaking to the side door. There was a back passage in their home, rarely used, and she took that to work her way slowly up the stairs to her room.

This must be her last risky decision, she told herself. No more. She did not want her parents exiling her to the country and cutting off her pin money.

Tonight's choice had been dangerous. Foolish, even. Her lips curved as she made it to her bedroom. And very, very worth it.

She opened the door to her bedroom. Warm light splayed against the floor. Jane had left the fire going for her. Not until she entered did she see her sister sitting on the bed, arms crossed, brow raised.

"Hello, Ingrid. Where have you been?"

Gideon could not believe his absolute stupidity.

He let himself into his house, mentally reviewing the previous hours. What had Ingrid been thinking? Had she made it home without being caught? He hoped so, for her sake but also for his. He did not want to lose his reputation as a valuable runner over her impulsive, foolish curiosity.

He stepped over a sleeping child who'd decided to plop himself in the middle of the floor. At the far wall, Petey's thatch of orange hair radiated in the flickering candlelight. The boy snuggled in a nest of covers, Sir Beasley snoring beside him. Another child huddled against the wall. Sarah and Anna curled together on the cot, sweet children who deserved more than a grimy cot for their slumbers.

Frowning, an ache pervading his chest, he shuffled around the room. He laid blankets over children who needed them, swiped pieces of bread and meat from the floor and dumped them into the sink. He'd have to clean it out tomorrow when he had a moment.

He found his way to his own bed.

For some reason none of the orphans ever claimed it for sleep. Whenever he returned home, morning or night, his bed waited for him. Neatly made, unrumpled. He half wondered if it was some sort of unofficial agreement the children had made to leave him a place for himself.

He sank onto the coverlet, stretching out his legs and looking up at the dark ceiling. He should have immediately noticed Ingrid when he first entered the carriage, but he'd been preoccupied by Lord Manning's strange behavior.

The additional funds for this new assignment had filled him with elation. He had not been observant, his mind cluttered with thoughts, excitement. He would see more of Ingrid. The elation of that had distracted him.

Her kiss tonight… He should not have allowed it. So innocent and sweet. Perhaps tonight had been the most severe testing of his will he'd ever endured.

He liked her in some elemental way he couldn't identify. He didn't enjoy the feeling. Not at all.

There had been an internal battle, and he'd almost lost. He should resign the position.

He should tell Lord Manning that he had other, more important, engagements.

He should never see Ingrid again.

He turned to lie on his side. He punched his pillow. Fluffed it. But his mind would not stop its ceaseless wanderings.

Feelings were not for him. Once upon a time, he had shunned commitments. That had changed with Petey and then with the others over time. Now his loyalties lay with the children. Only them.

Not a strange pianist who eschewed social norms for her own goals.

Even worse, she was a daughter of the peerage. So far removed from his world that it was laughable. His own mother had been betrayed by those very people. His jaw hardened.

All kinds of betrayals happened to all kinds of people. He was not fool enough to think evil only existed in the upper echelons of life. But at least the poor had their reasons for criminality. Often hunger. Often lack of education or moral upbringing.

What had been Lord Hawking's reasoning? All these years later, and Gideon could not shake his unforgiveness. It burned within, a boil in need of lancing. The man held a fortune. It would not have taken much to house Gideon's mother in a nice little cottage in the country. To give her a monthly stipend to care for their son, quietly, secretly.

His throat closed as his mother's face swam behind his closed lids. The gaunt cheekbones jutting from her once beautiful face. That hoarse, rasping cough. Consumption.

Fatal, but Lord Hawking could have made her comfortable.

The backs of his lids burned with exhaustion.

At least his mother had been released from her pain. Though his childhood had been challenging at times, he'd triumphed and managed to stay out of the prisons. His hurts had faded, and life had become comfortable until Lord Hawking showed up on his doorstep, claiming God had changed him. Asking for mercy. Requesting help.

Take care of his daughters.

Gideon grimaced. Was the man completely mad? He couldn't blame the daughters for their father's perfidy, but neither did that mean he wished to help the family. The illegitimate son introducing them to society? Even if Lord Hawking bequeathed him property and fortune, there would be plenty of families that would snub his sisters due to Gideon's situation of birth. Money could not buy complete acceptance.

Nevertheless, for a small moment he let himself imagine living in a house with plenty of food, plenty of beds for his orphans. What would that look like?

Then his mother's image interfered and he banished the betraying thought. To accept anything from Lord Hawking meant to absolve him of his injustice.

Time had helped heal the pain of losing his mother.

Time had not been so kind to Ingrid. She claimed to have held a grudge against her sister at one time. Yet, now they were close. Perhaps it had been easier for her to forgive her sister because she'd been just a girl? And the accident had been unintentional. She'd credited her faith, though. Forgiveness. A God who forgave and loved.

What did that mean? He shook his head as if it could calm the chaotic strumming of his thoughts.

No matter what, one lesson remained clear.

Love meant vulnerability. Danger.

And he had no intention of endangering anyone or anything, most importantly, his heart.

Chapter Sixteen

The next morning Ingrid stifled a yawn while heading down to break her fast. Between the kiss and Alice's late-night, nonstop lecturing, sleep had evaded her. Her sister had threatened to tell their parents. It took a great deal of talking before Alice promised to hold off on tattling for a time.

Ingrid rounded the bottom stair and made for the next flight of stairs. On every step a twinge reminded her to take care. When the injury had first occurred, she'd slept on a specialized bed in the first-floor study for two years until she'd managed to heal enough to use the stairs. Even then, her father had procured a handy chair to carry her up when necessary. She still used it once in a while.

Any pride she owned disappeared when her body acted the invalid.

She walked to the morning room where the scent of bacon permeated the air. Mother and Father both sat at the table. Beside them, Gideon attacked a plate piled with food.

Ingrid managed to keep her face impassive and ignore him as she went to the sideboard to inspect the morning's offerings, but her heart betrayed her. The traitorous organ began to thump in earnest. She frowned. The last thing she had anticipated was to see Gideon so soon. Did he think of their kiss when he saw her? Did he regret it? Should she?

She plucked a banana from the sideboard. "What is he doing here?"

"He is here to do his job."

She glanced at her mother, whose hands were folded in front of her and whose posture bespoke that of a queen laying down a command. She then eyed the man who was in the process of cleaning his plate.

"It seems he is here to eat all our food."

Gideon scraped the last bit of eggs onto his fork and popped them into his mouth. His eyes gleamed and she looked away, choosing to sit near her father.

"I sent a missive early this morn. The sooner we identify candidates, the sooner you two can get started. And Aunt Mildred will be here at noon to begin your chaperonage."

Ingrid rolled her eyes.

"Do not be disrespectful to your mother," said Father, his gaze not lifting from his paper.

"I am a little old to require a chaperone."

"It is the height of the Season. There can be not even a hint of impropriety. All social norms are to be properly observed." Mother reached for a tart. "Now, I have thought of several eligible men in need of funds. This list shall differ from the last as those were men I thought in need of love."

A laugh gurgled in Ingrid's throat. "And you thought me to be the best candidate to give them such an emotion?"

"Dear heart, you are lovely. Truly lovely. You have so much to offer the right man."

Except what many men wanted most. A child. Maybe more than one. The laugh shriveled away, dried and tired. She peeled her banana, feeling Gideon's attention upon her. She hadn't wanted to sit next to him, but sitting across seemed worse at the moment. Her position gave him a full view of her misery.

If she rented out her cottage to him, could those funds support her in Paris? Perhaps she need not marry after all.

"Why must Mr. West be present?" she asked. "Can he not wait in the study like any proper visitor? I'd like to eat in peace."

Gideon leaned back in his chair, relaxing as if he owned the place. His unruly hair shone like thickened chocolate, hued to a rich chestnut by the morning's sunrays. He regarded her soberly, his mouth thoughtful. His hands went behind his head as he studied her.

The audacity. She should not have kissed him. She skewered a glower in his direction. Her mother's hand went to her mouth.

"The thing I've always liked about Ingrid is her manners." Gideon's dimple appeared.

Father grunted. Or had that been a laugh? She shot him a glare but his head remained bent.

"Oh," said Mother, recovering with a shivery breath, "that's wonderful to hear."

"She's straightforward." Gideon's teeth gleamed. "One knows where one stands with her."

"And you like that?"

"Certainly. The level of artifice and lying I deal with daily makes your daughter a breath of fresh, jasmine-scented air."

Her eyes narrowed. Jasmine? Was he referring to her perfume?

He winked at her. Right in front of her mother. Groaning, Ingrid slapped the banana on the table. "Mother, please tell us your list."

As she listened to her mother prattle off an assortment of names, she tried to calm her racing heart. She should not be annoyed by Gideon. Not angry. But for some reason she *was* irritated. Kissing him had ruined her night's sleep. Potentially her reputation if he turned out to be a talebearer. One thought occurring to her last night was that people may not ask her to play at their events if word got out about her perceived loss of morality.

Another reason, perhaps, existed for her anger.

She'd been turning the introspection around, examining it on every side, and perhaps she felt angry because he had awakened a part of her she hadn't known to exist. What was she to do now? What was she to make of him?

"Well, what do you think?"

Ingrid looked at her mother blankly.

"About my list?" Mother tilted her head.

"There is nothing to think. My thoughts don't matter." Ingrid pushed away from the table, having lost her appetite. "You and Father could easily allow me to leave for the Continent. Instead, you are requiring me to be shackled to a stranger for life."

"Thank you for the breakfast," said Gideon, rising. "I have not had a meal this delicious in years." He slanted her a pointed look. "Would that my greatest hardship be a protective family."

A surge of hot anger rushed to Ingrid's chest. He dared judge her. Of all things. She could not even remember what she liked about Gideon at the moment. "Hunger is a small price to pay for freedom."

"Ingrid." Father spoke then, his tone warning.

She shrugged. "But you are right, I suppose." She turned to her father. "Thank you for the food, and thank you for keeping me from my goals in order to protect me. I shall find a husband post-haste who will do the same."

She walked out a little more forcefully than necessary.

Gideon did not understand her position. He had struggled, no doubt, but he had chosen his struggles.

She could always run away, she supposed.

Frowning, she made her way to the piano. That would break her mother's heart. Father's, too, if she was honest. Running away would bring stigma upon the entire family.

She was well and truly trapped.

Never anger a musician.

Gideon winced as the piano thumped violent notes throughout the house. Lady Manning sipped her tea and Lord Manning seemed not to notice the virulent noise. Their invitation to join them for a morning repast had arrived before dawn, and Gideon accepted because he was hungry. The children had finished off the food and he hadn't been able to get to the market.

"Shall I wait in the study?" He looked between the two people who had raised a decently stubborn young woman.

"Yes, that would be for the best," murmured Lady Manning. Her chin trembled as her gaze flickered to her oblivious husband.

Gideon rose, trying to ignore the plentiful food left on the sideboard. Where did rich people put their uneaten foods? Perhaps he could sneak down to the kitchens later and bribe the cook to let him take some home.

Pondering the thought, he went toward the sound of Ingrid's furious playing. She would not welcome him. He did not know why she was so angry at him. He'd kept her from a terrible mistake.

Because that was what further kissing would be.

A gargantuan bad choice.

He felt sympathy for her parents. Raising a curmudgeon looked to be a daunting task. He paused in the doorway to observe said being. Her eyes were closed. Her hair, plaited down her back, shone with health, and her fingers flew across the piano keys. One could go quite deaf listening to her.

He hadn't missed the shadows beneath her eyes when she came in to eat. Nor the droop to her lips. And though he had decided last night, in his exhaustion, to keep his distance, when he'd seen her this morning he had felt the most unwelcome urge to apologize.

He had made her unhappy.

It rankled.

He sighed deeply, leaning against the doorway and watching her play. That was the rub of it, though. He could not apologize for doing what was right.

He had never put a woman's reputation on the line, and he wouldn't begin now.

Straightening, he sauntered into the small room and came to a stop by her side. Her wild playing ended abruptly and her eyes opened. "What is it that you want from me?"

She did not sound angry, as he expected, but resigned.

"I would like you to look at me."

Her shoulders stiffened but she swiveled and looked up at him. Her mouth, too wide for petulance, remained flat and her irises, fringed as they were by dark lashes, held more blue than lavender this morning. Perhaps due to her day dress, which hugged her figure in beryl-colored swathes of cloth.

"Well?" she asked.

"I've never heard that song before."

"It is one of my *personal* compositions." Her emphasis on *personal* pointed out that he interrupted her.

"Absolutely lovely. The conservatory would be foolish to turn you away."

She did not even blink, only regarded him coldly.

He cleared his throat. "I have upset you."

"You needn't barge in on my playing to express the obvious."

"You call what you're doing *playing*?" He crooked a flirtatious smile toward her, hoping to coax a softening. But no, her arms crossed and her lips dropped into a distinct mew of displeasure.

"Yes, I do call it *playing*."

"It more sounded as though you were attacking that poor pianoforte." He reached over and ran a finger over the ivory keys, pressing gently down upon the G to elicit a rich note. "Dear Arabella, pay no mind to the lady. She is temperamental and she should not have taken her anger out upon you."

"You name instruments?"

"Don't you?" At her look of consternation, his grin widened. "What a sad household. Each lovely instrument relegated to anonymity. Not even deserving of a name to mark their uniqueness. Gus would be so disappointed."

"And who is Gus? And why should he care?"

"He's an older violin, beautifully wise, I'd say. Stays at my house most of the time."

"Gus is irrelevant. Have you nothing better to do than to criticize everything about me?" Her hands went to her hips.

"I am quite certain you are not to be following me about in my own home," she continued crossly.

"True. I was heading to the study, but the echo of your *playing* lured me here."

Her frown changed to a scowl and her chin lifted. "Find me a husband so that I may be free of your presence."

"If I rent your cottage, you shall not be free from me. How far is it from London?"

"A few hours on horseback."

"Perfect. Let us work up a contract."

"You must speak to my father, though. He will have the

papers drawn up." She folded her arms tightly against herself. "And so yes, I shall indeed be free of you."

Ah, the opening he wanted. Maybe even needed, for at the moment it took all of his willpower not to step forward, to pull her into his arms and to kiss the stubbornness from her lips. To remind her that she liked him, and that he liked her. To feel that emotional yearning within again, for he'd never felt such a kinship with any other before. He did not want to lose this strange, new feeling, much as it unsettled him.

Though they were of different classes and different breeding, and though they'd never see each other again after this job, there was an undeniable connection between them.

"You did not wish to be free of my presence last night," he said in a quiet voice so that any nearby servants did not hear. Most well-bred ladies might gasp, shocked that he'd mention such a thing aloud. Ingrid, of course, did not gasp.

It did not seem possible, but her chin lifted even higher. "That was last night."

"Mere hours ago, and yet your feelings have changed?"

"Most definitely." She eyed him. "I got what I wanted, and I learned what I needed to learn."

"How to properly kiss a man?"

Pink suffused her face, but her gaze did not waver. "I suppose."

Her tone sounded bored. Blasé. What did he expect? She belonged to the haute monde. He stepped back, alarmed by the disappointment coursing through him. He recovered enough to tip his head in her direction. "An apathetic response. Do not fear. It shall never happen again."

The sharpness of his tone landed cleanly, for her eyes flickered and for the briefest moment, she looked hurt.

Gideon grimaced. He moved to speak but a voice cut between them.

"Arguing with the help?" A woman, tall and lithe with elegant silver hair piled upon her head in perfect waves, sailed into the room. She looked him over, distaste twisting her mouth, and then turned to Ingrid. "I heard your parents have finally come to their senses. We shall leave at once."

"To where, Aunt Mildred?" asked Ingrid, her expression mutinous.

"Why, to Hyde Park. I have it on good authority that Lord Findlay is participating in a competition of sorts, and who better to cheer him on than an heiress? He would be most interested in a woman who can keep him in steady supply of excellent horseflesh." The woman's austere and almost severe face sharpened. "Come now. And you—" she gestured at Gideon without meeting his eyes "—you shall follow us at a distance and observe."

She took Ingrid's arm and they walked from the room. In that moment he was fully reminded of his place in Ingrid's world.

A place where he followed directions and did not have a name.

He tagged behind them. This had been his life, and though he did not quite agree with Ingrid's assessment of her station, there was something to be said about his own.

No one could link their arm through his and force him into a leg shackle.

Yet, Ingrid's stiff back, her prideful stance, struck Gideon as lonely. Despite his irritation at her, he hoped for Ingrid's sake that this Lord Findlay treated her well. She deserved camaraderie and respect.

That thought uppermost, he followed them to the carriage and sat at the top with the footman. Where he belonged.

Chapter Seventeen

The pianist needed better lessons. Ingrid cringed as the poor girl playing the pianoforte at tonight's rout hit the wrong note. Nevertheless, guests continued dancing and she continued playing. Ingrid pressed herself against a floral paper hanging on the wall, effectively avoiding eye contact with other guests. The room had become quite full for a simple rout. The hosts were no doubt thrilled at their event's popularity.

Alice came over, giggling. "Did you see Miss Lydia give Lord Dudley the cut direct?"

Ingrid shook her head. "I think I am done for the night."

"Is Aunt Mildred so bad?"

"I've danced four sets already, and she's filled my dance card. So yes." Her aunt took chaperoning to the extreme, and Ingrid had taken to hiding in her room during the day to avoid long conversations on wifely bearing and wifely skills.

Gideon had not been around. Ingrid missed him. She thought of the children every day but could not escape her aunt's proprietary clutch. She'd sent Jane over with goods a few times this week. Cook didn't seem to mind baking a little extra for "the babies," as she put it.

"I'm sorry, sister." Alice leaned in close. "She shall keep you safe from any impulsive decisions."

"If you are referring to my night tryst, either tell our parents or do not mention it again. Please." Her mind whirled with too many thoughts already. She didn't need to add the worry of whether Alice would keep her secret.

Her sister sighed. "I shall not speak of it unless it happens again."

A fair warning, though it brought disappointment. "Very well. When did you become so wise?"

"When I realized you're endangering my prospects." Alice giggled again. She sounded young, unfettered by dreams beyond her grasp. "Oh, look. It is the nefarious detective himself. He is rather handsome. I can see why you'd indulge curiosity."

Alice bumped Ingrid's shoulder, and despite herself, she smiled. "Shhh, sister."

"I'm off to dance more. Keep your conversation circumspect. You know Aunt Millie is watching." With an airy laugh, Alice fluttered off just as Gideon came to a stop beside Ingrid.

"Shall I investigate Lord Frasier? Your aunt thinks he is a nice man." Gideon scratched his chin, which had not been shaved recently and sported a bristly shadow that tempted Ingrid to touch it to see how it felt. She had not forgotten the sight of his bare feet, either. Men were such strange creatures.

"No, he is out of the question. Too young. What of Lord Harting's second son? Is he really looking for love or for a fortune?"

Gideon grinned. "Love. And I also heard from the ladies that Mr. Gaines is a serial womanizer. Scratch him off your parents' list. Then Sir Dudley. Well, you would not like him. He is known to be clingy."

"Ack." Ingrid scrunched her nose. "Why must this be so difficult? It can't be that hard to find a decent husband in search of a fortune."

"Lady Ingrid?" A gravelly voice, rich with masculinity, interrupted them. She turned and found a man with dark hair and hazel eyes watching her. "Though we have not been introduced, I know your mother and father. They assured me just a moment ago that you would not mind if I bent a social norm and introduced myself to you."

He was attractive, and his eyes held intelligence. "I am Lady Ingrid. And you are?"

"Sir Henry Lyons, at your service. I have a baronetcy a little south of London."

She raised her brows.

"But I bore you." Now he smiled, but he didn't have a dimple like Gideon. "I simply wondered if perhaps you might reserve a dance for me on your card."

She dug out her card and held it up. She wanted to tell him no, that she was done dancing, but before she could respond, he spoke.

"Perhaps the upcoming dinner spot?" He took in the empty spaces on her dance card and his smile deepened. There really was something very attractive about this man, and yet her heart remained in a normal beat. Just as she preferred. "We can get to know each other."

"I shall pencil you in."

"Thank you, my lady." He struck an elegant bow and left them.

Alice hurried over.

"He is very handsome." A happy lilt lifted her sister's voice.

"Yes," agreed Ingrid, watching the man's retreating form. "Do you know of him?"

"He's a widower. I believe he came to London specifi-cally to procure a wife."

"You think he's handsome?" Gideon sounded aghast and a scowl tugged at his features. "The man is shorter than you."

"He is not." Ingrid squinted at him. "Really, Mr. West. Shouldn't you be mingling? Or dancing or flirting or what-ever it is Bow Street Runners do when at a ball?" She waved a hand, ignoring the death glare he leveled at her. "Be off. I've a supper to attend."

She and Alice exchanged happy smiles. If Sir Lyons proved to be as promising as he looked, her future was set. Gideon could kiss some other silly female who might sneak into his carriage. She was done with that nonsense. She had given in to a weak moment. No more.

Alice had a potential suitor in mind and so did she. Gideon would use her cottage to care for the children. All of her worries could be set to the side.

Now her life truly was to begin.

Gideon's jaw hurt from gritting his teeth. Not shorter? Was Ingrid blind? Had she not dismissed a previous can-didate for her hand due to his disparate height? He ignored a woman to his left who kept smiling at him and trailed the sisters.

Lord Manning had given him a job. Find Ingrid a suit-able husband who would follow her to the Continent for a time and keep her safe. And that was what he would do. Who was this Henry Lyons with his fancy clothes and charming manners? He had managed to snag a supper dinner with Ingrid.

But not a dance.

That thought calmed Gideon somewhat.

Frowning, he followed the women to a corner where

Ingrid took a seat upon a chair, a look of such extreme boredom upon her face that he might laugh if he was not so irritated.

Alice flashed him a smile and then went to join a partner for a minuet.

Interesting that Alice had left Ingrid alone. Not only that, but she'd smiled at him while doing so. Curiosity piqued, he studied Ingrid. She did not see him. Her hair had been piled high tonight, pinned with sapphire barrettes that brought out the rosy hue to her skin. Her fingers tapped a rhythm at her side, perhaps silently mimicking the notes played by the orchestra. Gideon moved closer still until he lounged against the wall near her.

If others noticed, it might look as though he simply stood near her.

"He is shorter than you," he said.

"You again. Why am I not surprised?" Irritation edged her tone.

"Why are you so angry with me? I did nothing that was not asked for." He watched the dancers as they performed their minuet, silk dresses swaying, the gentlemen in perfect form.

"I'd prefer to forget what you did."

"Is that so? And what of your action?"

Her shoulders, all creamy skin and softness, visibly stiffened. "My action was unacceptable. I should not have been so forward, nor so presumptuous."

"Then why were you?" That question had burned in his mind. What had possessed a woman like Ingrid to sneak into his carriage? And for what? A kiss? It was so unlike the woman he'd expected, and yet, not. Because that kiss had confirmed to him that within Ingrid beat the heart of a woman in need of many more kisses. And he wanted to be the one to give them to her.

But a woman like Ingrid did not get kisses unless she was married. An impossibility for him. He pushed his mother's image away. He would never fall prey to such a weak emotion as love, nor legalize it with marriage. Look how that had worked out for his parents? And how many domestic disputes had he investigated? Far too many for him to put his trust in such a fickle thing as *love*.

"Why were you in the carriage?" he asked again, for she had not answered but instead looked out upon the room as though consumed by thoughts.

"Curiosity," she said at last, her voice quiet.

"You regret this curiosity, then?"

A long silence ensued. Her form, quite still on the chair, as if poised for flight. Was she longing for a curtain to hide behind? Or perhaps a pianoforte.

"I do not know." She turned to look up at him. "Why do you care? No doubt you have kissed too many women to count. Let alone remember."

"You sound bothered."

"Not in the least." Her eyes flashed and she resumed her previous position. "Find me a husband and pay the cottage rent on time. That is all I require from you."

Gideon shifted against the wall, turning ever so slightly so the gossips wouldn't presume them to be having a conversation for too long. That wouldn't do at all.

"I have spoken to your father. He is consulting with his accountants regarding a fair annual rent." He watched her posture, so straight, so firm. "Why not Lord Frasier? He's in line for an earldom, but the family funds are low. You like him and I happen to know he's a man of good character."

"He will want children."

"That is a problem?" The minuet ended and a bell sounded for supper. His cue to leave.

"Yes." She rose, her tall form still shorter than his own height. Alice threaded through the crowd toward them. Ingrid faced him, searching his eyes as if she wanted to say something.

"You like children," he said. "Are you going to dismiss all candidates who want heirs?"

"Yes." She nodded, but there was something about her eyes that caught him. Or perhaps the shape of her mouth. Sadness, he thought, and a sudden urge to take her hand pressed upon him.

Someone stopped Alice to conversate, and he took the opportunity to move closer to Ingrid.

"Why?"

"My goals do not allow for their presence."

"You can play piano and still be a mother."

The tip of her tongue touched her lower lip, hesitant, then retreated. "Perhaps I do not want to be a mother."

Surprise rippled through him. He hadn't anticipated that, simply based on what he'd seen of her interactions with children. "Yet, you are wonderful with children. Mine adore you. And all those presents you keep sending."

"Yours." Her mouth melted into a sort of sorrowful frown. "Please give them my regards."

"Ingrid, Mr. Lyons is on his way," put in Alice, who had reached them slightly breathless and most definitely flushed. "To take you to supper." She stopped, glancing between them. "Is everything well? Your hip?"

Ingrid nodded in a slow, dullish fashion. Her eyes had glazed over in a way Gideon did not like. He could not tell if he had hurt her with his words or if her body pained her.

They turned to go.

"I will tell them," he called out, earning a glance back from the lovely lady who twisted his insides and stole his sleep. "The children. They miss you."

Her eyes flickered an acknowledgment, and then Mr. Lyons reached them and they continued into supper. Suppressing the irritating jealousy that plagued him, Gideon pivoted and headed toward the servants' quarters.

He did not like this baronet. An obvious fortune hunter looking for a mother for his children. Ha. He had crossed many men off Lady Manning's list for Ingrid, and this Lyons would be no different.

He frowned as he loped out of the house, into the damp fog of a London summer night. As long as the man did not call upon Ingrid tomorrow, he might have time to investigate him. It did not bode well that Ingrid seemed to like him, which convinced Gideon that he should attend their every meeting. She was too naive. Intelligent, but naive. He should be there to run interference, if necessary.

Unfortunately, Bow Street had an assignment for Gideon in the morn and he'd have to leave Mr. Lyons to his machinations for the day, hoping Ingrid might see through them. Perhaps she'd even turn the man away.

The thought brought a grin to his face as he hailed a hackney for home. Time to start packing for the cottage. If all went well, he'd be there in a fortnight.

Chapter Eighteen

Were there truly no acceptable men in London? Ingrid perused the paper Gideon had given her, his notes scratchy letters on the sheet. The carriage rocked gently. Aunt Mildred sat across from her, knitting and thankfully, not speaking.

Alice peered over Ingrid's shoulder.

They had received an invitation to a house party at an estate a day's drive away. Aunt Mildred insisted they go as the guests consisted of gentry who would gladly take Ingrid's money.

She just wanted it all to be over with.

It was the beginning of June and she was no closer to finding a match than when her parents issued their decree.

Alice laughed, pointing to one of Gideon's sentences. "Look, he says the man's oversized mustache will tickle your face too much."

"This is ludicrous. I must speak to Mr. West. I expect better reasons than these." She rapped the ceiling of the coach and it slowed to a stop.

"Whatever are you doing, child?" Aunt Mildred eyed her sternly above the rims of her spectacles.

"I'm straightening our investigator out." The man

should be sacked. Yet, a pang struck her squarely in the stomach at the harsh thought. If fired, she would never see him again. And how would he care for the children? She opened the carriage door and carefully leaned out. "Mr. West, I require your presence in the coach."

Aunt Mildred popped Ingrid on the arm with her knitting needle. "That commoner is not sitting in here with us."

"I need to speak to him." She moved out of striking space, settling against the cushioned squabs and straightening her skirts.

"Well, I never," Aunt Mildred sputtered but Ingrid ignored her. She grew tired of butting up against the woman. Her aunt was to chaperone, not dictate, and yet she'd tried to control everything from Ingrid's breakfast chocolate to her taste in dresses.

"I'll sit by you, Aunt Millie," Alice said brightly, jumping up and crossing over to their aunt's side.

Which meant Gideon would sit next to Ingrid. Throat tight, she eyed the opening to the carriage. Within a moment he appeared. The wind had tousled his hair and there was something very wild about him. A raw, masculine charm that immediately took her thoughts back to the last time they'd shared a coach seat.

She looked away, keeping her gaze focused upon a space above Aunt Mildred's head as Gideon settled beside her. He closed the coach door, rapped the ceiling and their journey continued.

"Hello, ladies," he said in a deep and decidedly playful tone.

"Mr. West. So nice to see you again." Alice dipped her head, acting as if they had not just seen him nights ago at the ball.

The night he'd asked Ingrid about children. Her throat grew even tighter and the tips of her ears burned. Why had she not answered directly? Why feel shame over something so outside her control?

Her aunt did not deign to return Gideon's greeting. Another mark against her, in Ingrid's opinion.

"I have been summoned." He leaned back, his body long and lean, taking up more space than she liked. "For what momentous reason have you taken me from fresh air and thrust me into this darkened, slightly stale carriage?"

Aunt Mildred made a sound of disapproval. Ingrid swept a glare across his irritating smirk. Alice simply watched, the barest hint of a smile tugging at the corners of her mouth.

"You are being rude on purpose," Ingrid accused.

"Well, whyever shouldn't I be?" He dimpled at Aunt Mildred, who sniffed and turned her head. "Not a single person in this carriage is paying me to go to a country party. A house party, mind you, in which I have to wear clothes your parents provided. They really are desperate to marry you off."

"Need you remind me?" She crossed her arms, glaring. "That is precisely why I have called you in here."

The carriage jolted and her knee bumped against his. Hastily, she scooted farther into the corner.

"I suppose I should count myself so lucky to mingle with people more along the lines of my lowered social status. Gentry, tradespeople and a few titles. Who do you think they have in mind for you at this particular party?"

"Men with mustaches."

His brow rose. "Indeed."

"Yes," she said in a tone altogether snappish. "And I don't care if their mustaches grow to their ears." She held up the paper, tapping the ridiculous thoughts he'd penned. "You are to cease your meaningless reasons why I will not like someone and find an adequate gentleman of whom my parents will approve."

"This man must be willing to travel to Paris with you."

"And no children."

"Right." He nodded, but she detected a quizzical look in his eyes. "And will the esteemed Mr. Lyons be attending?"

"He will. In fact, he is who I prefer. Note *that*." She shoved the paper at him, but the carriage bumped again, throwing her against his broadness. He caught her, though Alice did not do so well with Aunt Mildred. Her aunt's knitting and spectacles scattered across the seat. As those two sought to unentangle themselves, Ingrid gave herself a moment to enjoy the strength of Gideon's arms around her.

How strong he felt, and his mouth merely inches from hers. Their eyes met and in that space of time the strongest certainty swept through her that she wanted to kiss him again.

"Oh, I shall help you find everything, Aunt Millie." Alice's overly loud exclamation broke into Ingrid's reverie, and she jerked away. She could not breathe. Everything within her screamed to be close to Gideon.

She squeezed her eyes shut, huddling into the corner and counting to one hundred until her breath slowed and her pulse stopped knocking within her neck. Opening her eyes, she observed Aunt Mildred gathering her knitting, spectacles askew across her nose. The carriage had resumed its movements.

She snuck a look at Gideon, only to find him staring at her with such a serious expression that a little dart of alarm stung her.

"You appear stressed, Mr. West." Alice sounded sympathetic. "Are you worried over your children?"

"A little. Their manners are nonexistent. I asked a neighbor to check in on them."

"How many children do you have?" asked Aunt Mildred.

"As many as need food and a place to sleep. Most of them are orphans."

Aunt Mildred sniffed again. "Orphans. Why aren't they in a home? Surely, they'd fare better than wandering the streets." Her fingers twitched within the blanket she knitted.

"Sadly, few orphanages are better than the streets," said Gideon, "and the children lack food and clothing. They often run away. Better to brave the unknown than to be trapped within a place of brutality and starvation."

"I hardly doubt that is the case." Now Aunt Mildred's eyes lifted. "I give to several charities a year and they all appear to be doing an excellent job." Aunt Mildred's chin waggled, if such a sharp jut as hers could be considered to waggle.

Gideon bent his head in consideration of her words, but his gaze twisted to Ingrid, and a heaviness lurked within it. "Would that all charities hold to honesty, but there are many who mislead those with generous hearts."

"You speak as if from experience," Ingrid said slowly, realizing again how little she knew of this man beside her. His mother had died... Had he been an orphan on the streets? Her heart wrung, for Petey's face flashed before her, followed by Anna's and Sarah's. Surely, he had not.

"Your aunt in not wrong in her perceptions of me," he answered. "No matter my parentage, I did live on the streets after my mother died, and I saw firsthand the perilous conditions these children are subjected to."

"How ever did you survive?" Alice's wide eyes and the admiration coating her words almost made Ingrid smile. Her sister had experienced very little of the world outside her privileged circles. And so had Ingrid, at her age.

Though a difference of only five years separated them, at times like this, the gap felt greater.

"By my wits and charming manners." Now Gideon's teeth showed.

Ingrid snorted. "I doubt that."

"I am also known to be adept with a dagger."

"Oh, will you show me?" Alice leaned forward.

"Hush, child." Aunt Mildred eyed Gideon with suspicion. "Do you tell tales, sir? I do not like the thought of my money being misused."

"I wish I told tales." He sighed in a heavy way, his teeth disappearing behind a frown. "Unless you do a thorough search into the operation of a charity, or unless you know those running it well, your funds are likely to be misappropriated."

The carriage stopped and Alice drew back the curtain. "Oh, I think we are here." She beamed at them and Ingrid could not help but smile back at her sweet sister. She shot a secret peek to Gideon, who assisted her aunt with packing the darning while a footman helped Alice alight from the carriage.

Gideon climbed out next. He helped Aunt Mildred, who in a shocking move, smiled at him. Then he held out a hand for Ingrid. She scooted to the door, checking that their footman had placed a special box for her to step on. He had not. The ground greeted her, muddy and ever so far away. Her cane had been stowed with the baggage.

"I shall lift you out," said Gideon, a mischievous smile splaying across his face.

Gideon saw the uncertainty creeping into Ingrid's features. She clutched her reticule, searching behind him. Dusk had arrived, and the innards of the carriage darkened by the second. He had sent the footman to help unpack the baggage, though. What he wanted most was to put his hands around Ingrid's waist and lift her down.

He wanted to kiss her.

Which was why the sooner he found her a husband, the better.

He crooked his hand at her again. "Come, I shall not drop you."

"Very well." She had slipped her gloves on, and grasping his shoulders, allowed him to help her out of the carriage. He lowered her to the ground. Instead of allowing his hands to linger upon her waist, he immediately released her and stepped back.

She brushed her skirts, not meeting his eyes. "Thank you, Mr. West. That will do."

"I shall see you at supper, Lady Ingrid." He bowed.

"Lady Ingrid!" A shout cut the air, coming from the steps of the massive estate behind them. He hadn't had a chance to look about, but now he took in the freshly manicured lawns, the looming Elizabethan architecture and the multitude of carriages pulling into the circular drive.

He found his invitation odd and had not believed Lord Manning at first that he was to be a guest. Lady Manning insisted that her friend Lady Danvers held an event every year and invited those who lived nearby. She said Lady Danvers would find a Bow Street Runner a delightful addition to her party.

Not only that, but she had an odd number of guests. He'd bring it to even.

Shaking his head, he watched Mr. Lyons head toward them.

A plan was afoot, but he did not know what it might be. Lady Manning exhibited all the signs of a meddling mother. Nevertheless, Gideon could not turn down the extra coin Ingrid's parents offered, nor the opportunity to engage in social entertainment. The plentiful food was reason enough to go.

"Lady Ingrid, so good to see you again." Mr. Lyons bowed and Ingrid offered a curtsy, her dark hair shining beneath the lit torches as she dipped down.

"I did so enjoy our ride in Hyde Park the other morning. Perhaps we shall have opportunity for another ride?"

"I will insist we create an opportunity." The man gave her a grin that set Gideon's teeth on edge. He held out his arm. "May I escort you in?"

"Why, yes, I'd be delighted." She glanced at Gideon, two spots of color rising to her cheeks. "Have you met Mr. Gideon West?"

"I saw him at the ball, I believe. Sir Henry Lyons." The baronet reached out a hand, and Gideon met it. His firm handshake and direct eyes irritated Gideon. Surely, Ingrid would not marry him.

"Gideon West."

"How do you know Danvers?" asked Lyons.

"Mr. West is a special friend of my parents', who are great friends with Lord and Lady Danvers. They could not make this weekend and so they sent us in their stead." Ingrid tapped Lyons's arm. "Let us go in."

Lyons swept a gaze over Gideon that was neither condescending nor haughty, but thoughtful. "Interesting. You look familiar to me."

Gideon forced a starched smile. "I work for Bow Street. You've probably seen me at one time or another."

"Maybe."

He did not like the introspective arch of Lyons's brow. Dusk settled more deeply on the lawn and they moved up the stairs. The carriages dispersed, servants scattered to their assigned quarters and the other guests joined them as they entered the home.

Gideon lost sight of Ingrid and Lyons. If he wasn't mistaken, she deliberately escaped him. All for the better, he supposed. Kiss or no, he had no mind to encourage a relationship. He shuffled into the house with others.

Multiple maids and manservants greeted them. Gideon handed his overcoat to a smiling footman and then milled into a room to the right, where pastries and drinks graced a long table. His stomach rumbled, tantalized by the scents permeating the room.

Two lavishly clad footmen stood on the other side of the table, handing out dinnerware. At the far end of the rectangular room, a large punch bowl awaited guests.

"Lemonade?" A maid sidled over, brown eyes twinkling.

"Thank you." He took the cup, sipped and walked to the corner where he might observe the guests more fully. With his free hand, he reached into the pocket of the stylish vest gifted to him by Lady Manning, and withdrew a note. Lord Manning wanted him to study Lyons and two other eligible men. A Mr. Barley who owned a nearby mill but struggled to turn a profit due to aged technology, and a Lord Early from Northern England who was rumored to be in town in search of a rich wife.

He plucked a tart from a tray as a footman swept by. Living the good life, he thought wryly. All of these people here for a weekend, enjoying unlimited fare and entertainment.

Lyons and Ingrid entered. The man stood an inch taller than Ingrid, proving Gideon wrong. He had put in a few light inquiries and heard back only good about Lyons. Now to keep an eye on the other two. A man's treatment of servants often said much of his character.

As the guests mingled, laughter and conversation filled the room. He grinned at Ingrid's bored expression, located Alice chatting with her aunt near the scones, and then Lord

Hawking came into view. A petite blonde, surely barely out of the schoolroom, hung on his arm.

Scowling, Gideon crossed the room.

"Mr. West. Good to see you here." Lord Hawking held out his hand, but Gideon refused to shake it. "Have you considered my offer?"

"My answer remains the same." Gideon swept a cutting glare at the earl, then turned his attention to the young woman. She looked young, barely old enough to attend a house party with a much older man. Would Danvers countenance such a blatant breach of morality?

"You assume much, judging by your expression." Lord Hawking's arm moved protectively over the girl. She studied Gideon as well, her blue eyes steady and direct. Noting him, he thought, as her gaze traveled his visage.

"Rachelle, how good to see you here." Alice bounded over, trailed by Ingrid.

"And you." The girls hugged and Gideon shifted on his feet.

He had misread the situation, but how? Ingrid came to his side, the corners of her lips tugging ever so slightly.

"You look put out," she said beneath her breath.

"This is not my ideal place to be."

"Nor mine," she agreed, then dipped a slight curtsy to the earl. "Lord Hawking, you are looking much better since the last time I saw you."

"All praise must go to Rachelle. She has doggedly nursed me back to health." The man bestowed an affectionate look upon that girl that caused an uncomfortable squeeze to Gideon's stomach. She looked too young to be a nurse.

She laughed, her open nature easily expressed in that single exhalation. "He is concerned that I shall become a bluestocking. He dragged me here on pretense, claiming fatigue."

Alice giggled. "Fathers can be the worst. Come, let us see what this weekend's events are to be. I do so hope for a foxhunt."

They meandered off while Gideon processed the information that had just knocked him over the head. He felt frozen in place, his mind clobbered. Miss Rachelle, his half sister. Lord Hawking and Ingrid engaged in conversation but Gideon remained mute. That bright girl might soon be a poor relation, relegated to live off the good intentions of relatives when her father passed.

Had Hawking planned this meeting?

And more than that, did Rachelle know of Gideon's identity?

"Is Miss Rachelle out for her first Season?" inquired Ingrid, drawing his attention back to their little huddle of three.

"No, this is her third. She is simply accompanying me for exactly the reasons stated. The girl's nose is too often buried in books. I fear she shall not procure the match needed for her to live her life in comfort."

"A common fear among fathers," stated Ingrid, her gaze flickering to Gideon.

"It is my hope to relieve this fear. I have three daughters, and my health is not good. They will need someone to watch over them."

Gideon's cue to leave. He would not allow Hawking to guilt him into doing the very duty Hawking had himself failed in. But as he left the room, he felt Ingrid's stare. He passed Alice and Miss Rachelle on his way out. They spoke animatedly in a corner of the room, their giggles innocent and joyful. The girl, his sister, appeared happy and at peace.

What would happen to her should he continue to refuse Hawking's request? Resentment pressed heavy upon his shoulders, joining the other responsibilities there, and to his great and utter consternation, he didn't know what to do.

Chapter Nineteen

This weekend could not end soon enough.

Ingrid hobbled across an emerald hillside with a group of guests who'd decided to have a picnic. Lady Danvers insisted they see the new folly her husband had constructed upon the grounds. She claimed it to be the most extravagant folly in all England, incorporating unique designs and a maze of great proportions.

The sun beat upon Ingrid's bonnet as she traipsed after the group ahead of her. Staying longer at this estate could not be an option. Not with Alice and Aunt Mildred constantly pushing her to be more social. She'd managed to beg off the dance last night, but today's event remained a necessity.

Aunt Mildred had taken great pains to remind Jane to dress Ingrid in her prettiest clothes. She half wondered if her aunt might arrange a tête-à-tête in which Ingrid found herself alone with some eligible, impoverished man. A proposal ensured by ruination. She laughed at the thought, lifting her dress to step over a rock.

Thankfully, her body cooperated today.

The sky, a clear blue, predicted good weather. Not enough to entice her to stay out, though. Perhaps if some left the picnic early, she could join their retreat. Surely, Aunt Mildred would let her go. She glanced ahead, noting Sir Lyons walking with Alice and Lord Hawking's daughter. Beside them, Aunt Mildred spoke with Lady Danvers. Gideon marched to the left, conversing with an older gentleman from Northern England.

She'd spoken with him yesterday afternoon. A nice enough person, though she could not recall his name.

Whoops and cheers erupted from the group as the folly came into view. Situated upon a verdant rise in the landscape, the looming structure mimicked a Greek temple, complete with pillars and stairs. Behind it, one could see the tall hedgerows, which must make up the maze. Little glints of reflected sun winked at them from the folly's jeweled ornamentation.

"Lady Ingrid Beauchamp?" A gentleman clothed in a navy blue superfine walking coat, joined her. His gray whiskers lifted in greeting.

"Yes?" She swerved another rock, her cane a help. She almost hadn't brought it, but one could not be too careful on a country jaunt.

"Nasty things, these rocks. I see you've brought assistance." He pointed to her cane. "How are you enjoying the party?"

"The Lord and Lady Danvers are generous." It was the nicest thing she could think of to say.

"Were you not playing the pianoforte this morning?"

"I was." They moved carefully up the hill toward the folly.

"I am a great fan of music," he continued, obviously determined to carry this conversation himself. "Handel, was it not? Your mastery of his pieces is astounding."

Not Handel, but she dipped her head nevertheless, a

happy warmth invading her chest. "I'm sure I am not deserving of such high praise."

"But you are." Gideon joined them, his deep tones sending a ripple of pleasure through Ingrid. "You should hear more of her playing, Mr. Barley. She is a prodigy."

A laugh broke loose. "Really, Mr. West. You exaggerate."

"You have heard her play?" Beside her, the man slanted a look to Gideon that felt a tad hostile. Though Ingrid was not the best at deciphering the emotions of those around her, she detected a sudden tension.

"She is a family friend," Gideon said blithely. "Here, let me help you here."

Before she could react, he touched her elbow and guided her over a particularly patchy stretch of hillside.

"I see." The man's posture bespoke irritation. "Lady Ingrid, I have been remiss. May I introduce myself?"

She stopped and pulled her arm from Gideon's grasp, annoyed that his gallant gesture awakened some long dormant feeling within. "Please, do." She smiled at the man, shading her eyes where her bonnet failed to do so.

He was not a bad-looking sort. Well-trimmed whiskers, a strong jaw, and he did enjoy music, even if he did not recognize Beethoven. His eyes were not as deep a blue as Gideon's, though. More the color of a shallow pool of water on a sunny day.

"Mr. Charles Barley. I own a lumber mill a few kilometers away."

She tilted her head. "You are neighbor to Lord and Lady Danvers, then?"

"For all my life." They continued walking, closing in on the folly. Gideon, wretched man, did not move from her side. Mr. Barley twirled his mustache. "I grew up with their children. Do you know this area well, Lady Ingrid?"

"No. I spend most of my time on my family's country

estate near Wales. They drag me to London for the Season every year, unfortunately." They walked up the steps and immediately the cool shadow of the high ceiling blanketed them. She focused on heading toward the food.

"You do not like the Season?" he asked.

She shuddered. "That supercilious time of year when parents marry off their daughters as if they were Herefordshire cows up for bid?"

Gideon coughed, and she shot him a glare. Mr. Barley had a stymied expression upon his face. No doubt he went to London specifically for wife-finding. Sensing she'd made a social faux pas with her words, she tried to smile at the poor man. Her lips stretched but did not quite curve.

"I am not social, so no, I do not like the Season," she said in a strained tone. She plucked a cucumber sandwich from a tray a servant held, stomach growling.

"Oh, look. There's Mr. Connors." Something akin to relief flashed across the man's face. "I've been needing to speak with him. Perhaps you will grace me with a dance later."

"Perhaps." Or perhaps not. She bit her sandwich.

Mr. Barley bowed quickly and left her.

Gideon coughed again, though it sounded distinctly like a smothered laugh. She frowned. He looked exceptionally handsome today, which sparked further irritation. His hair had been neatly combed, and the clothing her parents lent to him fit his figure to perfection. She took another bite, determined to ignore him, and looked over the group gathered within the inauthentic Greek temple. Aunt Mildred was not being near as careful in her chaperonage as Ingrid had expected her to be. She swallowed the rest of her sandwich.

Gideon snorted.

Sighing, she turned to him. "Snorting is most ungentlemanly." She aimed a highbrowed look at his forehead, over which an errant curl of hair lay in charming rebellion.

"But you have already noted that I am not a gentleman," he rejoined, that confounding mouth of his quirking upward. "And may I point out that you have an unladylike appetite."

"I'm hungry."

"Is that why you were so rude to poor Mr. Barley?"

She glared at him, now thoroughly annoyed. "Rude? I daresay that is an overstatement."

"The man was clearly out to get to know you. The least you could have done was indulge his curiosity."

"He thought I played Handel this morning." A servant hovered nearby and she grabbed another sandwich. They were too delicious to resist. "He said nothing interesting to which I could reply."

"Neither did you," Gideon pointed out. A condescending smirk tugged crinkles around his eyes.

"I do not need to say interesting things. My wealth is interesting enough." She huffed a breath. "Come, Gideon. Do you truly think he will leave his lumber mill to live in Paris with me? No, I need someone unencumbered by such responsibilities. Furthermore, I do not understand what you are about at the moment. My parents are not paying you to criticize my every move." She crossed her arms, scanning the large space now filled with ladies and gentlemen. Tables and chairs had been set up at the far end of the room. She spotted two different arched doorways leading to alcoves in the folly.

A small breeze riffled through the area, bringing with it the tantalizing scent of arriving food.

"Oh, I know what I'm being paid to do," he said, amusement layering his voice in such a rich fashion he might as well just outright laugh at her.

"Mr. West." Lady Danvers beckoned them from where she stood at a nearby table. "And Lady Ingrid. Join us."

Reluctantly, she followed Gideon to the table where her aunt and sister had already found their places. Mr. Lyons smiled from his place beside Alice, and Lord Danvers dug into the sandwich tray as if he had not eaten in years.

Lady Danvers preened like Alice's cat after being fed hot mutton when they reached the table. "I was ever so pleased when Lady Manning suggested your presence, Mr. West. Having an uneven party can be tediously inconvenient."

A servant pulled out two chairs beside each other. Ingrid and Gideon both sat down. The informality of the party allowed such a thing. She took another sandwich from a tray in the middle of the table.

"I am most happy to be here," Gideon said in a polite way. "It is not every day I am invited to enjoy good company and delicious food."

Lady Danvers giggled, positively giggled, and brought out a fan to presumably cool the flush staining her smooth cheeks. "Yes, yes, my dear Lady Manning mentioned your occupation. A runner, are you? How ever did that come about?"

Ingrid peeked at Gideon's profile, noting his open, slightly flirtatious, grin. He truly did enjoy being here. He liked people. Fascinating. How did a man who spent his days steeped in darkness, investigating vices and arresting criminals, retain a liking for humanity?

Alice, who sat across from her, winked, and the sandwich lodged in Ingrid's throat.

Sputtering, she reached for a napkin. Gideon stopped midsentence to snag a cloth for her and thrust it into her hand. She pressed it against her mouth, eyes burning.

"Here." Gideon once again came to her rescue with a

goblet of lemonade. She grasped it and sipped, willing the irritation in her throat to cease.

"Oh, my. Are you well?" Aunt Mildred spoke from beside Lady Danvers.

Ingrid nodded, studiously avoiding looking at anyone.

"To continue," said Gideon, thankfully bringing everyone's attention to himself, "I was a very naughty little boy who lived on the streets."

"Good gracious." Lady Danvers's hand went to her neck. "What of your family?"

"I knew only my mother. My father left us when I was young, but I scarcely remember the man. Nevertheless, bad times befell us, as they often do to the poor."

Maids placed plates of salmagundi in front of them. A great relief filled Ingrid as she noted the lack of anchovies upon the popular salad. She dug in, but Gideon kept talking. "We found ourselves on the streets, my mother stricken with consumption, my father releasing all responsibility of me to her."

"A terrible thing," muttered Lord Danvers.

"Agreed. Fathers who abandon their children are the worst sort of creatures."

Between bites of salad, Ingrid slid a look at Gideon, who had spoken more loudly than necessary. He had that hardened tilt to his chin again. Shaking her head, she speared a piece of boiled egg. His bitterness might destroy him, but she knew not how to help him.

Prayer, perhaps. That had been her relief. Mayhap it would prove to be his.

Throughout lunch Gideon regaled his table with tales of danger and criminality. He starred as the hero in all of them, of course. And as he ate and spoke, Ingrid's presence remained a constant beside him. Soon, the meal ended and Lady Danvers stood, clapping her hands.

The guests turned to her, including Lord Hawking and his daughter, who sat only feet away at another table. Jaw grinding, Gideon focused on the lady who took ultimate delight in addressing her guests.

"We've a maze, everyone, but take care not to lose yourself within." She wagged a finger and several people laughed. "We've also set up a sack race at the other end of the folly, and kites near the pond."

People began to stand, excitement filling the air with a sort of crackling energy that put Gideon in a better mood.

"My lady, how about a sack race?" A young bloke with shocking red hair stood before Ingrid. Stifling his grin, Gideon noted her blank look and deduced that she could not recall the gent's name.

"Thomas Dagbert. We sat next to each other last night at dinner."

"I remember, Mr. Dagbert." She dabbed at the corners of her lips in a delicate way, much more delicately than how she attacked food. One did not expect a lady to be quite so hungry, but then again, Ingrid was no ordinary lady.

"You may call me Thomas," he said with a bashful smile. Poor sot.

"Thomas, thank you for the invitation, but I must refuse."

"Kites, then?" Hopeful, persistent chap.

"No, I think I shall sit that out. I believe Sir Tuckerson has a daughter in need of a partner." She pointed to a slip of a woman standing near a wall.

Luckily, Mr. Dagbert didn't press his luck and bowed out gracefully.

"No kites? What do you plan to do?" Gideon stood, offering his hand to her, grinning when she took it more forcefully than needed.

"The sack race is out of the question, and running after a kite proves equally problematic." She stood, and the pressure she put into his grip made him wonder if perhaps she needed more help with movement than she cared to admit.

Ingrid's aunt sauntered over just then, eyes as beady as a hawk's. "I've a mind to fly kites. Join me, Ingrid."

Something a little stubborn and downright frightening crept over Ingrid's face. He shoved his hands in the pockets of his trousers, wondering if he might be about to see a clash of iron wills. Her chin lifted to epic proportions.

"I think not, Aunt."

The woman's steel brows rose.

"Mr. West has so kindly offered to escort me on a short walk about the grounds."

"Alone." Her aunt's eyes narrowed and a chill stuttered down his spine. Lord Manning's sister had a most daunting effect upon a man's courage.

Ingrid fingered the pretty pink lace at the waist of her dress. "It is a picnic. No one shall bat an eye and we will be in perfect sight of all."

"Hmm." Her aunt managed to concoct a foul look, which she dispensed equally upon them both. "See that nothing untoward happens to Lady Ingrid. She may be marrying for practicality's sake, but her sister still hopes to make a love match."

"Where is Alice?" Ingrid's brow knit.

"With Lord Hawking's daughter, exploring the maze." With a haughty sniff, the woman trounced off.

Shaking his head, Gideon extended his arm and to his surprise, Ingrid took it.

So she wanted a walk. He would give her one, and while out and about, get her take on the various potential bridegrooms present.

Chapter Twenty

They descended the stairs at the north end of the folly. A warm breeze brushed Gideon's face and promised a fair afternoon. Not a cloud in sight, and the pond, which seemed more like a small lake, twinkled with tiny diamond ripples. Some guests already had their kites in the air, the colorful cloths zigzagging across the sky. Faint shrieks wafted over from where the sack races ensued.

"A stroll, perhaps." Ingrid's arm moved ever so slightly within the crook of his elbow, evidence of her uneven gait. She used her cane in the other hand. "I must move after that meal."

"You did seem to enjoy it."

"I didn't realize you grew up on the streets."

He schooled his features to stillness even as surprise undulated through him. "Are we delving into heavy topics during our stroll?"

"If you care to oblige me."

To his surprise, as he swept a glance over her flushed cheeks, he realized that indeed, he did very much care to oblige her. Tucking her arm nearer to his, he aimed their walk in the general direction of the pond.

"You shall cause talk with all this arm holding," she murmured.

"Not enough to harm Alice's pristine reputation." He maneuvered her around a rock jutting up from the grass.

"What was it like growing up on the streets?"

"Why do you ask?"

She shrugged in a feminine way, and a hard tightness squeezed at his chest. This woman, daughter of a wealthy earl, would always be out of reach. He must remember that. Throat dry, he removed his arm from hers.

"We near the lake," he said in answer to the surprise that flitted across her pretty face at his arm removal. Not popularly pretty, but uniquely pretty. "I do not wish to tempt the gossips."

"I ask about your childhood because I think of the children often." She chewed her lower lip in an oddly endearing way, then let out a soft breath of air. "I worry for them."

How had this woman snuck past the hardness he'd built around his heart? He hated how he felt the sadness in her tone, felt it to his very bones. He hated that the more he came to know her, the more he wanted to know her.

They meandered to the water's edge, stepping over pebbles and soggy dirt. "My childhood was much like theirs. Dirty and hungry, begging for scraps and picking pockets."

"How did you end up turning to the runners rather than to a life of crime?"

"My life of crime ended abruptly when an old constable caught me in the act of filching a pie from his kitchen."

She gasped. "You broke into someone's home?"

He lifted a shoulder, looking out across the pond. "A hungry boy does what he must, and the window had been left open. I smelled the pie over the refuse on the street. Boysenberry." He closed his eyes in search of the memory.

"Is that why you help the children? And what did the constable do?"

"You are very curious today, Lady Ingrid."

She slowly bent. She used her cane for balance and picked up a smooth pebble, turning it over in her palm. "You intrigue me."

"And here I thought no one could tear your interest from your piano. What a pleasant surprise."

"I am not so sure about *pleasant*." She held the stone out to him, the slim length of her fingers capturing his gaze. "Tell me more, and I shall teach you to skip rocks."

He laughed and took the stone. "What makes you think I don't know how to already?"

"You're telling me a street urchin has time between crimes to skip stones?" Her brow arched and the supreme confidence infusing her posture almost made him want to let her believe what she would.

"The constable did not turn me in," he said instead. "It turned out that his elderly sister, whom I had assumed to be his wife, had been watching me skulk about for days. Normally, we street rats don't stay in the same place for long, but I'd found that their particular street lacked other criminals due to the constable's presence." He fingered the stone, marveling at its smooth, oval shape, wondering if it would be up for the task of proving the overly confident Ingrid wrong. "Therefore I'd been stealthily robbing carriages, pickpocketing and begging when I could find an easy mark. She liked my dimples."

Ingrid made a sound that denoted irritation.

"And so," he continued, drawing his arm back, "she baked a pie, opened the window and waited." He released the stone, grinning as it skipped not once, not twice, but thrice across the waters.

Clapping sounded behind them. Several guests cheered

him on, lauding his skill, to which he offered them a gallant bow. He faced Ingrid for a similar applause.

She crossed her arms, the cane tucked betwixt her rib cage and right arm. Meeting his triumphant smirk with speculation, she said, "And then?"

"What, my lady? You cannot pause for a moment to admire my talent?"

"I believe you admire yourself enough for the both of us."

He chuckled at that. "You may be right. Nevertheless, I ate that entire pie and then the constable and his sister invited me to live with them. They'd provide food and a room if I'd perform general chores about the house that they were growing too old to do. We often went to the countryside for picnics and to visit their friends."

"They had no servants?"

He gave her a look that caused an attractive flush to rise to her cheeks.

"Where are they now?" she asked, moving on from her incorrect assumption.

"The sister, Betty, died a few years after taking me in. The constable followed in my twentieth year."

"That is very sad," she said as she carefully stooped and picked up another stone. "And your father?"

"My sire lives." He could not help the coldness that entered his voice.

"I see." She aimed, swung and her stone sailed cleanly through the air before cutting across the surface of the lake in four clean skips. "Can you best me, runner?"

"I can and I will." His pulse picked up as the wind riffled through her hair, as the sun drew sparkles from her eyes.

"You may try."

Just as he was about to toss the stone, she said flippantly, "And do tell me more of your father. His eyes are very like yours, are they not?"

His stone hit the water with an unremarkable splash, and promptly sank. If he said he didn't recall, it would be an outright lie.

"There is no need to answer," she said softly. "But the resemblance, once one sees it, is startling. Is there really no way for you to forgive him, Gideon?"

It was as though the stone had sunk in his stomach rather than in the pond. His innards roiled and he stepped back, done with stone skipping.

"He wants me to care for his daughters when he passes. Yet he could not care enough for me to keep me from the streets." His quiet words cut as surely as a blade, for Ingrid winced before picking up her skirts and turning toward the grassy hill leading to the folly.

"That is a difficult proposal to consider," she said. "Will you help him?"

"He let my mother die. He abandoned me." He followed her to the slope leading away from the pond. "Where are you going?"

"Alice is waving to me. She looks quite frantic."

He looked up. Indeed, Alice waved at them in quick succession.

"Something is wrong." Ingrid stepped faster, then faltered with a short hiss of breath.

Gideon put his hand on her arm, stopping her. "You will hurt yourself. Stop here and I shall run up to her."

Alice was already sliding down the slope toward them. Warring emotions crashed within Gideon as he went to meet her. The always-present bitterness colliding with concern for Ingrid, the uneasiness mixing with fear for the future.

Ingrid's sister met him and kept going toward Ingrid.

"What is wrong?" he asked, keeping pace.

"It is Rachelle."

"Lord Hawking's daughter."

Alice gave a terse nod, almost tripping over a rock. He did not often think she and Ingrid were alike, but in this moment he saw that the sisters shared the same single-minded persistence. It shouted in Alice's footsteps, in her hurried and precise manner. "She is lost in the maze. We were separated. I fear for her. A man followed us."

Gideon grabbed her shoulder, as impolite as it was to do so. He swung Ingrid's little sister around, noting the fear in her dark eyes, the tremble to the mouth that was not quite as wide as Ingrid's. "Elaborate."

Alice gave him a stark look. "We heard footsteps. We were not afraid at first, but then Rachelle told me that she is quite scared of Mr. Barley."

"Barley," Gideon bit out. He knew he had not liked that man.

"We began to run, but somehow, and I do not know why, we separated. I lost her. I…" Alice's voice dropped. "I worry that Barley has caught her. That he means to ruin her. The man is in great debt and has been hounding after her in London."

"And her father does nothing?" The incredulous tone to Ingrid's question jolted Gideon into action.

"We must find her," he said in a clipped tone.

"But we cannot alert others to their absence, nor to the potential ruination occurring. It is Barley's plan. It must be." A tautness strung Alice's words together in tight, staccato beats. "We must find them before anyone else."

"Shame on Lord Hawking." Ingrid hooked her arm through her sister's.

"Oh, no, Ingrid," Alice protested. "The earl is lovely.

She could not tell him, you see. His health is not good and the care of three young daughters weighs on him daily."

Ingrid made a noise that sounded near to a growl. "We shall find them. Mr. Barley will not succeed."

Gideon pressed ahead, his gaze scanning the land in front of them. Counting the guests. There had been a total of fifty to this country party. From what he could see, ten milled around outside the folly.

It took a good deal of self-control to keep their amble relaxed but they finally reached the maze without alerting the guests as to the precarious situation.

"Shall we split up?" asked Alice. The maze stretched before them, lush and thick. Lady Danvers had not exaggerated its size.

Gideon looked at the sisters. "If you encounter Barley, what will you do?"

Fright washed over Alice's countenance but Ingrid's expression took on that of a warrior. She jabbed her cane in the air. "He will not dare cross us."

Would Barley harm them? A man of low character did not care whom he hurt in pursuit of his goals. Though Gideon wanted to split up, he could not risk these ladies' safety. "Lady Alice, take us the way you remember."

They turned into the maze, but it did not take long before Ingrid stumbled.

Eyes wide, face a little pale, she shook her head. "I am so sorry, but I cannot run."

"Slower is better," Gideon said, wishing suddenly that he could take her pain. That he could wrap his arms around her and carry her wherever she wished. "We shall listen for rustling."

"It is I who is sorry," he heard Alice say quietly from behind him.

"Hush. No more apologies." Ingrid's forceful tone crinkled Gideon's brow. Ingrid could have spent her life blaming Alice for her injury. But she'd found a way to faith, somehow.

He peered through the thick shrubbery lining the maze's passageway. The fragrant leaves tickled his face, but alas, he could not see through the natural wall. They continued, coming to the first fork. He looked to Alice.

Her teeth tugged at her lower lip. "I think I turned left on my way out."

"Right it is." Gideon cut over, double-checking Ingrid's face for signs of stress, but her color had improved. "Stay together, and listen for abnormal sounds."

Ingrid followed Gideon at a distance, the tall athleticism of his frame bolstering her courage. She did not think she could take Barley physically, but she planned to verbally assault him, that odious fiend.

She skirted a root, ignoring the telltale twinge that predicted a few days' worth of hot compresses and time in her bedroom chair when she returned home. She wanted to ask Alice many questions, such as how the girls were separated in the first place. She wanted to ask Gideon how he felt protecting a girl who was likely his sister, if she was right that Hawking was his father.

The truth had bludgeoned her during luncheon. Gideon's voice had risen in his distaste for the father who'd left his family, and shortly thereafter, someone at a table behind her let out a guffaw of grating proportions. When she looked, she found that Hawking had not joined the laughter at his table. Instead, he had been staring at Gideon, a great sorrow in his deep and soulful blue eyes.

Eyes that bore an uncanny resemblance to Gideon's.

Could it be that Gideon was the illegitimate child of an earl? Though illegitimate children were not uncommon,

Ingrid's understanding was that men of standing quietly provided for their secret children. And if Hawking had abandoned his son and mistress, no wonder Gideon harbored ill feelings for the man. How very ironic that he now helped to keep his enemy's daughter from ruination.

They took the next right, Gideon following Alice's hand signal.

Ingrid studied the back of his head. His dark curls brushed the lapel of his coat in charming abandon. He walked in a steady, resolute manner. Stalking his prey. His shoulders broad, his strides long. What must he be like on the streets, hunting wicked perpetrators of crime?

Alice loped beside him, her sweet sister's hair escaping its pins and spiraling out from her hat. Ingrid touched her own hair, finding it in place beneath her bonnet. Jane had done well.

As they moved farther into the maze, a knot formed in her stomach. Would Barley truly compromise Hawking's daughter if he found her?

She trailed her fingers across a sheet of ivy draping the hedgerows, seeking to bring her mind back to the present. Dark green leaves relaxed beneath her fingertips, pliable and warm from the sun. In the maze cool shadows traded turns with sun-kissed patches of nature.

The space between Ingrid and the others lengthened as their paces picked up and hers slowed. She pressed her palm against her hip, wishing for the thousandth time that she had not ridden in the carriage that day so long ago. But she could not wish that her sister had not stolen her spot, for that would mean wishing this pain upon Alice. And not only the pain, but the deadness of her womb.

That, she could never do.

And in a way one could not anticipate, the valleys of her life had brought her closer to God. To peace.

A sound reached her, a little whisper that frolicked across the maze in hushed undulations. Ingrid moved more closely to the hedgerow, attempting to peer through its coiled leaves. When that didn't work, she pressed her ear to the shrubbery.

The voice grew clearer. A man. She beckoned for Gideon and Alice to listen, but they had rounded left at the next corner, not knowing she had stopped. It took only a moment to debate her next move.

Using her cane, she navigated the length of the hedge-row and turned right. The opening ahead carved a dank and fearsome terror into her mind. Who would she find? And what circumstance?

A thump and the sound of a quickly hushed cry tugged her forward and into the opening. She raised her cane, knees trembling.

Barley's back was to her. He held Rachelle by the hair. Her eyes shifted toward Ingrid, round and unseeing. It was her face that terrified Ingrid more than anything. Her skin was the color of old egg whites. Gray and clammy.

Ingrid quickly put her fingers to lips, motioning Rachelle to silence. She did her best to move forward quietly, arm raised. One good whack should do it, she'd think. This ne'er do well wouldn't know what hit him.

She swung hard, praying for strength and aim and hoping she didn't hit Rachelle instead. The cane connected with the side of the louse's head in a shuddering contact that rippled up to Ingrid's shoulders. He let go of Rachelle, though.

"Run," Ingrid said to the woman as she lifted her arm back again despite the hot arc down her hip.

Barley was already recovering. Pressing a hand against his temple, he lumbered toward Ingrid. She swung the stick again, harder, and managed a rather sound thud against his skull before he yanked the cane right out of her hands.

An *oomph* sounded behind her. She glanced back and saw that Rachelle had run into Alice. Gideon stormed forward, his expression hard and dangerous and dark.

"Go," he bit out, and the two girls pivoted and fled.

Not Ingrid, of course. She did not know that she could even walk.

She slowly limped backward, even as Gideon passed her. His fist jabbed Barley squarely in the nose. The man swayed. One more punch, and Barley crumpled to the ground.

They had to get Rachelle back to the outing, and quickly, before anyone happened upon them. One wrong look and a gossiping biddy would assume the worst. No one cared whose fault the attack was, only that an unmarried lady had found herself in the tenuous position of being alone with a man.

And the punishment meted out by a stringent, unforgiving haut monde?

Immediate marriage or ruination.

Ingrid would not allow it. She and Alice would create a reason for Rachelle's dishevelment. No one would know what happened this day, because they would concoct a story beyond refutation. And let that greedy, vile louse Barley dare disagree.

Gideon turned to look at her then, just as her silly leg gave out and she dropped painfully to the ground.

Chapter Twenty-One

Ingrid's collapse stuttered Gideon's heart to a stop. He hurried to her, bending and taking one of her hands. It was far too cold.

"Gideon." Her eyes searched his face. "How could this have happened?" Her words caught, snagging on the pain.

Before him sat another Ingrid. He had met the haughty pianist, the austere lady, the kindhearted teacher, the passionate woman.

But now she was the grieving human whose fingers clutched his shirtsleeves, a fragile bird in search of a sturdy place to land. He gulped down the jagged, painful lump in his throat and touched her face.

She blinked slowly, one iridescent tear lodged upon her eyelashes.

He dropped to his knees. Brushed his thumb against her lids, and then pulled her into an embrace. His heart bumped crazy in his chest but he only tightened his hold. She buried her face into his shoulder and for a long moment, he breathed jasmine and shattered innocence.

Nuzzling his nose against her head, he relished the feel of her arms encircling him. This felt right. Too right to ignore. She uttered a long, shaky exhalation and pulled her head up. He cupped her face, his fingers rubbing patterns against her temples.

In the shade of where they sat, her irises were gilded lavender. He lowered his head and touched his lips against hers, slowly, with care. And then again, feeling the warm softness of her breath as he kissed her tenderly.

A suspicion he'd been fighting to ignore for weeks welled up, and he could no longer deny the truth: he loved Ingrid.

Well and truly loved the exasperating woman.

Feeling shaky, he disengaged himself though he could not bring himself to look away from her beautiful features. "All will be well," he said, his voice hoarse. "We must get you out."

As though a shade had been drawn over a window, the vulnerability upon her face disappeared, replaced with sheer stubbornness. Her shoulders went back, her chin up.

"What of that swine?"

"Leave him to me. Can you find your way back?"

She nodded, taking his hand as he helped her to her feet. She heavily favored her leg, even after he handed her the cane. She turned and limped toward the small entrance. Ducking beneath the low-hanging leaves, he followed her to the left.

They moved into the maze corridor. Alice and Rachelle met them halfway.

"Lady Ingrid is in need of assistance," he told them.

She did not deny his words but leaned on her sister. "We shall say Alice had a scare."

Gideon nodded. "I will leave you ladies to the details while I take care of Barley."

And he would do his best to forget that he'd kissed Ingrid.

He looked at Rachelle, whose visage remained pale. She shivered from shock.

Who would protect her if Hawking died? What of her other sisters? *His* other sisters.

As though hearing his thoughts, Rachelle reached out and squeezed his arm. "Thank you," she said in a low tone. Alice shot her a look of concern.

"I need to speak with Mr. West." Rachelle tipped her head. "Privately, please."

Alice nodded and helped Ingrid slowly walk to the next turn in the maze.

Rachelle turned so that her back was to the sisters and looked up at him. "You look like my father."

He waited, for she'd endured a great trauma today and though this was the last thing he wished to speak of with her, his wishes were not important at the moment.

She wet her lips. "I remember you."

He tipped his head. "Impossible."

"Not impossible. I am two and twenty. You must be less than thirty. Though I may have been quite young, it is forever burned within my memory."

"What is?" His voice cracked, brittle, but she did not flinch.

"You." Her tone wavered, thickened by emotion. "Standing in the rain on our doorstep. Just a little boy with dark hair. And my father was so very cruel. I do not remember his words. Only that you looked at me, and I could not tell if your face was wet with tears or rain, only that your eyes looked like Father's. Like mine."

Gideon inclined his head. "Your memory serves you well."

"I always wondered as to the identity of that little boy. And then I saw you here. I heard you laugh." She reached up to touch his face, her fingers much too cold. "How is it possible that a stranger laughs just like my father?"

His gaze flickered beyond his sister to where Ingrid watched him with sympathy.

"My brother," breathed Rachelle, her eyes still dry. She hadn't cried, he realized, and that seemed worse than anything. "You have saved me from that greedy, wicked man. I shall not be utterly ruined in society. What was planned for evil shall be turned to good." She blinked once, twice. "Because of you, I will return home unscathed, at the very least, by gossip. And I shall not have to marry that..." She trailed off, the words shuddering and trembling into silence. "Mr. West, whatever happens after this, I need you to know something."

She took his hands. Clutched them, really.

"Since I saw you on our doorstep, I have not ceased praying for you."

"What did you pray?" Foolish to ask, but he wanted, he needed, to know.

"I pray that you will have a family. That you are loved." With that, she patted his cheek as a mother would a son, and joined the other ladies.

He took a second to watch them leave. He did not like the look of Alice's wan features, nor the way Ingrid limped. But he could not help them at the moment. He had to figure out this business with Barley.

It took some time and effort, but the man finally roused. It did not take much in the way of conversation for Barley to realize he should leave the country for an extended vacation. As much as Gideon wanted to arrest him, he could not. They left the maze together. Barley made his excuses to anyone who happened to stop them, citing an unfortunate run-in with a hedgerow to explain his bloodied visage and reason for leaving the country estate early. It took over an hour to escort the man out, to see him and his servants and his luggage off the property, and then another quarter hour to confer with Lord Hawking about a plan.

This situation had changed something within him, and he could not expose Rachelle to any scandal whatsoever, not with her family in such a vulnerable place. Should Hawking die, and should Rachelle bring disgrace to the family, who would care for her and her sisters?

No one, because no reputable household would want gossip attached to them. The girls would be on the streets, or relegated to a cottage in the country, living on whatever pittance a guardian decided to give them. The unjust way of the world he lived in. But he could make sure Barley never hurt anyone again.

He *would* make sure of it.

His gut churned. It quite suddenly occurred to him that in his great anger, the bitterness so often riding his shoulders had lifted. He had felt, even, a small measure of compassion for Hawking. He managed to defer his personal feelings toward the man during conversation.

It was decided that if Barley returned to England, Hawking would call in all his debts and leave him penniless. Should Hawking die, Gideon would carry on the promise in his stead.

Gideon left the man in his room to search for Ingrid.

Though they'd been moving slowly, surely they had arrived at the estate? Or perhaps they'd stayed longer at the luncheon to make a good appearance?

He went down to the main hall just as the front doors opened and Ingrid's aunt burst through, followed by Lady Danvers.

"Make way. There has been an injury." Lord Danvers pushed through and beyond him, Gideon could see a small group of people halting up the steps.

He backed up. "What has happened?"

"The ladies had a fall in the maze."

And then there they were, Ingrid's arms resting on Alice and Rachelle's shoulders. From a different room, servants filled the hall. Jane was among them. He caught her eye and nodded toward Ingrid.

They came into the great hall.

"Jane knows what to do," said Ingrid loudly. "Please, I am fine. Just an old injury."

With a nod from Lord Danvers, the guests filed back outside and the servants dispersed.

"Are you sure, my dear?" asked Lady Danvers in a kind voice.

"I could use assistance." Rachelle removed Ingrid's arm and carefully gave her to Jane. Once again, Gideon saw the sweetness in his sister, and his heart twisted. She took the attention from Ingrid to save her embarrassment.

"Of course, darling. Let's get those scratches cleaned up. You all took such a tumble. I feel positively terrible. You must tell me where in the maze is such a rough spot…" Her voice trailed off as she led Rachelle away.

The hall grew quiet.

"What is wrong, Lady Ingrid?" Gideon's gaze roamed over her in search of rips in her dress, tears, but all looked to be in place. Yet, Alice and Jane did not let go of her, and the ever-present cane was noticeably missing.

"Just a bit of stiffness, sir," said Jane.

The fact that the maid spoke for Ingrid was alarming enough, but add to that the pasty tincture of Ingrid's skin, and he could only presume that her collapse in the maze had more to do than shock. She'd grievously aggravated her hip.

He held out his hand. "Let me help you."

She shook her head, dark strands curling over her shoulders. "I need no help, Gideon."

Gideon watched through hooded eyes as Jane assisted Ingrid up the first set of stairs. Each step took longer than the last.

In a quiet voice, Jane mentioned something about a chair.

"No," said Ingrid, her voice the sharpest he'd ever heard. Her gaze skittered back to him, a flush spotting her too pale cheekbones. "Why are you following us? Gawking at me?"

He paused on a step.

"Go." She waved her hand at him as if he was a servant.

But he was not her servant. She needed help. Anyone could see that. His spine straightened. And no matter his parentage, his class, he was not hers to command. Jane kept her gaze down, her face also pink, and suddenly, Gideon realized they were embarrassed.

Or perhaps the maid felt bad for Ingrid, which meant that Ingrid's great pride had been pricked.

They reached the first-floor landing. Ingrid rested against the wall, her lips a drained pink. Gideon crossed his ankles, leaning against the stair banister with folded arms. He let his gaze travel Ingrid languorously, from the top of her mussed hair to her slipper-clad toes. Her resulting scowl told him she noticed.

"Tell me about this chair."

"There is nothing to tell," she snapped. "Did I not order you to leave?"

"You certainly did." His eyes roved her face, remembering too clearly their brief kiss, the way she felt in his arms. As if she belonged. Swallowing back the thought, he focused on the present. On the very stubborn, cantankerous lady in front of him. "Did I not tell you that I am not your servant?"

"I know that." Crisp and sharp, yet strain filled her words.

"But it could be arranged," he continued, giving her a slow wink.

"I don't have patience for your flirtations, West. The chair is a ridiculous way to help me upstairs. I'm not using one, Jane."

"But my lady, please." The maid's mouth pursed in disagreement.

Gideon should have watched Ingrid more carefully in the maze. She should have stayed behind. But then who would have so soundly hit Barley with a cane? He'd sported an impressive knot on his head.

Footsteps sounded behind them as her aunt came up the staircase. "Ingrid, we are bringing a chair to take you to your room. I will brook no argument."

Ingrid's lips firmed, almost flattening, and her eyes flashed. Oh, his darling Ingrid.

He did not want to love her. Everything within resisted. What good could come of such a silly emotion? And yet, he did, and his heart, which had been aching for hours, began to throb anew with sorrow.

"Please, Aunt Mildred. No." Her voice dropped, infused almost with…desperation?

Gads, he wanted to reach out and touch her cheek. To still the trembling that radiated her body. "Is it so difficult to accept help?"

"Yes," she whispered.

"She doesn't want the chair," he said to Jane. "Why?"

"It's bumpy, sir. It causes more pain but she needs it because when her leg is aggravated, she cannot lift it to go up the stairs." Jane still looked nervous, as if the admission betrayed a confidence.

"I shall crawl," said Ingrid in a tight voice. But she was slowly sliding down the wall, unable to hold herself up any longer. Utterly ludicrous to wait for her permission.

He stepped forward and hooked his right arm under her arms, creating support. She sagged against him, her left hand curling around his neck.

He glanced at the aunt, whose own expression carried a great deal of sympathy.

"Permission to assist?" he asked the woman.

She nodded in a stiff manner.

Gideon put his head near Ingrid's. "My lady, you are in grievous straits. Allow me to assist you."

"How do you mean?"

"Will I cause you further pain if I carry you?"

A faint sheen of sweat beaded her upper lip. He thought she might blush at his words, but she did not. Her lids were heavy, pale curtains over her eyes. A faint throb of pulse moved at her neck. "You are ridiculous."

The words lacked rancor.

"Jane, can I carry her without harming her further?"

The maid wet her lips, glancing at Ingrid as if fearing for her job. Ingrid, however, seemed lost in her own wan world. Her body had begun shaking.

Gideon had never been in chronic pain, but he had suffered a knife wound at the age of ten and four that had become infected. The agony had turned him sleepy and shivery.

Jane came forward then. "Put your arm here." She took his left hand and, forcing him to bend, brought it behind Ingrid's left leg. "Slide your arm under both of her legs, and then lift her slowly and carefully. In a smooth movement, if possible." Her gaze flickered up and down his body. "You are big enough, I think, to carry her easily. You must know that each step shall be a jostle. But perhaps less painful than the chair."

"If she has medicine, get it," he bit out.

Ever so carefully, he swooped his arm beneath Ingrid's

legs, then rose as smoothly as he could. Her skirts fell over his arms as he lifted her off the ground. Her head nestled against his neck, and besides her quick intake of breath, he thought he managed to lift her without worsening her pain.

He walked to the next set of stairs, the ones that led to the third-floor east wing. The guest suites.

He lifted his right foot until it joined his left on the step.

And then he carried his lady up the stairs.

Ingrid pressed her nose into the hollow at the base of Gideon's throat. His skin, warm, comforted her. Sandalwood and a musky smell that she did not dislike surrounded her. His arms held her in a most gentle way, and though her head throbbed with bright stabs of lightning, and though her entire right side felt afire, there was finally a relief of sorts.

The farther he moved up the stairs, the more she relaxed against him. Her arms wrapped around his neck. This was not the first time she'd been carried upstairs. Though not often, the help had been needed in the past.

But this was the first time that she felt so completely aware of the man carrying her. His breaths, moist exhalations against her forehead. His fingers gripping her legs, and her body ensconced in his arms. Safe.

She swallowed tightly, for her throat constricted and tears threatened.

Humiliation and comfort. They should not coexist, yet in this moment they did. The part of her that railed against his help had quieted, soothed into tameness. Even the cramping in her hip had slowed, mellowing into a sort of bruised ache.

It did not compare to how her heart felt, though.

Trampled on. Ripped open and sore. Raw.

Paris awaited her, but in going she would leave Gideon

behind. The children. Her family. All that she'd ever cared for, as long as she could remember, had been playing the piano. Living had always been something she observed from a distance.

But in these past months, a change had occurred. She'd come to care what happened in the lives of others. It was a most inconvenient sensation.

Would she even be able to make Paris by end of summer? A hot burn trailed down her cheek as a tear escaped her closed lids. She'd planned to leave by summer's end. But with no husband in sight, that seemed improbable. And now that her body betrayed her again…

"Where is your room, my lady?" Gideon's words fell near her forehead, his lips grazing ever so closely to her temple. If she turned her head just the slightest, if she lifted her face, she could take a kiss, a comfort she craved.

Instead, she said, "Fifth room on the right."

Thankfully, he heard her despite the threadiness of her voice. Even her throat betrayed her.

Gideon stopped at her room and the door squeaked open. Someone walked into her room and lit the candles. She could not bring herself to open her eyes. Not only because of the megrim, but because to see any sort of sympathy or compassion upon Gideon's face threatened to whittle the last of her dignity to nothingness.

And that, she could not bear.

So she listened, curled up against Gideon's chest, as the coverlets were turned. His heart beat against her ear, sure and strong. Like the man himself. The illegitimate son of an earl. Not quite a commoner, but not quite a peer. Nevertheless, a man who had overcome his childhood to become a respectable Bow Street Runner.

Pain turned her thoughts hazy. Waves of slow, rolling aches undulated through her lower back, to her thigh, down her leg.

Gideon gently deposited her on the bed. She opened her eyes, relieved the room was dimly lit. Jane hovered behind Gideon, the warming pad in her arms. Her aunt stood at the base of the bed.

Jane moved beside Gideon and set the pad on the bed. "I've brought you a tonic to ease your pain." She reached for a cup another maid held out, and then gave it to Ingrid.

A strange thing, how pain affected a whole body. Ingrid's arms felt like overstretched string. Her limbs, shaking and unsure. She took the draft, relishing spicy warmth as it slipped down her throat.

Everything felt a little off. Unsteady.

"Gideon." Ingrid found her voice. He turned, and to her dismay, sympathy etched itself upon his features. "Please do not look at me so."

"And how would you have me look at you?" He leaned forward.

She smiled, though it did feel as though it wobbled a bit. "You know how I want you to look at me."

His brow scrunched, and then his dimple appeared. He glanced at Jane, who had moved to a chair near the bed's headboard. "What exactly did you give her?"

"Valerian root, sturdy English tea and a bit of rum."

How handsome he looked in candlelight. A soft yellow spilled across his features, carving his face like a sculptor carving Adonis. She almost flexed her fingers toward him, but stopped herself. Working class. A man with a career.

He did not belong in Paris, and her parents would never approve marriage between them. She, a proper heiress, and he a pauper. A man of the streets.

"How are the children?" Sleepiness pulled at her eyelids, coaxing them to close. She fought the sensation.

"Those street urchins." He chuckled. "They make do. We are to be out in a fortnight, you know."

"Out?" His face blurred, and with a start, she realized her megrim had eased into a faint throb.

"We shall speak of it later."

"I miss the children. Jane, do you miss them?"

"Is she always like this?" Gideon's face wavered into view as he came closer, his eyes a brilliant blue.

"A little extra in the tea this time, sir. To soothe the muscle pain," came Jane's voice from far away.

"Gideon." Ingrid drew a deep breath, willing herself to stay awake, to focus on him. "The children…give them my love…how I wished for children."

"You deserve children, my lady." Surely, his face so close to hers was not proper. "I shall find a husband for you, and you will have a multitude of babies to love."

Was she crying? She could not tell. A pleasant, cloudy numbness tingled her cheeks. "You are kind, but I cannot have children. My womb is injured, you see."

Was he squinting at her again?

"Lady Ingrid," Jane's voice drew near. "Sleep now."

And she did.

Chapter Twenty-Two

Ingrid's injury kept her from rejoining the house party. The aunt kept Gideon apprised of her health but did not allow him to visit her. Gideon didn't push the matter. How could he, knowing that his heart had become irrevocably involved. He did, however, delve into the list from her parents and indulge in some gossip about men in search of wives.

He would find Ingrid the perfect husband. At the end of the weekend, the Danverses lent him a horse to ride home.

He returned to London armed with information on husbandly prospects. When he walked into his home, five unruly children greeted him. Petey and his dog among them.

Massaging the back of his neck, he surveyed the room and its contents. Clothes spilled out of luggage and stale bread littered the floor. "Where is my broom?"

Petey lifted his shoulders. "I think some 'un came in and stole it."

Anna hovered in a corner, Sarah next to her. Two little boys with soot on their noses sat on a pallet near the wall. He frowned. Soot meant they'd already been pressed into cleaning chimneys. A sad lot for ones their age, and dangerous.

"Listen, I've got to go and get payment. This place needs cleaning and packing. Do any of you have clothing?"

As one, the children looked at each other.

"We wear what we's gots from Miss Teacher," said Anna quietly, fingering her curly dark hair. "Is Miss Teacher coming back?"

"No, but she sends her regards to you all. She said she misses you."

"Think she's sitting at 'ome eating pies and drinking chocolate," Petey said in a sullen, bitter voice.

Gideon thought better than to chastise him. The boy was still smarting over Ingrid's absence. He would talk to him later, try to help him understand.

"I have to vacate the premises soon." He eyed the kids. Only five. It saddened him. "Does anyone here have a parent? A family?"

Petey shook his head. "My da is dead and my mum run off on me."

"I ran away from the orphanage. Been there my 'ole life," said one of the new little boys. He thumbed in the direction of the child next to him. "This 'un, too. We got tired of 'unger and beatings."

"I see." Gideon looked to the girls. "And you?"

Sarah stared at the floor. "Auntie kicked me out. Said she didn't have enough food to feed me."

"My mother be dead, about two months now," put in Anna. "Never knew a papa."

"Very well." He nodded, though the pit of his stomach ached for them. "Pack your things. I'll return tonight with a broom. You all must be here to leave next Sunday. Otherwise, I'll have to go without you."

"Where are we going, Gideon?" Petey pet Sir Beasley in jerky, quick strokes, betraying his nervousness.

He shook his head. "I have a possible cottage lined up in

a village outside of London. It's my intent to find schooling for you—"

"Schooling?" interrupted Petey, his nose scrunching into furrowed rows of freckled skin. "We don't want no schooling."

Gideon stifled his laugh, covering it with a stern look. "Do you wish to be a criminal, then? To sound uneducated and boorish?"

Petey flapped a hand. "I don't need book learning. I 'as my smarts."

Anna snorted. "That 'asn't helped ye much now, aye?"

"First things first. Book learning will keep you all from sounding like pirates." Gideon grinned and tossed a pillow at Petey.

The boy dodged, as Gideon knew he would.

"Fine, but what of food? Are ye going to feed us?"

"Yes, but I'll require that you behave for whoever teaches you and that you keep the place kept up. Not like this." He swept a hand out.

"I want to go with you," Sarah said quietly, sliding her thumb into her mouth.

Gideon so badly wanted to hug her and assure her that all would be well, but time would do that for him. "Sunday," he reminded them. "I'll be back later tonight."

"With more treats?" Petey's eyes lit up.

Gideon chuckled. Lady Danvers's cook had been happy to give him some pastries and scones for the children. "Maybe."

He spent the next days finishing up a case and filling out paperwork. Always paperwork. On Thursday, he hailed a hackney because a thick moistness swelled in the air. No doubt rain was on its way. The hackney stopped in front of him. He climbed up, giving the address of Lord Manning's town home, and settled back in his seat. Hopefully, the rain waited until he reached his destination.

The horses trotted through the streets, and Gideon withdrew the letter his mother had written Hawking all those years ago. It had been burning a hole in his pocket, in his soul, but he'd decided that if he was to be known to his sisters, he needed to understand more of what had happened so long ago. Forgiveness for Hawking eluded him, but perhaps he could grow to care for the women related to him by blood.

Seeing Rachelle's distress, her lack of protection, stirred his sense of honor. Changed his mind. He would care for his half sisters.

Avoiding the letter solved nothing and since he couldn't bring himself to toss it in the oven, he might as well read it.

He unfolded the paper carefully, noting the creases, as if Hawking had read it over and over again.

Dearest John, father of our child,

I did not think I asked too much of you. Certainly nothing deserving of your abandonment. A love such as ours requires its own place in the world. Your wife does not need you as I do. Come to the Continent with me. You said that you loved me when you promised me forever.

I did not mean what I said that terrible night. I will not tell your family about us. Please forgive me. Please come back. Wesley has been asking for you. He should be your heir, and you know this is true, but I shall not press.

If only you would return, darling.

At the very least, let us have a conversation. Our son deserves that much.

With utmost passion, the woman you claimed to be the love of your life,

Cecilia.

Gideon frowned, refolding the paper and staring out the window at the shadowed buildings the hackney passed. The letter brought more questions than it answered. For the longest time he'd held his mother up as a paragon of innocence in all that had transpired. This letter sowed uncomfortable suspicions.

When the hackney stopped in front of Lord Manning's town home, he jumped out, paid the driver and then rapped on the front door. The clouds above darkened the afternoon, and a distinct scent of coming rain permeated the air. The butler opened the door and silently ushered him into Lord Manning's study.

The man himself was absent, and so Gideon sat in a chair and waited. The office, filled with books and richly decorated furniture, only served to heighten his nerves.

He'd determined several acceptable husbands for Ingrid. Now for payment. He tapped his knees, staring at the paperwork littering Lord Manning's desk.

Behind him, a hiss of sound tickled his hearing as the door opened and footsteps trod into the room. Lord Manning and his wife entered, both with most stern looks upon their faces.

He rose, offering the countess a respectful bow.

"You've news?" Manning did not sit at his desk, choosing instead to stand in front of Gideon.

"I have candidates who would suit Lady Ingrid well, if she'll have one."

"Splendid." Yet, Lady Manning did not look happy. "Who are they?"

Gideon gestured to the seat behind the desk. "Would you prefer to discuss the gentlemen from the comfort of your seat? I had to hunt outside your list as I became aware of new parameters."

"Parameters?" Lady Manning moved behind her husband's desk and Lord Manning took a seat.

But before Gideon could elaborate, the sound of piano rioted throughout the house. Ingrid's parents exchanged a glance.

Gideon sank into his own chair, watching them closely. He'd expected elation, but maybe they hadn't expected him to find anyone for her? Most likely they did not want Ingrid leaving England, no matter what. A violent E note filtered into the office.

Lady Manning's fingers twisted in her skirts. Lord Manning glowered.

"I take it Lady Ingrid has recovered from her muscle strain?" asked Gideon.

"Not quite, but she insisted on getting out of bed. Is there a chance, West, that you might tell our daughter you found no success in your endeavors?" Lord Manning's fingers drummed against the desktop as his gaze found Gideon's.

He felt his brows lift. "You are asking me to lie to Lady Ingrid?"

Her mother moved forward. "Normally, we eschew untruths." Her violet eyes, so like Ingrid's, held sadness. "But she is determined to go to Paris. Her father and I simply do not think her body could take the travel. Why, even coming and going from our country estate taxes her so. Can you imagine sailing across the Channel, navigating a new country? And though we engaged a French governess, Ingrid's mastery of the language is atrocious."

"I think you underestimate your daughter," he said in a quiet tone, though he himself held reservations.

Another note crashed through the house, a particularly vicious G, if he had it correct.

"She is overly optimistic." Lord Manning stood. "I've

a notion, suddenly. Come, we shall speak to her. Present the suitors to her yourself."

Gideon could guess Manning's notion: when presented with suitors, Ingrid would reject them. Gideon half thought she might as well. Would she really shackle herself to a husband for life, just to teach at a Parisian conservatory?

As they neared the room where the piano lived, the music grew louder. Ingrid was at it today, he thought ruefully. Did she know he might arrive? Did she remember what she'd told him?

He'd ruminated on her words during his quiet hours. She claimed to be unable to have children. If that was true, did it influence her aversion to marriage?

He had modified his list in the past days. One thing he'd discovered…he did not want Ingrid to marry.

But what other options did she have?

Certainly not himself.

Ask her to marry a man who spent all his money on orphans, whose parentage was not even legal? Sighing, he followed Lord and Lady Manning into the study.

Ingrid's fingers flew across the keys, long practice and uninhibited passion propelling their movements. Chopin flowed through her: long, sharp, high, low, waves and waves of sensation to drown every thought. Her fingers slowed as she neared the end of the piece, plucking out the final notes with crisp clarity.

The last note, a steady A, lingered like the scent of lilies before trailing into silence. Clapping startled her, and her eyes flew open. Mother and Father, wearing smug little grins, sat upon the sofa.

And Gideon…he clapped heartily, admiration upon his handsome features. And a touch of something else, perhaps, in the lift of his lips, the crinkle of his eyes. She'd missed his face. That mussed hair. The grin that knew its own charms. Even more, she'd missed his artistic appreciation of her skills. As much as her family liked her music, they were not musicians. They could not pick up on the subtleties of a note held a fraction longer than usual, of a key pressed more ardently than called for.

But Gideon could.

He saw more than anyone had ever seen. The very thought terrified. Goose bumps rose on her arms. She dropped her hands, eyeing the trio. They could only be here for one reason: to present prospective bridegrooms. Panic rose in her throat, tightened her windpipe until for the barest hint of a second, she could not breathe.

She did not even like dancing with peers she'd known her entire life. How would she embrace a stranger?

There must be another way. But as she looked into her father's resolute face, she knew there was not.

Her parents hovered like the ducks at the Round pond in Kensington Gardens over ducklings. They would never let her out of their sight. Not without protection. Though Rachelle's horrific experience remained fresh in her mind, it did not quell her desire to leave. Even her body, achy as it was, had not changed her mind.

The invitation lay open on her dresser. Every day she reread it, hoping against hope that the conservatoire would not turn her away when they discovered her to be a woman.

"Join us, Ingrid." Mother patted a spot next to her on the couch. With an enigmatic expression, Gideon also sat.

Gritting her teeth, less from pain and more from the great irritation her parents continuously caused her, she slid carefully from the piano bench and limped to the couch. Yesterday had been her first day out of bed, and that only for a short play of the piano.

She rubbed at her thigh as she lowered herself to the

couch cushion. She then placed her palms upon her knees and waited for her parents to speak. Gideon looked to be holding back a smile, which annoyed her no end. It was there in the crook of his lips, a betraying twitch at the corners of his mouth.

He must find this entire husband fiasco supremely funny. She had found it amusing at first, when she thought she'd had the upper hand.

"I am surprised you have not yet escaped the coop, Lady Ingrid." He tipped his head in a teasing manner, and beside her, Mother inhaled sharply.

"Do not think I haven't considered it," she said in an overly saccharine voice. Both her parents seemed to be gasping for oxygen. "If I did not want to terrify and disappoint my parents—" she shot them an arch look before returning attention to Gideon "—I would do so. It seems that though they believe in following the heart's lead, they never intended for me to truly follow mine."

"Cutting words, daughter." Father's voice held disapproval.

"The truth is often sharp," she replied.

"Well," said Gideon with a lazy grin, "I've excellent news. There are men galore in need of fortune, and a few of them are prone to traveling. I've made certain they've good character and that they are not in need of an heir."

"How efficient of you."

"I am nothing but effective, my lady, which is why your parents hired me."

"Humble as well." She pressed her lips together. So he did remember that she'd spoken of her barrenness. He'd believed her, too, enough to find candidates who did not need children. She could feel her parents' gazes burning into her.

"You told him?" asked her mother in a quiet voice.

"I have wondered in the last few days why Ingrid's condition was not disclosed sooner." Gideon steepled his fingers and tapped the tip of his nose, an altogether sober expression crossing his face. "Did you not think it pertinent? Did you not consider that a man might wish to know she could not produce an heir?"

She gulped because a sudden onslaught of emotion threatened to choke her.

"Her situation is not certain, only suspected," said Father. "And due to the sensitivity of the topic, her mother and I did not think it necessary to disclose until a bridegroom was found."

"I see." Gideon brought his hands down and looked to her. "What is your reason for secrecy?"

She blinked. "I did not wish to marry, and then I did not care to divulge my private circumstance."

He nodded slowly. "As it is, I devised a new list." He rattled off the names. "All of these men already have heirs or do not have titles. Do you have a preference, Lady Ingrid?"

She took a quick breath. "No. Just choose one for me. I shall show up for the wedding."

"Ingrid, you must be involved." Mother slapped the couch, much too forcefully to Ingrid's way of thinking.

"Why?"

"To see if you are compatible."

"I believe Lady Ingrid will get along with anyone on my list," put in Gideon. "They are all interested in music, each plays an instrument and they are known to be kind men."

He had only said five names. She'd met all but one of them throughout the years. "You see, he has said it himself. I am not necessary to this arrangement. Secure me a husband, for I am to leave before autumn."

A sort of shock spread across Gideon's face. His brows lifted. His jaw dropped for the briefest of moments before closing, turning his jawline into stone. He stared at her in a far too intense manner. Disbelieving?

"Manning, may I speak to you?" Mother stood abruptly, her fingers snagging Father's shoulder. "In the hall, if you will."

They bustled out, Mother speaking in hushed, unhappy whispers.

"I really do not care for the look you are giving me," said Ingrid to Gideon.

"You, on the other hand, wear a particularly attractive scowl this fine afternoon."

Hotness seeped into her cheeks. "Frivolity. Have you nothing of substance to say?"

He leaned forward, resting his elbows on his knees and giving her a smile that sent delightful shivers to her toes. "I could say that I long to give you a proper kiss."

"Still a sentence of nothing but fluff."

"And yet you like it."

"I do not."

"Do, too."

"Why are you so very immature?" She glanced at the door, which her parents had left cracked. Their voices filtered in, muted and impassioned.

"Why will you not admit to your feelings?" How did one's eyes manage to sparkle in a dull room? Yet, his did precisely that.

Oh, her foul mood. Her irritable nature. She wanted to respond to him with a smile, or some witty remark, but her tongue cleaved to the roof of her mouth and her spine felt ramrod straight. Instead, all she could think of was the way he was looking at her.

She swallowed hard, her fingers clasping together in her lap. He truly did want to kiss her.

"Fine," she said, voice taut. "We share an attraction. What of it?"

He shrugged, grinning and leaning back in his chair. He stretched his legs before him. "I must say, your parents are unaccountably upset."

"They are," she murmured, trying to adjust to his sudden conversational shift.

"You'd think they'd be thrilled. Tell me, my lady, do you suppose they did not expect you to agree so handily to marrying a stranger?"

Chapter Twenty-Three

Making Ingrid blush was pure delight. Gideon adored the high color in her cheeks, the disapproval she tried to express in the purse of her mouth and yet failed to do. He was certain pleasure lit her eyes, even as her arms hugged her body as if to ward off flirtations, as she liked to call them.

She blinked slowly, her dark lashes a lovely fringe around her eyes. He did not think she even knew her own beauty. Or perhaps she did not care.

A pang inched through his chest, slow and creeping, as he watched her considering his words. Hadn't he known her to be dangerous from the beginning? He hadn't protected himself thoroughly, and now he might go the way of his mother. Loving someone beyond his reach. Outside his realm.

His previous levity faded.

One day, and soon, a different man might make her blush. Kiss her senseless. Feel the warmth of her smile.

Why not him?

"You do not need to stare at me so. I am contemplating an answer."

"Am I staring?" He allowed his mouth to curve, though within his heart thumped in painful beats.

"I suspect you are right," she continued as though he hadn't answered. "My parents made an agreement they did not intend to keep. I daresay they'll keep me safe until I die of parental asphyxiation."

The overly dramatic comment elicited a surprising chuckle, easing the disappointment that had flooded his system. He wanted nothing more than to gather his money and leave.

Even as the notion crossed his mind, he realized it was not entirely true. He did want something more. He wanted to pull the woman sitting across from him to himself. He wanted to lay waste to her defenses, to kiss her until she melted, to slide a promise of forever upon her finger.

But he could not even afford a ring.

What life could he offer her? If he accepted Hawking's proposal, if he took over his lands and money, then he'd be a man Ingrid could marry. Illegitimate, yes, but still somewhat acceptable.

Ingrid seemed lost in thought, her focus on the doorway where her parents' voices could still be heard engaged in impassioned whispering. She was unaware of the trajectory of his own thoughts, her proud profile set in concentration.

"What if they do not let you go? Are there musical conservatories in England?" He needed to distract her. Or perhaps he simply wanted her eyes on him. Her attention.

Slowly, she faced him. "There are music conservatories in many countries. I preferred the Parisian one for its reputation and elite composers. If they reject me, I suppose I shall apply to others. I could always sell my cottage."

All of his romantic leanings toward her stuttered to a halt. "But you told me that you'd rent it to me."

"I have been thinking of how to acquire my own funds. You know I truly don't want to marry, Gideon."

"You will renege on our agreement?" His words whipped from him.

Surprise rounded her eyes. "Have you not enough money to secure another cottage?"

"Money, I have. Time, I do not." Irritation bit at him, sharp. His fingers curled around the edge of the couch cushions so tightly his knuckles ached. He should have anticipated this. One could not trust the ton. "You are thinking nothing of how this will affect us."

Ingrid frowned. "But there are plenty of cottages for you. If I sell mine, I shall have funds to do what I wish and live elsewhere."

"Will it be enough to hire a companion? Servants? It most certainly won't buy your parents' forgiveness from the beau monde when they find out an earl's daughter has run away to teach music."

"You speak sharply, Gideon."

"I am not the one who changes my mind on the whim. Who goes back on my word."

Ingrid's mouth flattened. "I will do what I must to follow my dreams."

"At what cost?"

"I haven't made a decision," she bit out. "The cottage is near Hawking's estate. I'm well aware that if you rent it out, you shall be able to care for the children. But you could also accept Hawking's proposal. Forgive him. Live at the estate. Do not pretend you have no means, Mr. West."

"You speak of something you cannot understand." Yet, he felt guilt as he said it. She understood far more than he gave credit for. Would she really snatch the cottage away at the last minute, though?

"If I sell the cottage and embarrass my family, put you and the children out, for the sake of my music, what does that make me?" Her eyes flickered, clouded with what looked like sadness. "You are telling me that I should marry rather than go back on my word."

"Do you even have legal right to sell the cottage?"

"A woman has so few liberties that I simply do not know." She sighed heavily. "I voiced a potential option, and you are quite angry over it."

It was his past, he wanted to tell her. He disliked how people with means so easily walked over those without.

But she continued speaking. "I suppose marriage is the price I must pay for a semblance of freedom. And I will be no different than other women in my circles. My family is strange, you see. My parents were a love match and you know the notions they subscribe to. Alice is the same."

"Not you."

She laughed without humor. "No, I am the odd one in my own family. In my circles, even. I do not fit and I never have. I cannot reason why I should object to a loveless marriage."

He did not like this sadness of hers. Despite his anger at her fickle notion of selling the cottage, every inch of him wanted to go to her, to scoop her in his arms as he did when he'd carried her up the stairs. He would kiss her forehead, her mouth. He would show her that love was real, that it could exist between them.

And he'd be exactly like his mother. Wanting what he couldn't have. Pining. Love had destroyed her.

"I think the right man will not care what he can get from you, only what he can give to you. What he can build with you. A life filled with happiness and understanding."

"Mr. West, are you a romantic, then?" Her smile trembled.

"A realist." He straightened. This went too far. He did not wish to discuss love anymore with a woman more deeply attached to her pianoforte than to people. An angry

thought, but frustration continued to sizzle through him.
"If you are not going to rent the cottage to me, I must
know now."

"I need time."

"I do not have time."

"Meet me there in two days. I shall tell you then."

"We'll see." He left the room, passing her parents in
the hall. They tried to stop him, but after some back and
forth, he finally received his money. Frustration at how
close he was to losing the cottage churned his stomach.
He'd trusted Ingrid on her word alone.

A mistake he should never make again.

Nevertheless, he found himself traveling to Lord Hawking's estate on the second day. His inquiries into other
lodgings had been fruitless. He wanted to check on Rachelle anyway. He didn't like worrying over her and yet he
could not stop.

His carriage pulled into the estate's drive. He'd brought
all of the children with him so that they could also see
the cottage. Perhaps a part of him hoped to influence Ingrid's decision.

The carriage followed a long, oak-lined road and drew
to a stop in front of an impressive set of steps. The estate had been built in the Elizabethan era and conformed
to the architecture of that time. He tamped down his rising bitterness, focusing instead on helping the children
alight. He'd written ahead to warn Hawking of his plans.
Servants emerged to take their luggage, but Gideon kept
his bag. He only had one, after all. Dusk had fallen, spilling shadows about the landscape. The tall oaks edging
the property stood like shadowed sentries guarding the
house. The regal double doors opened and three women
rushed toward them.

He waited at the foot of the stairs as Rachelle descended. The other two remained at the top. Were these his half sisters then?

"What is this?" asked Rachelle, straightening and eyeing the children with a timid sort of curiosity.

"I'd like you to meet my little family."

Gideon gestured to the line of five children who fidgeted beside him. Sarah had her thumb in her mouth again, and Petey held his dog close to his face.

Rachelle eyed the group as if she'd never seen such a thing before. "How do you do?" she asked in a strained way.

The children looked at her with something like awe upon their thin faces.

"Is you a lady, too?" asked Petey, leading the group as usual.

"I suppose so. And are you a gentleman?"

Petey's chest puffed out. "That, I am."

Anna swatted his arm, her dark eyes dancing with indignation. "Are not! The carriage ride was 'orrid. This chucklehead thought it a merry idea to pinch me."

"You got me back, didn't you?" Petey glared at her while holding his arm up to show a good-size welt.

"Oh, dear," murmured Rachelle, her eyes lifting to Gideon's.

He shrugged. "They still have much to learn about becoming a lady or gentleman. Did Hawking prepare rooms or am I to take them to Ingrid's cottage?"

"She's here?" Sarah's quiet voice spiked up.

"Perhaps." He glanced at Rachelle questioningly.

"Not yet." She suddenly grinned at the children. "Shall we surprise her when she arrives?"

The resounding whoops resulted in a skirmish. Gideon grabbed Petey by the collar and moved him to his other side.

The ladies who had waited at the top of the steps decided to descend at that moment.

"Mr. West, these are my sisters." *And yours* she seemed to say with her eyes.

"How do you do?" The shortest one, the only one with dark hair like him and a dimple in her cheek, cut a quick curtsy. "I am Elizabeth, but you may call me Lizzie." She had inquisitive eyes, their color a dark blue in the deepening evening.

He dipped his head in greeting.

"Let us move into the house. I do believe a mosquito just bit me." The other sister, perhaps the youngest one, spoke in a surprisingly husky voice. She led them with a firm stride, and Gideon held back his smile.

The children bounded up the stairs, giggling and happy to be free of the long carriage ride.

If he took on the responsibilities Hawking wanted him to, he'd have to keep an eye on that youngest sister. A look of mischief stamped her mouth. He followed everyone into a great hall decorated with family portraits and a rounded staircase leading to the second floor. He swallowed back his envy, pushing the bitter feeling down. These girls were not to blame for his childhood poverty.

The children stopped in amazement.

"Where is your father?" His gaze cut to the sides of the halls, to the closed doorways.

"Upstairs in his study." The youngest girl slanted a look toward Rachelle. "He has taken a turn for the worse and is weak. You've come at the proper time." Then she looked at him, her eyes a startling ochre that contrasted with her fair coloring. "I am Deidre. I'm told you are a special friend of Father's?"

Gideon wandered down the hall, looking at the portraits, ignoring her question. "Am I to understand that when your father passes, you shall lose this home?" He pivoted, eyeing each girl carefully.

"No. This estate is not Hawking Hall. It is unentailed. It shall pass to whomever Father states in his will," said Rachelle.

Gideon hated that his stomach knotted at the thought of seeing Hawking. He felt like a young lad again, hungry for the safety of his father's love.

And why had Lord Hawking turned him away in his greatest hour of need?

His sisters ushered the children through another door, and he numbly followed, hoping he could find the strength to move past his anger.

The strength to be the brother, the father, everyone needed.

Where to find such strength?

Unbidden, Ingrid's face came to mind. She had found her strength in faith. But how could he find such a thing? Where? His lack of belief was a yawning cavern within his soul that he did not know how to fill.

He banished the image of Ingrid from his thoughts. He did not know how to believe. And he would not be her husband. He could not.

Squaring his shoulders, he continued onward.

Chapter Twenty-Four

Gideon spent the night in the cottage. Ingrid had sent servants ahead to ready the place. Morning came soon enough, and he expected to be summoned to see Lord Hawking or Ingrid. Instead, servants brought sweet rolls and coffee, and he heard nothing else.

The children had already tromped outside to explore the rolling hills and the pond.

He ate and then stepped outside, stopping to fully feel the rising sun on his cheeks. His mother's letter lay tucked within his jacket's pocket. He started for the perimeter of the property.

Ingrid's cottage nestled on a grassy two-acre plot with large oaks for shade and a small garden behind the cottage itself. Perhaps there were fish in the pond. He'd have to see about having it stocked.

As the mist lifted, birds began to sing around him. A rabbit darted into the grass as he approached the group of children running toward him. He could get used to this. Live in the country. Travel about for investigations but set the children up with a nanny. Depending on what Ingrid might charge for renting the cottage, this might be a viable plan.

It would be easy enough to let Hawking's daughters run their own home and he could accompany them to London every so often. See that they had good Seasons, find them caring husbands.

Hard to believe he even allowed himself to entertain these thoughts. Yet, he did, the fresh country air cleansing more than his lungs. He did not expect to like Hawking, nor respect the man he used to be. But the earl wanted to do right by his daughters. And from the single letter Gideon had reread over and over, it sounded as though he'd wanted to do right by his wife.

Who had *not* been Gideon's mother.

Being out here almost made him want to believe that God cared for him after all. That perhaps the hurts of his past had been used to prepare him for the present.

But could he truly believe? He searched the bright cerulean of the sky, wondering, the tiny flutter in his chest something a bit like hope.

"Gideon, Gideon." Petey ran up. "Lady Ingrid is here. Come see."

He patted the boy's head, his thoughts tying into knots. What would she say? How would he feel? Could he keep himself from confessing all?

The children increased their speed, their yells growing louder. His breathing quickened as they neared Hawking's estate. There she was, standing with the other ladies, her cane setting her apart.

After the initial teary hugs, his sisters and Alice left to feed the children sweets.

"They've just eaten," he called out, but was rewarded with a dismissive wave of hands and lots of giggles.

Leaving him and Ingrid quite alone.

"Mr. West." Ingrid eyed him carefully, her hat slanted in a jaunty way across her face.

"Lady Ingrid." He swallowed back the words yearning to spring to his lips, for he longed to pull her to him. Yet, he could not. No, he could offer her nothing. "Have you come to a decision regarding your cottage?"

"I—" Her voice faltered. "Do you think a heartbeat can strangle a person?"

"I'm quite sure it cannot." Where was she going? What thoughts hopped through that beautiful mind of hers?

"My hands are clammy." She looked down as though seeing them for the first time. "I am more nervous than I have ever felt. The ride gave me a good time to think, you see. There is an obvious solution to my husband predicament. I do not know why I did not see it sooner."

Oh, no. She could not mean what he thought she might.

"Not once have I ever thought to be more intrigued by a person than my piano. And yet my feelings have been deepened." She searched his eyes, her look direct and strong.

This felt a pivotal moment. A moment that terrified him. A moment he wanted to hold on to with every ounce of love in his heart.

But no. What would her family think? What of the conservatoire? Sweat gathered at the base of his neck.

"Don't," he said, his voice sounding strangled even to his own ears.

"Don't what?" She lifted her chin so that he could fully see her face.

"Don't complicate this," he bit out, hating the tautness in his voice. He drew in a deep breath. He should just walk past Ingrid. Walk right past her, into the house.

But he found himself chained to where he stood. Hooked by the look in her eyes, the promise that lit her expression. Panic spiraled through him. It almost seemed… dare he think it…that she might say she loved him. His chest squeezed painfully. He thumbed his trouser pockets, forcing himself to step back again. He needed space.

"We are quite alone, Mr. West." Ingrid moved forward, following him. "I confess that I have missed the children more than I anticipated. In fact, there is a quite painful feeling within me at the moment. Do you feel it as well?"

Feel? He searched for an answer. "I am beyond happy to hear you missed them. Does this mean you'll let the cottage to me?"

"The children…they are so happy." Her mouth trembled, a surprising movement that caught him off guard. "Yes. This is the perfect home for them. I'm certain we can find them a tutor."

"We?"

Her gaze clouded. "I feel quite clearly that *we* is the correct word."

But he did not feel that clearly. And what were all these feels she kept throwing about? "They are not your responsibility. You are their music teacher, nothing more."

"Nothing more?" An expression that lived somewhere between aloofness and sadness crept across her face. "I do not think that is true."

"Do you want to be more? They are orphans, Lady Ingrid. I am a commoner, as you have called me. A Bow Street Runner. You receive more pin money in a month than I make helping the constabulary in two months. What is it that you're playing at here? Rich earl's daughter saves the poor orphan children?" He whirled from the wounded look upon her face, shoving his hands through his hair and despising himself. But it could not be helped.

The rich, they moved through the world as though they owned it. They took what they wanted and only gave when they wished. No matter how generous Ingrid's heart, how deep her faith, she lived a different life.

"That is unfair, Gideon." Ingrid's arms crossed, the cane secured beneath one elbow. "For one, your father is an earl. Your illegitimacy does not change your bloodline. Secondly, there is but one Savior." Her gaze narrowed. "I like the children. I love them, in fact, and I wish to remain in their lives."

"And how do you intend to do that?" He bolstered himself to say what he must. "Are you not leaving for your conservatoire?"

"Well, yes, but I shall visit."

"Really?" He raised a brow, eyeing her closely. "And what if you are hired? And what of your injury? Will you truly be motivated to travel back and forth from Paris? What do you think it does to these children when someone gives them grand hopes, only to let them down? Think of how easily you told me you'd rent the cottage, only to change your mind when you felt like it."

"It was a thought, Gideon. How long will you hold that over me?" She fidgeted, her tongue flicking out to wet her lips.

Gideon groaned. "You've no idea, have you? Children need constancy. Stability. Petey was disappointed after he missed your last lesson and you had gone for good. He is already growing a grudge against the nobility."

"He is not the only one who nurses a grudge." Her jaw lifted, though uncertainty lent a small quiver to her chin. "Never have I seen such arrogance."

He barked a short laugh. "Never? That is immensely difficult to believe as you are surrounded by people who are nothing but conceited."

"Do you wish to have a row?" Ingrid sniffed, her tone taking the snooty inflection that so often amused him. Not right now. No, at this very moment everything within felt afire. Raw and vulnerable. As though he relived his mother's duress. How she'd loved Hawking, and what had he done? Removed himself from her life. Abandoned Gideon. He could not let the same thing happen again.

"No, no, I do not wish to fight." He turned to the house, but she touched his arm, stopping him.

"Gideon, there is more to be said."

He shook his head, staring at the ground, realizing the sun bled higher into the sky. Noon loomed.

"I think I deserve a reason as to your harsh words." Her voice, strong and clear, washed over his uncertainty, his regret. He sighed and faced the lovely lady with the purple eyes who had intrigued him from the moment he'd met her.

"You know Hawking is my father."

Her head tilted. "Yes."

"When I was around ten, my mother breathed her last. I came to Hawking. I begged him to take me in as a servant, a stable boy. Anything. But I made the mistake of telling him that I knew who he was. That my mother was dead." Gideon paused, because even though this had happened so long ago, he still felt that little boy inside him. Cut to the quick by his father's abandonment. "She pined for him. She prayed every night he'd come back to us, save us."

Ingrid nodded, but he did not think she understood. He wasn't sure he even did. "Ingrid, you are a kind woman but you live a different life. Add to that your personal goals, and surely you see that insinuating yourself into the children's world will only hurt them."

"You are telling me to leave."

He rubbed the back of his neck, his fingers kneading the tight muscles as if he could force out an adequate response. "No. Just…move with care. Do not make them love you if you plan to abandon them."

"But is not your complaint that your father left? I am not going to do the same."

"Are you saying that you'd give up the Paris Conservatoire, the place for which you labored for years over your compositions, in order to be with the children?" He felt his cheeks tugging into a glower. A dark and visceral anger spread through him. Was she so blind? Did she not see what she was saying? And even still, the tiniest kernel of hope lay somewhere within, wondering if she'd actually do such a thing. Leave her dreams. Her plans. All that she'd been waiting for since the moment she learned to play piano.

And could he truly let her?

What did he know of dreams? He'd been living day by day for so long, the only dream he'd entertained included providing a home for the orphans. Playing them the violin at night. Seeing them well fed and educated.

Ingrid's face had grown shadowy despite the sunlight. She chewed her bottom lip, torn in her desires. He couldn't help her.

He could influence her, though. Easily, though one would not guess that the indomitable Ingrid could be easily swayed. Her posture bespoke indecision.

Would she really want her life to include a clan of unruly children? Or a lovesick by-blow who wished she'd been born to a low birth so that he could gather her in his arms and profess his love?

"There are many dreams to be had," Ingrid said softly. "I have come to the realization that the conservatoire is only one fulfilling part of my life. While piano provides a great deal of pleasure to me, so do many other things. A piano does not offer hugs. Nor love."

"If you stay, you will change your mind." As his father had.

"I am quite stubborn."

And that was the rub. She was, but so was he.

What did it matter if he loved her? That he could now provide a home? Until lately, this lady had never wanted a home. She'd wanted music.

He crossed his arms, firming himself to say what he must. "This is all shiny and new to you. Like a Christmas bauble to play with."

"You think me so shallow?"

"I think you young, filled with idealism."

"This is offensive, Gideon."

"And I shall be more offensive yet." He had to be. What greater heartache than for Lady Ingrid to stay, to perhaps even accept an offer of marriage, and then in so many years hence, fall to boredom and dissatisfaction.

Sucking in a quick breath of air, he spoke the words he hoped would sever her from his life completely. "Go, Lady Ingrid. Marry and go. We do not need you here."

She blanched, as he'd known she would.

"But do you want me here?"

He paused.

She leaned upon her cane, her body sagging in a way that almost broke his resolve. "Very well. Say it clearly, since I'm quite positive the children want me and it is you who does not."

He had to say it. He had to. He bid his mother's wan image to mind, his father's cruel features as he closed the door. He drew upon every ounce of anger he'd ever held within, yet his eyes stung and his mouth refused to form the words he must speak to keep her from staying.

Her mouth took on a grim set and there was something of a shattered look to her eyes as she slowly blinked, assessing him. "Very well," she said in a whispered breath. "So be it."

She departed, just as a cloud drifted across the sun and cast the world into shadow.

Chapter Twenty-Five

"**W**hy did you leave Hawking so early?"

Ingrid felt Alice's gaze as she settled into her place at the piano in the study.

"Hello, Arabella," she said quietly, touching one ivory key with her forefinger, relishing the smooth coldness soon to be warmed by hours of playing.

"Ingrid." Alice came farther into the room. "The children were saddened by your absence."

"They're all absolutely fine and in no need of me." Indeed, she'd left Gideon standing in the yard, went inside and found the orphans enraptured by Rachelle as she read them stories from an old book while they scarfed down treats. She had not seen Rachelle look so at peace since before she'd been attacked.

Gideon was right.

They did not need her, nor would they want her. Ingrid had said hello, but only Petey waved to her.

The next morning had been similar. Servants, both of Lord Manning's and Lord Hawking's, worked together to fix up the cottage, bringing in more beds, scrubbing floors. The children helped, their little faces alight with joy. Ingrid had experienced a most terrible urge to sob as she watched them.

To think that she'd almost told Gideon that she loved him. Had almost willingly given up all that she'd worked for to be there with them. He'd stopped her in such a cruel way. Her throat closed just thinking about his words. His face.

He did not want her to love him or the children.

He did not want her, period.

Oh, he had not been able to say it but some things did not need utterance. Her chest clenched, a vise of sorrow wrapping about her heart. She pressed D# minor, holding the key as the lament of her heart spilled out with the mournful note. What had she expected? That he'd jump to be with her? All because they'd shared kisses? Music?

He cited their stations in life as a detriment. He said nothing of love. He did attempt to speak to her the following day, but she'd felt so frozen, so completely wounded by his words, that she'd only given him a dismissive look. She'd refused to meet his eyes or entertain conversation.

What could he possibly say to undo the horrible fact that he'd told her to leave? He thought her feelings ephemeral, that she simply indulged him and the children as idle curiosities soon to be bored of. How cynical he was. How much deeper his bigotry lay than she had realized.

She pressed the D# Minor again.

Alice sat beside her, knocking her finger off the key. "Whatever is the matter with you?"

"Nothing."

Alice sighed gustily. "Please. Nothing? You are in a sour mood. I shall get to the bottom of your dank spirits."

"How was Rachelle when you left?" Ingrid stared at the piano, willing the heaviness in her chest to recede.

"She has lost weight and has trouble sleeping. The children have lifted her spirits. Once she met them, she did not leave their sides, nor they hers."

"For the best, I should think."

"How sad you sound." Alice went to put her hand upon Ingrid's, but Ingrid pulled away. She did not want sympathy.

"Are you bothered that the children like Rachelle?" asked Alice.

"Of course not. I left early because I was not needed. All is in order."

"And now you may focus upon a quick marriage and then Paris. So why are you so sad? What happened?"

Ingrid shook her head. "Nothing to speak of. Absolutely nothing."

Which was the worst of it all.

"Oh, girls." Mother flounced into the room, her happy, uncomplicated face welcome for its distraction. "I am positively delighted. We've been invited to an exclusive musicale this Friday." She clapped her hands, oblivious to the tension between her daughters.

Practically skipping across the study, she glided to the windows and drew the drapes. Sunlight radiated into the room.

"I'm so happy to see you back, Alice." Their mother ran a finger along the rim of the window. "This needs to be dusted. Oh, a Mr. Traversy would like to call upon you, Ingrid. I believe he's an excellent candidate for your heart."

Ingrid slid off the bench carefully to join her mother. "I do not think I can marry."

"But why?"

Ingrid stared out the window, which faced the busy streets of London. So many people going about their business.

"He is a perfect match for you."

"Is he?" Ingrid wet her lips, pressing them together tightly as if it would stem the tears springing to her eyes. Alice came to her side, so that they were three women at a window. A few passersby glanced at them. One man doffed his hat.

"I have discovered a most inconvenient feeling that has changed my mind."

Concern washed over Alice's features. "Is this why you are so sad?"

"Ingrid is sad?" Mother touched Ingrid's shoulder. "Irritable is more your style, darling. What is wrong?"

Alice chose a chair nearby and pressed her chin into her palms, introspective. "I believe she may have a broken heart."

Ingrid shook her head. "Nonsense. But it is true that I've developed an unfortunate affection which shall affect my ability to marry." Broken heart, indeed. She did not believe in such things, though the organ beneath her ribs throbbed as though it had been twisted and abused.

"Really?" Mother's face lit.

"Mother," scolded Alice. "How can you smile?"

"My plans have come to fruition after all."

"What plans?" Ingrid eyed her mother.

"Just let me ask you this. Did you turn Mr. West down, or did he reject you?"

Ingrid inhaled deeply as her mind tried to sort her mother's intentions. "No one rejected anyone." Not in the traditional sense.

"How very odd." Mother's mouth skewed. "Perhaps we did not push you together enough."

"We?" Ingrid folded her arms against herself, wishing to be back at the pianoforte and pounding out a vigorous solo.

"It is just that I saw you two at the ball, you and Mr. West, and it was quite obvious that there was a spark between you." Mother faced Ingrid fully, her eyes a deep lavender that matched her dress. "Mr. West looked so familiar, and it did not take long to discover his parentage, nor that Lord Hawking has determined to lay a good deal of money on him, as well as land. But you know all this, do you not?"

Ingrid nodded slowly, dumbfounded by the turn of the conversation.

"The thing is, daughter, you are unconventional and it is highly doubtful just any man might catch your eye. It has been quite the dilemma for your father and me. But Mr. West, oh, charming, dapper man that he is, snagged your interest quite quickly."

"He did not."

"To my mind, he is the perfect match. I saw how he looked at you. I deigned to keep you two together, and you both fell in perfectly with my plans. I truly did believe searching for a husband would bring you to each other." A hint of a frown appeared between her eyebrows. "It seems my plans have gone awry. Your father will be so disappointed."

Ingrid should be shocked, she really should be, but she could not shake the hurt dragging at her emotions. Like mud caked to skirts, slogging her movements, her responses.

"Mr. West and I are socially incompatible," she said tiredly. "Your scheming has come to naught."

Alice covered her mouth at Ingrid's words, though she could not tell whether her sister stifled a laugh or covered a frown.

"I intend to travel to Paris, but I cannot marry. You are right in one thing, Mother. This spark I feel for Mr. West has ruined all others for me. Please do not ask me to marry another." She hated how she fumbled those last words.

"But darling, have you spoken with Mr. West? I'm quite certain your fortune is exactly what he needs to help with all those babies. Just think of the good works he could indulge in." Mother sniffed, a look of satisfaction smirking about her cheeks. "I'm certain he has an affinity for you as well. Tell me, do you love him?"

"Love has little to do with compatibility," Ingrid said stiffly, determined that no more words tumbled or fumbled or otherwise emerged in any sort of weak way. "I cannot find it within myself to marry anyone at all."

"But Paris." Alice faltered, glancing between her mother and Ingrid.

"I suppose if you and Father do not support my travels, I shall have to go without your blessing."

"And how do you suppose to do that?" One of Mother's dark brows rose.

"I will find a way. Ladies do not quit." She ignored the traitorous feeling within that she'd quit on Gideon. It had not taken much, after all, for her to walk away from him. A few well-placed words, aimed in the most likely way to cause pain. She'd given him what he wanted, the thing he asked for, that she leave and hurt no one in the process. Perhaps her submission showed the measure to which she esteemed him.

How it hurt, though.

And how many hurts could one person sustain in a lifetime? Surely God had a plan, but at this very moment, she felt quite alone. Sighing, she looked down at the Oriental rug festooning the wooden floor.

"I shall speak to your father." Mother's voice drifted over, hardly piercing the fog of sadness overtaking Ingrid.

"His Lordship shall see you now."

Gideon looked up from his place near the piano. He

and Anna had practiced a simple duet together. Her face beamed with both health and cleanliness. In the days since they'd arrived, life had unaccountably changed for the better. With fresh meals, servants galore and three sisters who adored the children, the orphans had never known a better life. Rachelle even coerced each and every child to take a bath, though Petey had yowled the entire time.

His mongrel had done the same.

Gideon closed his violin, nodding to the servant who'd come to fetch him. He hadn't been to the main house since Ingrid left. His mind swept to that day and his chest knotted. The look on her face... But he'd had to do it. She would be fine. She would change her mind and go to Paris and be happy without them.

Maybe it was presumptuous of him, but he'd seen enough of human nature to understand the fickleness of emotion.

"Did I do well, Mr. Gideon?" Anna smiled, showing off a gap where she'd newly lost a tooth. Her joy when Rachelle gave her a farthing for it had made Gideon grin for hours.

"You are a budding musician." He patted her head.

She scooted toward him and in a surprising movement, wrapped her arms around his waist. "I'm sorry you're sad." Her words, muffled as they were, surprised him.

He hugged her back, noting the frail bones of her shoulders. That would be remedied soon enough. "Why do you think I am sad? Look at us all. Out of London, in a beautiful home with three doting ladies who keep bringing us puddings, custards and flummery. There is nothing to be sad about."

She pulled away, her dark eyes huge and fathomless as she stared up at him. She brought her finger to his face, touching lightly near his mouth. "I 'aven't seen that dent in your cheek."

He tried to smile, he really did, but his mouth failed to obey. He settled for giving her one more hug before sliding off the piano bench. "I'm to see the earl now. I'll be back in the evening, but then I must go to London for work."

"Who'll watch us?" Her brow knit and her bottom lip trembled.

"We will figure out something." His sisters, and how strange that felt to think, had told him their old nanny lived in a small cottage on their father's estate. She might help with the children for a small stipend.

He left Anna and trudged toward the Hawking estate. Before long he found himself escorted by a staid butler to the earl's bedchamber. Someone had drawn the drapes, allowing afternoon sunlight to splash against the giant bed situated in the middle of the room. Huddled within the middle of that bed was the earl.

His hair straggled in thinning strands over his head. The bed engulfed his frame. Gideon swallowed the sharp lump that had risen to his throat and followed the valet to a chair, which had been placed beside the bed. A soft, rich blue quilt tucked up beneath the earl's chin. His lids fluttered when he saw Gideon.

"Forgive me," said Lord Hawking in a voice that sounded as though a stiff wind could blow it right out the window. "I have been unable to regain my strength. Wycoff."

The valet went to his side. Minutes later Lord Hawking sat upright, propped against his white thistledown pillows. His cheekbones jutted out unnaturally, the skin that stretched across them an unnatural pink. The flesh beneath caved inward. Gideon did not relish the unwelcome rush of pity that filled him.

He wanted to hold on to his bitterness, his unforgiveness.

The memory of the earl's dismissal burned brightly in his mind. He forced himself to recall the look in the man's eyes as he'd shut the door in his face. Now did not seem the time to ask why, and yet that was the question that would not leave him be.

"You have come." With his change in position, Hawking's voice grew stronger. "I hoped you might."

"For Rachelle." Gideon sat in the chair provided, resting his elbows on his knees and leaning forward. "And Deidre and Lizzie. I'm doing this for them and no one else."

"What of your charges?"

Gideon's jaw tightened. "Let us speak instead of your health. What is your prognosis?"

"Not good." Hawking's eyebrows looked as though they had not been trimmed in a month. They drooped low. "Perhaps tonight. Perhaps a sennight from now."

"I see. What must I do?"

"It has all been done. My solicitors, my attorneys, all have copies of my will. The title shall go to my nephew, along with most of my estates. But this one remains for the girls, and I've a fortune set aside for all of you." Hawking groaned, his breath shuddering out almost like a death rattle. Gideon did not like to hear it.

"Are your plans also written? What you want for your daughters?"

"You will have control of their fortunes until they marry. And you are set to inherit this estate."

"No."

"Yes. Wesley..." Hawking coughed, long and hard. Wycoff brought a porcelain bowl and Gideon averted his eyes, his desire to correct Hawking's use of his childhood name smothered beneath an overwhelming sorrow. When the earl recovered, he stretched out the arm nearest Gideon.

The thick, dusky veins on his withered skin spoke to his illness. His palm opened, beseeching. "Please," said Hawking. "If you cannot forgive me, please accept my remorse."

"It is difficult," acknowledged Gideon with a grudging tone. "How does a man turn away a son?"

"There has not been a day gone by that I have not regretted my hardness of heart." Hawking blinked as a tear slipped down his cheek. "After you left, I hired someone to find you. We searched London for three years. I was so afraid my wife would discover the truth, but after I turned you away, I admitted my perfidy to her. You had disappeared, though. Lost in the London slums. Perhaps dead. I did not know."

"A kind constable and his sister took me in."

Hawking's lids fluttered closed. Had he fallen asleep? His arm still rested on the top of the bed, reaching for Gideon. Beseeching. But finally, the old man stirred. "My thanks to them. I will repay."

"You cannot. They have been dead a great many years. It is too late for repayment, Hawking."

His eyes opened, their blue tone striking in the sunlit room. "You are a hard man, West."

"I take after my sire."

A harsh almost-laugh burbled out of Hawking. "My detectives told me you are a good man, also. You will care well for the girls."

"I think I have shown my caring. Barley, by the way, has left England. Your funds ensured that he will be followed long enough to scare him into appropriate behavior."

"My heart…broken for Rachelle."

Gideon nodded. In this, at least, he shared a commonality with the man. "She will be safe and have a good life."

"You cannot forgive me, then?"

Forgive him? The very idea still felt so foreign.

"I want to but…" He met Hawking's tired gaze.

The earl nodded slowly, his body slouching into the bed. "With the little time I have left, I shall pray for you. If God can change one such as me…"

God again. Why did Providence so suddenly urge His followers to pray for Gideon? Yet, the more he heard those words, the more something hard and brittle within began to soften. To bend.

"I have had trouble with faith. My mother prayed, to no avail."

"And yet you said kind people took you in. That is not to no avail."

Gideon shrugged, though Hawking's words pricked at him. "Pray all that you want, then. Perhaps the Lord will gift me belief, for I certainly have no power within myself to fabricate such a faith."

The distress on the earl's features tightened Gideon's throat, for he had not expected to find himself in sympathy of the man. He stood.

"Let us make amends," he said. "Forgiveness is a heavy hand that I fear I may never play."

"The fault is mine. But until you forgive, the burden will be yours."

Gideon swallowed hard. "So be it."

He left the earl and readied for his trip to London.

He had done what he set out to do. The orphans were safe, his position secure.

Why did he feel so empty, then?

Chapter Twenty-Six

"You are more of an idiot than I ever supposed you to be."

Gideon pivoted at the feminine voice that interrupted his search for missing paperwork. Lady Alice lounged against the wall, her pristine apricot dress out of place in the bustling Bow Street office. Her lady's maid twisted a kerchief, nervousness plastered across her face. Runners bustled about, filling the office with the steady hum of noise that often comforted Gideon.

Lady Alice, unlike her maid, did not look nervous. She actually looked quite cross. He had not known Ingrid's sister possessed the ability to exhibit such a mood.

He dropped his gaze, continuing his search amongst the piles of documents littering the desk's surface. "What do you want, Lady Alice?"

"What do you think I want?" A rustle of skirts, and then the sound of her plopping down in the chair on the other side of the desk added to the noise.

"Evidently to express your opinion," he muttered. He sifted through a pile near his ink blotter. Where was the Simpkin's case? He'd solved it last week but the constable was demanding usage of notes for evidence in the trial.

"Will you please look at me, Mr. West?"

Sighing heavily enough so she'd note his displeasure, he met her very serious eyes. A jolt of sadness bolted through him. Despite her eye color being brown rather than lavender, her expression bore enough resemblance to Ingrid that regret powered through him in sudden, painful waves.

Regret and longing and a terrible notion he'd made a mistake he could never fix.

Hadn't that been his fear these past weeks? He'd gone round and round in his mind what he should have said differently. Maybe he should have encouraged Ingrid to speak her mind, or better yet, kissed her.

But he'd been terrified, not only of what she might say, but of his own response.

Then she left the next day, and he was saved the bothersome chore of investigating his feelings on the matter. A week later Hawking passed away. Gideon's days were filled with planning the funeral, comforting the family, settling the finances. Before he knew it, a month had passed.

During that month Rachelle found joy with the children. She came to him one afternoon, her once happy mouth now set into a thin line, and asked him if she might live at the cottage to care for the orphans.

Her request seemed an answer to his unspoken prayers.

She moved into the cottage as a sort of parental tutor for the children, and they were delighted. She was more religious than Gideon expected, and he found himself listening to readings from the Bible at night, prayers at meal times. Despite what Barley had done to her, she harbored no resentment toward the Lord. They spent many evenings discussing religion, faith, and somehow, a new and unexpected belief burgeoned within his soul.

By the time all accounts and family business were handled, Gideon realized that with what Hawking had left him, he no longer needed to work. Despite his full purse, an uneasy restlessness still drew him to London every few days. He often rode past Hyde Park, wondering if he might encounter Ingrid.

He'd even spied out Gunter's, telling himself he merely craved a cherry ice.

The bookstore drew him, especially the large one with all the cheap sheet music.

But not once in these almost two months had he seen Lord Manning's daughter.

Now her sister sat across from him, disapproval dragging her brows together and pursing her lips.

"I'm sure you can see that I am busy. Speak now, please." He knew he sounded grumpy. The children had remarked upon his snippiness multiple times. He had often thought to himself that the wealthy had nothing to complain of.

And he still mostly believed that, but he had also discovered that a full stomach did not ease the ache of a hungry heart.

"You are too busy to speak to the love of your life's sister?" Alice arched a fine brow, her scowl somehow transforming into a smirk.

He had no response for the silly, girlish comment, but nevertheless, he felt the muscles in his back tense.

"I have come to a realization." She tapped a gloved finger against her chin, gaze speculative. "Humans are far more complex than I gave them credit for, and love is far more messy than I realized. Have you ever read the novel *Pride and Prejudice*?"

"I can't say that I have." He gave up looking for the papers and leaned back in his chair, pasting a bored sneer onto his face.

"For shame, Mr. West. It is not like you to look at people in that manner."

Shame, indeed. He grimaced, trying his best to clean the sneer from his features. She was right. He did not normally condescend to others. He had just been in a foul mood for so long.

Almost three months long.

"Much better. Frowns are far friendlier than sneers." Lady Alice's gaze perused him. Thoughtful. "The book is a most popular story amongst the ladies of my acquaintance. Its characters have been on my mind greatly these past few weeks. You see, Ingrid is packing for Paris."

"That is good news," he managed to say, though his mouth felt dry as dust at her words.

"One would think so. Yet, she is as miserable as ever. I have tried to speak to her, but her pride is immense. I fear she hasn't heard a word I've said."

He crossed his arms, hoping to hide the storm of emotions exploding through him. "That does not sound like a problem for me. I hunt criminals, not pride."

Alice grinned then. "You are not as funny as you used to be."

"That is right. More of an idiot, less a comedian." He scowled. "You have made your opinions known. What is your purpose here?"

She reached into her reticule and drew out a pile of envelopes. She placed them on the desk, and with a sinking feeling, he guessed what they were.

"Imagine my surprise when Rachelle came to visit last month." She pushed the letters toward him.

"She did?"

"Yes, and she brought all those children." A hint of humor filled Alice's voice. "Not only children, but these love notes. They were found wedged within some trash."

"I know where they were." He frowned. He'd deliberately thrown them out. "I didn't think her one to dig through garbage."

"The redhead, Petey, I think, thought he might find something interesting in the garbage of a wealthy estate."

He glared at her and she grinned wider.

"Don't be so stuffy, Mr. West. Now, I read these and quickly realized that you obviously had not. Or you would not be so prejudiced against us all."

He eyed the letters. He did not want to read them. What would that accomplish? To open old wounds, to dig through painful memories. No. He meant to move forward with his life.

Alice shoved them closer to him. "Go ahead. Take them. I can hardly believe that I must behoove myself to stray from my own satisfactory life in order to help you and Ingrid fix yours, but I daresay some people can't see the forest for the trees. Do you understand what I am telling you, Mr. West?"

He shook his head, slowly reaching for the letters. Throwing them away had been impulsive. Now that some time had passed, a tiny part of him longed to read them.

"You should thank Rachelle when you go home," Alice continued. "When do you mean to leave London?"

He glanced up, noting her determined air. "Tomorrow, I think. The children expect me."

"What if I told you that I think my sister expects you to come after her?"

"Is she not betrothed?"

"She is not. And her pride has assured her that she needs you less than you need her. And your prejudice has convinced you that no one of her station could possibly be honorable enough to keep a vow." She edged forward, her fingertips splayed against his desk. "Read the letters. Quit being a stubborn oaf and at least tell my sister goodbye. At least have the strength to look her in the eyes and tell her you don't love her."

"You've grown bold this summer." Gideon eyed the girl whom he'd always thought to be a bland shadow of Ingrid. He should have known better.

"Bold and impatient. Not the best qualities in a lady, but there you have it." She stood suddenly, her face taking on a disquieting look. "I expect more from you, Mr. West. Much more."

She turned and in five seconds flat, it was as though she had never been there chastising him. And for what? His prejudice?

He touched the letters, his heart thumping so hard he could hear the pounding in his ears. Could Ingrid really be waiting for him?

He'd been so certain that her presence in his life could only one day bring pain. But he was already in pain, even with newfound faith. Every day, remembering her smile, her haughty tone, her sweet affections. He had played the coward in chasing her away. Too fearful of repeating the past, instead of trusting in the depth of character Ingrid had shown him throughout their interactions.

He scooped the letters into the pocket of his jacket. One way to find out.

Before she left for good.

"What time did you say the sailboat departs?" Mother bustled into the room where Ingrid sat at the pianoforte.

She'd been staring at the keys for nigh on an hour now. After many long and drawn-out conversations, she'd finally convinced her parents to allow her to travel to Paris. There'd been a great deal of back and forth with the ironing out of details and making promises of safety. Her parents consulted with a family friend who owned a home on the Boulevard de Capucines. They'd kindly agreed to take Ingrid as a guest.

She should be overflowing with joy.

Frowning, she pushed C minor. The key of lament. Of longing.

"Ingrid?" Mother neared, her face marked with concern. "Your sailboat?"

"A fortnight, if the weather permits." Crossing the Channel could take as little as three hours if the weather was perfect but more often than not, crossing from Dover to Calais took longer due to weather. She'd need to get a room at a local inn if there were any delays.

And a new maid. Jane had left three days ago to help her mother with the new baby. She would not be going to Paris after all, but she'd agreed to come back if Ingrid returned.

Mother plopped beside her and perfume enveloped them both. "I have not seen you smile in weeks."

"I have much to think about." One would presume she'd be thinking of her compositions, creating new ones and practicing night and day. Instead, her thoughts circled and circled around Gideon and the children. Had Sarah stopped sucking her thumb? Had Anna learned a new song? Was Petey being kind to the two little boys who'd joined the family?

Thankfully, Rachelle had visited with them. They did not stay long as they had a full schedule of sites to see as part of their lessons. They'd invited her to come along, but Ingrid declined. Their presence rent her heart into pieces. When they left, Petey and Anna both cried, though he'd swiped his eyes quickly. Ingrid herself had to blink forcefully to restrain her own tears.

It was for the best she told herself, moving on to the lovesick C# minor. *Comfort me, Oh Lord, in my distress.* Prayers continually poured from her soul, searching for an answer from Him, a confirmation that she did the right thing in going to Paris.

Mother laid her palm over Ingrid's knuckles, stopping the tune she'd begun to pick out. "I do not like to see you this way. It reminds me of the days after you were injured."

Ingrid sighed, hating how heavy her heart felt. As though it might fall to her stomach, or perhaps turn to stone. An impossibility, and yet she could not deny sorrow's ponderous burden.

Where had she gone wrong? Perhaps she should have encroached upon Gideon. Touched his hair, poured out the words longing to be released. *I love you.*

Insist that he listen.

But he had stepped back. He had even looked somewhat alarmed.

As though he had not expected her to feel for him. As though they had shared nothing special.

Their relationship had *felt* special to Ingrid, but these past months had told her very clearly that she had been deluded. It had not been special.

Mother picked up her hand, cradling it. "Darling, your soberness is alarming. Have you changed your mind? Do tell me you'll stay in London. That you'll give up this silly dream. Most likely the conservatoire will not even accept a female composer."

Ingrid snatched her hand away. "I have to try. I will not give up."

"I am happy to hear that." The deep, familiar voice washed over Ingrid's senses so quickly that for a moment dizziness buzzed within her mind. Vaguely she felt her mother stand.

Ingrid wet her lips, willing her mind to escape the fuzzy joy that immediately fogged her brain. Gideon walked into view, his hair combed neatly and a single red rose dangling between his long fingers.

"Might I speak to your daughter?" he asked Mother.

Her mother sputtered. "But what of Lord Manning? Have you spoken to him?"

Gideon inclined his head. "I have."

Mother clapped her hands before regaining a semblance of propriety. "I see. Yes, I see very clearly." She cleared her throat and then fairly floated from the room.

Ingrid took a deep breath. A wavering, unsteady breath.

"My lady, how lovely you look today." Gideon came to sit beside her on the bench. He laid the rose on the keys in front of Ingrid. "Do you like flowers? I confess I do not know, and it bothers me no end."

"I do." She touched the petals. "What are you doing here?" How she longed to stare at him, to drink him in until her senses overflowed.

"Today I came to realize a grievous flaw of mine."

"Just one," she murmured.

"One of a great many, my dear." He turned his body to face her, and as if pulled by invisible strings like those puppets she'd seen as a child, she faced him as well.

His eyes were strong and blue and ever so clear.

"There is a book called *Pride and Prejudice*," he said.

"Yes. Alice is a great fan. I have not read it myself." Ingrid felt her fingers twisting into knots. She forced them to lie still, though her heart fluttered beneath her ribs as if a captive struggling to break free.

"Apparently, there are two characters beset by the great vices named in the title. Alice seems to think we are like those characters." The corners of his eyes crinkled in a most adorable way, and she wished to touch the laugh lines fanning his cheeks.

She inhaled shakily, forcing her mind to the matter at hand. "What has Alice to do with this?"

"Your sister believes herself to be a word of warning, forced to point out all of my monumental failures."

Ingrid's lips twitched. "Did she chastise you?"

"Most soundly."

"Oh, dear. Alice is very good at giving one an earful."

He put his hand beneath his coat and then drew out a pile of letters. "She also brought me these." His smile wavered. "Letters from my mother to my father."

"I am sorry for your loss." Rachelle had passed on the news of Hawking to Ingrid. "How do you fare?"

"I could not forgive him when he asked, if that's what you mean. But now there is something within that wishes to be clean of the past. The letters…" He placed them at the top of the pianoforte. "They present a deeper view of my parents. I shall never understand their choices, but it is difficult to hold anger against them any longer. Forgiveness may not be so out of grasp as I once assumed."

Ingrid dipped her head, happy that he'd come to this understanding, but wondering why he'd told her. Why he was even here, causing her heart to ache even more. "I am happy you've found peace."

"Ah, but that is why I am here." He took her hand, his fingers warm and gentle and ever so missed. "I have not had peace for almost three months, madam."

"Why?" she whispered.

"Because I am a big-headed fool, that's why. A scared, cowardly—"

She put her finger over his lips. "Enough. Only I am to call you names."

His teeth gleamed beneath her fingertip. "As you wish, my lady."

"Go on, then." Her nerves felt afire. She moved her finger away, but he grabbed her hand and nestled it together with the other.

"I knew a very long time ago that you were trouble."

The flutters increased, spreading to her stomach. Heat warmed her face.

"Trouble that endangered my heart, until I could not but be certain that I loved you more deeply, more fiercely, than I have ever loved another." His eyes shadowed. "I felt certain that you could not love me in return. Or that perhaps you'd fancy me for a bit but leave when you became bored. I based this supposition upon my observations of human nature." His hand tightened around hers, imploring. "And upon my understanding of my father's abandonment. The letters showed me that Hawking put himself in a bad position. Ultimately, he stayed with his wife because he loved her greatly. He confessed to my mother that he had always loved his wife. That he had done us wrong and would help us. She refused his help. She was angry that he chose his wife over her."

"He still turned you away," she said in a quiet tone, even as her pulse thrummed hungrily through her body. Gideon had said he loved her. Should she say it back?

"He did, to his dying shame. But—" Gideon's eyes crinkled once more "—after some prayer, I have realized that my biases against the haute monde is ruining my life. Particularly, the life I wish to share with you."

"Oh." She could hardly breathe.

"Lady Ingrid, never have I felt the pangs that I feel with you."

"That sounds most uncomfortable."

"But I believe you know of what I speak. Do you not?" His thumb drew a circle against her skin, a light caress that brought goose bumps to her arms.

She nodded slowly. "It is true. I have also suffered such pangs."

"And have you ever felt or can you possibly ever feel more for me than a companionable friendship?" He searched her face, his hands traveling to her forearms, his thumbs still brushing against her skin in an achingly tender way that shortened her breathing.

"What do you suppose, Mr. West? That I would kiss a companionable friend with such earnestness? My pride would never allow such a thing."

"I thought not." He grinned then, his smile more beloved to her than she'd ever believed possible. "But will your pride allow marriage to a mere Bow Street Runner?"

"I believe, sir, that I could be convinced. You see, I love you also. Intensely and wonderfully more than I ever imagined possible. I love your children as well." She hesitated. "You realize that I may never conceive?"

He chuckled. "I have more children than I know how to handle. And I love you for *you*, not for what you can give me." He touched her cheek gently. "Believe me when I tell you this, Lady Ingrid Beauchamp: I desire to be with you no matter what, until the end of my days."

"Excellent. When can we be married?" She leaned forward, intending to steal another kiss, but he halted her with a gentle palm that cradled her cheek.

"I shall procure a special license. But my dearest Ingrid, I intend that you fulfill your journey to the conservatoire."

She drew back and laughed. "Well, my dearest future husband, did you think our marriage would keep me from my dreams? We shall bring the children with us. I'm positive you can hunt down criminals in Paris."

They laughed, and the deep loneliness that had lived within Ingrid for so many years disappeared, leaving her with a joyful certainty that life with Gideon should always be challenging and wonderful and full.

He kissed her then, a true kiss that filled her heart with music.

Their love was a song without end, and she intended to listen to the melody forever.

* * * * *

Dear Reader,

How funny it is to think that I found a few chapters of this story languishing away on my hard drive since 2014. If you read The Matchmaker's Match, you'll know there was a Bow Street Runner in that story, as well as an epilogue referencing a pianist with a limp. Fast forward almost seven years later, and that detective and that pianist evolved into the characters of this story. I had a lot of fun writing it. Who knew grumpy, straightforward heroines could be so amusing? And charming heroes still need redemption?

Writing two broken characters' love story filled my heart with hope and joy. Their banter made me smile as I wrote it. Then of course that plucky brood of children... I wish I could give every hungry, lonely child a home.

Thank you for reading this book! I enjoy connecting with readers. Feel free to find me on Facebook, Instagram, Twitter or my website, jessicanelson.net.

May your faith in Jesus fill your life with peace.

Sincerely,
Jessica (Nelson) Hamm

PS: Yes, I have recently married my very own hero! Another surprise, but there you go. Life is full of those. Happy reading!

Get 4 FREE REWARDS!

We'll send you 2 FREE Books plus 2 FREE Mystery Gifts.

FREE Value Over $20

Both the **Love Inspired®** and **Love Inspired® Suspense** series feature compelling novels filled with inspirational romance, faith, forgiveness and hope.

YES! Please send me 2 FREE novels from the Love Inspired or Love Inspired Suspense series and my 2 FREE gifts (gifts are worth about $10 retail). After receiving them, if I don't wish to receive any more books, I can return the shipping statement marked "cancel." If I don't cancel, I will receive 6 brand-new Love Inspired Larger-Print books or Love Inspired Suspense Larger-Print books every month and be billed just $6.49 each in the U.S. or $6.74 each in Canada. That is a savings of at least 16% off the cover price. It's quite a bargain! Shipping and handling is just 50¢ per book in the U.S. and $1.25 per book in Canada.* I understand that accepting the 2 free books and gifts places me under no obligation to buy anything. I can always return a shipment and cancel at any time by calling the number below. The free books and gifts are mine to keep no matter what I decide.

Choose one: ☐ **Love Inspired**
Larger-Print
(122/322 IDN GRHK)

☐ **Love Inspired Suspense**
Larger-Print
(107/307 IDN GRHK)

Name (please print)

Address   Apt. #

City   State/Province   Zip/Postal Code

Email: Please check this box ☐ if you would like to receive newsletters and promotional emails from Harlequin Enterprises ULC and its affiliates. You can unsubscribe anytime.

Mail to the **Harlequin Reader Service:**
IN U.S.A.: P.O. Box 1341, Buffalo, NY 14240-8531
IN CANADA: P.O. Box 603, Fort Erie, Ontario L2A 5X3

Want to try 2 free books from another series! Call 1-800-873-8635 or visit www.ReaderService.com.

LIRLIS22R3

Get 4 FREE REWARDS!

We'll send you 2 FREE Books plus 2 FREE Mystery Gifts.

FREE
Value Over
$20

Both the **Harlequin® Historical** and **Harlequin® Romance** series feature
compelling novels filled with emotion and simmering romance.

YES! Please send me 2 FREE novels from the Harlequin Historical or Harlequin Romance series and my 2 FREE gifts (gifts are worth about $10 retail). After receiving them, if I don't wish to receive any more books, I can return the shipping statement marked "cancel." If I don't cancel, I will receive 6 brand-new Harlequin Historical books every month and be billed just $6.19 each in the U.S. or $6.74 each in Canada, a savings of at least 11% off the cover price, or 4 brand-new Harlequin Romance Larger-Print books every month and be billed just $6.09 each in the U.S. and $6.24 each in Canada, a savings of at least 13% off the cover price. It's quite a bargain! Shipping and handling is just 50¢ per book in the U.S. and $1.25 per book in Canada.* I understand that accepting the 2 free books and gifts places me under no obligation to buy anything. I can always return a shipment and cancel at any time by calling the number below. The free books and gifts are mine to keep no matter what I decide.

Choose one: ☐ **Harlequin Historical**   ☐ **Harlequin Romance Larger-Print**
                    (246/349 HDN GRH7)   (119/319 HDN GRH7)

Name (please print)

Address   Apt. #

City   State/Province   Zip/Postal Code

Email: Please check this box ☐ if you would like to receive newsletters and promotional emails from Harlequin Enterprises ULC and its affiliates. You can unsubscribe anytime.

Mail to the Harlequin Reader Service:
IN U.S.A.: P.O. Box 1341, Buffalo, NY 14240-8531
IN CANADA: P.O. Box 603, Fort Erie, Ontario L2A 5X3

Want to try 2 free books from another series? Call 1-800-873-8635 or visit www.ReaderService.com.

Get 4 FREE REWARDS!

We'll send you 2 FREE Books plus 2 FREE Mystery Gifts.

FREE Value Over **$20**

Both the **Harlequin® Special Edition** and **Harlequin® Heartwarming™** series feature compelling novels filled with stories of love and strength where the bonds of friendship, family and community unite.

YES! Please send me 2 FREE novels from the Harlequin Special Edition or Harlequin Heartwarming series and my 2 FREE gifts (gifts are worth about $10 retail). After receiving them, if I don't wish to receive any more books, I can return the shipping statement marked "cancel." If I don't cancel, I will receive 6 brand-new Harlequin Special Edition books every month and be billed just $5.49 each in the U.S. or $6.24 each in Canada, a savings of at least 12% off the cover price, or 4 brand-new Harlequin Heartwarming Larger-Print books every month and be billed just $6.24 each in the U.S. or $6.74 each in Canada, a savings of at least 19% off the cover price. It's quite a bargain! Shipping and handling is just 50¢ per book in the U.S. and $1.25 per book in Canada.* I understand that accepting the 2 free books and gifts places me under no obligation to buy anything. I can always return a shipment and cancel at any time by calling the number below. The free books and gifts are mine to keep no matter what I decide.

Choose one: ☐ **Harlequin Special Edition**
(235/335 HDN GRJV)
☐ **Harlequin Heartwarming Larger-Print**
(161/361 HDN GRJV)

Name (please print)

Address   Apt. #

City   State/Province   Zip/Postal Code

Email: Please check this box ☐ if you would like to receive newsletters and promotional emails from Harlequin Enterprises ULC and its affiliates. You can unsubscribe anytime.

Mail to the **Harlequin Reader Service:**
IN U.S.A.: P.O. Box 1341, Buffalo, NY 14240-8531
IN CANADA: P.O. Box 603, Fort Erie, Ontario L2A 5X3

Want to try 2 free books from another series? Call 1-800-873-8635 or visit www.ReaderService.com.

HSEHW22R3

HARLEQUIN
PLUS

Try the best multimedia
subscription service for romance
readers like you!

Read, Watch and Play.

Experience the easiest way to get
the romance content you crave.

Start your **FREE TRIAL** at
<u>www.harlequinplus.com/freetrial</u>.